Received on:

DEC 0 4 2012

Green Lake Library

NERVE

NERVE

JEANNE RYAN

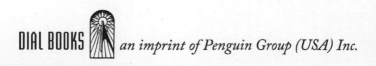
DIAL BOOKS *an imprint of Penguin Group (USA) Inc.*

DIAL BOOKS

An imprint of Penguin Group (USA) Inc. · Published by The Penguin Group

Penguin Group (USA) Inc., 375 Hudson Street, New York, NY 10014, U.S.A. · Penguin Group (Canada), 90 Eglinton Avenue East, Suite 700, Toronto, Ontario, Canada M4P 2Y3 (a division of Pearson Penguin Canada Inc.) · Penguin Books Ltd, 80 Strand, London WC2R 0RL, England · Penguin Ireland, 25 St. Stephen's Green, Dublin 2, Ireland (a division of Penguin Books Ltd) · Penguin Group (Australia), 250 Camberwell Road, Camberwell, Victoria 3124, Australia (a division of Pearson Australia Group Pty Ltd) · Penguin Books India Pvt Ltd, 11 Community Centre, Panchsheel Park, New Delhi - 110 017, India · Penguin Group (NZ), 67 Apollo Drive, Rosedale, Auckland 0632, New Zealand (a division of Pearson New Zealand Ltd) · Penguin Books (South Africa) (Pty) Ltd, 24 Sturdee Avenue, Rosebank, Johannesburg 2196, South Africa · Penguin Books Ltd, Registered Offices: 80 Strand, London WC2R 0RL, England

1 3 5 7 9 10 8 6 4 2

Library of Congress Cataloging-in-Publication Data

Ryan, Jeanne.
 NERVE / Jeanne Ryan.
  p. cm.
 Summary: As a player in NERVE, an anonymous game of dares broadcast live online, high-schooler Vee is unhappy to be watched constantly but finds it exhilarating to be paired with handsome Ian taking ever riskier dares—until the stakes become too high.
 ISBN 978-0-8037-3832-4 (hardcover)
 [1. Risk-taking (Psychology)—Fiction. 2. Games—Fiction. 3.Fame—Fiction. 4. Internet—Fiction. 5. Adventure and adventurers—Fiction.] I. Title.
 PZ7.R9518Ner 2012
 [Fic]—dc23
                        2011048055

For James, my grand prize

prologue

prologue

It took three days of waiting, but at four a.m. on a Sunday, the street in front of her home finally emptied of all Watchers. Maybe even crazies needed to sleep once in a while. She could use some rest too, but more than that, she craved freedom. It had been almost a week since she'd left her house.

She scribbled a note for her parents, threw a pile of gear into her car, and sped off, peeking into the rearview mirror all the way out of town and throughout the two-hour drive to the Shenandoah. The countless times she'd ridden these roads with her family had been filled with games, singing, videos, and sometimes just daydreaming, but this time, it was with a rising sense of panic.

Ignoring years of training by her parents to check in with a ranger when she reached the park, she left her car near the most deserted trailhead she could find and took off on a path where the foliage was on the verge of being overgrown. By early afternoon, she'd have to settle on a spot to set up camp. For now, she just wanted to disappear into the greenery. If she could evade the Watchers for a little while longer, this greenery would bring her some measure of peace, at least for a few days.

Her backpack weighed heavy on her shoulders as she pounded up the rocky hillside, pushing past ferns and catching the occasional drops of dew that lingered on the leaves. The rushing sound up ahead spurred her on with the promise of a waterfall. It would be a blessed distraction from the constant rumination that had taken over her thoughts for the past twenty-three days. Damn game.

She swatted a low-hanging branch, dumping water and leaves on her head. Whatever, it wasn't as if anyone were around to witness the bits of foliage plastered to her skin and hair. But the thought of other people led immediately to insistent, unwanted images. And fears. Fears that lived at the edge of her consciousness and seemed to take physical form, this time in the sound of soft footfalls behind her.

She stood stock-still, waiting, praying that the sound had been just her imagination. Her brain betrayed her a lot lately. Stop. Focus. Think.

The footsteps halted for a moment and then picked up again, faster. Yes, there was someone behind her. What now?

Hide behind a bush and let the person pass? It had to be

a random hiker, probably looking for solitude the way she was. Still, concealment sounded like the best plan. She raced ahead to gain some distance and tucked herself within the arms of a lush rhododendron.

The footsteps became louder, their heaviness suggesting someone large. Was this the "consequence" those jerks who ran the game threatened if she didn't make herself available to the fans? But no one could expect her to make nice with the jerks who called at all hours, the creeps who'd follow her into bathrooms, or the sickos who created that horrifying website with crosshaired images of herself and the other players. When she'd found that, she invented an illness that kept her home for the past week. But she couldn't hide forever. And it wasn't like she could get restraining orders for the whole planet.

Her breathing became quicker and shallower as whoever was behind approached. The steps were rhythmic, measured. Maybe they weren't human. Funny, how the possibility of a black bear concerned her less than if the intruder were a fellow hiker. Or maybe the footsteps weren't even real. This could all be a dream, manipulated in the same way her every waking thought had been during the game, and even after. It was getting harder to figure out what was truly happening. Like the note she'd found in a magazine when she'd snuck out to the mall: *Dear Abigail—The game isn't over until we say it is.*

How could anyone have known she'd visit that particular store, and glance at that particular magazine? Yet, by the time she'd ripped through every other magazine on the rack, to see if any others had been tampered with, she'd lost track of the offending note altogether, as if it never existed. Probably stolen by one of the unknown "we" who spied on her every move. That was the worst part, not knowing what her enemy looked like, while her own image was available to all, like a perverse kind of trading card.

Now the footsteps were joined by whistling. Even her active imagination couldn't conceive of a scenario where an animal knew the tune to "Somewhere Over the Rainbow." Her eyes welled up as she willed herself to believe that this person was simply a trekker in a good mood.

The footsteps halted. She crouched deeper into the foliage as the bushes nearby rustled.

A deep voice said, "I know you're here."

Her gut went to jelly. She pressed herself into the tree behind her, wishing she'd climbed it instead. There was no one around for miles, and a quick peek at her phone showed no reception. Figured. Her phone only delivered misery these days.

The branches of the rhododendron she was hiding within parted to reveal a man with a face like a pit bull and breath that smelled like bacon. Oh God, not knowing what her tormenters looked like had been better. This image would play a featured role in nightmares for the rest of her life. However long that was.

His meaty hands pulled the branches farther apart. "Why not come on out, sweetie? Make things easier on both of us."

Every muscle contracted and her knees almost gave way. The total dread rising in her belly was worse than during the last round of the game, when she'd faced a room of snakes. To think that that used to be her biggest fear in the world.

Despite the shudder racking her chest, she somehow found the strength to say, "Leave me alone, asshole."

He startled. "No need to get nasty. I've been your biggest supporter."

Her eyes darted through the shady undergrowth. Only one option held any hope. She let her pack slip from her shoulders to the ground before springing toward the thinnest section of branches. But there were still enough to scratch her arms as she bashed through them onto the trail. Unfortunately, the man blocked the path leading back toward her car, so the only option was to head farther into the hilly forest.

She ran, followed by thundering footsteps behind her. All sounds soon became absorbed in the crashing waterfall ahead, which sprayed her face with a fine mist as she approached the rickety-fenced overlook. The only way forward was down a steep, rocky cliff, boulders thick with moss.

From behind came discordant whistling in a pitch that cut through the sound of the water. She turned to face the man, whose pockets bulged with jagged shapes that brought to mind the various weapons in a game of CLUE. Not that he'd need a candlestick or knife, with his arms as thick as the nearby tree trunks. What did he want? Was he a rabid fan who'd decided to punish her for missing the "epilogue" broadcast with the other players the night before? She'd watched it, hand held to her mouth, as her fellow players joked and laughed despite the twitches in their cheeks and the dark circles under their eyes. Yet none of them would answer her texts afterward, as if associating with her were more of a threat than whoever was haunting them. It was insane. No one had said anything about follow-up videos or stalkers when she signed up to play.

She climbed over the fence, trying to keep hold of the slippery metal. Could she make her way down to the river without breaking her neck?

"No need for that, Abigail." The man grunted and reached into his pocket. "Just come back here and work with me. We could capture something that no one else has, earn a thousand credits."

Credits? He must be one of those crazies who captured video of the players for no other reason than to earn the respect of his fellow Watchers, which was awarded in the form of votes, or credits. If there were a way to measure her terror, this guy was hitting the jackpot. The pervs got off on that. But would this guy take things a step further? Her throat tightened at the thought. Deep breaths. Concentrate on a way out.

He cocked his head at her, as if considering lighting and

composition. Was it possible that all he wanted from her was a picture? Her breath caught as he slowly withdrew his hand from his pocket. All she could think of was how odd that her life didn't flash before her eyes. What she remembered instead was an old movie she saw in eighth-grade English class, *The Lady or the Tiger?* It had ticked her off that the film left the audience in the lurch. Why couldn't they just pick an ending?

And now, in front of her, a stranger could be pulling out a camera or a gun, depending upon what he wanted to steal, her image or her life. With a sob, she realized that part of her wished for the option she wouldn't have dreamed of choosing before she played the game, just so the horror, what had become her reality, would end.

His hand popped out of his right pocket, clutching a camera, tiny and black, like a cute little bug. She exhaled and choked back a sob. So, a picture after all. Maybe, if she tried really hard, she could fake a smile and this would be over. She could run down the trail, drive like a demon back home, and hide in her room for the rest of the day. Or longer. The Watchers would have to lose interest in her eventually, especially when another game, with a new cast of players, took place.

"Smile pretty," the man in front of her said.

She stared at him and tried to raise the corners of her mouth. A bead of sweat rolled down her temple, followed

7

quickly by another. A few more seconds and this would all be over.

Click.

She exhaled. Okay, if that's what he wanted, fine. Well, not fine, but survivable.

And then, with a lopsided grin, the man reached into his other pocket.

one

I'm the girl behind the curtain. Literally. But after I open
the grand drape for Act Two, I'll have forty minutes to
kill, no more costume changes or makeup to coordinate
unless an actor needs a quick repair. I take a deep breath.
For opening night, things have gone smoothly, which
worries me. Something always goes wrong the first show.
It's tradition.

I debate between heading to the girls' dressing room,
where the talk will be about guys, or staying out in the
hallway, where I might actually run into one, well, one in
particular. Since the guy in question has a cue in ten minutes,
I choose the hallway and pull out my phone, even though
Ms. Santana, our drama coach, has us under threat of death
to keep them off during all performances.

Nothing new on my ThisIsMe page. Not surprising, since most of my friends are in the play or the audience. I broadcast a message:

STILL A FEW TIX LEFT FOR THE NEXT
TWO SHOWS, SO BUY ONE IF YOUR BUTT
ISN'T ALREADY HERE!

There, I've done my civic duty.

Along with the message, I post a picture I took before the show of my best friend, Sydney, star of the play, and myself. The photo's like something out of those contrast books from preschool, she, the golden Hollywood Barbie hovering next to me, the retro Blythe doll, with pale skin, dark brown hair, and eyes a little too big for my face. But at least the metallic shadow I borrowed from the cast's makeup kit makes them look bluer than usual.

An ad for Custom Clothz pops up on my phone, promising to demonstrate how great I'd look in their latest sundresses. Summer clothes are wishful thinking in Seattle, especially in April, but a lavender one with a full skirt is too cute to resist, so I upload a photo of myself and fill in my height: five four and weight: one-oh-something. As I'm debating what further measurements to enter, a familiar laugh booms out of the guys' dressing room, followed by its owner, Matthew, who sidles up next to me so our shoulders are touching, well, my shoulder to his football-team-honed biceps.

He leans so his mouth is inches from my ear, "Thirty-four B, right?"

Ack, how did he read my phone so fast? I shift it out of his vision. "None of your business." More like 32A, anyway, especially tonight with my filmy bra that doesn't claim to perform miracles.

He laughs. "You were about to share it with total strangers, why not me?"

I flick off the display. "It's just for this dumb ad, not a real person."

He flips around so we're face-to-face, with his forearms pressed to the wall on each side of my head, and then says in his silky voice that always sounds like he's letting you in on a secret, "C'mon, I really want to see you in that dress."

I tuck my arm behind my back. "Really?" My own voice is squeaky vinyl compared to his. Lovely.

He reaches around me and slips the phone from my fingers. "Or maybe something, you know, more comfortable." Sliding back into position beside me, he pecks at the phone and holds up a picture of my face superimposed on a body wearing white lingerie. The bust appears larger than life size, well into the D range.

A burning creeps up my neck. "Funny. How about we do one of you now?"

He starts to unbutton his shirt. "I'll model in person, if you like."

The hallway becomes stifling. I clear my throat. "Um, you need to stay in costume, so how about we start with the virtual you?" Boy, could I sound any less appealing?

His eyes twinkle greener than usual. "Sure, after we finish playing dress-up with virtual Vee."

We huddle next to each other as he selects various slips and bikinis. Every time I try to pull the phone away, he laughs and tugs it back. I try a different tactic, nonchalance. It almost works when I surprise him with a quick swipe. Not fast enough to get the phone away, but at least I hit the right part of the screen, closing the dress-up site. It's replaced with an ad for that new game called NERVE, which is basically truth or dare, without the truth part. Under a banner that says LOOK WHO'S PLAYING! pop up three thumbnail pictures of kids completing various missions.

Matthew's eyebrows rise. "Hey, let's check out this girl doing the pretend-to-shoplift dare."

He tilts the phone so we can watch a video of a multi-pierced female stuffing bottles of nail polish down her cammo pants. Um, even if she's just pretending, it seems like a felony to stick any merchandize down those pants. And how does she get through airport security with all those safety pins along her jawline? As if she hears my snarky thoughts, she turns to the camera and gives it the finger. The image zooms in on her wolflike features, causing my shoulders to stiffen. With a smirk, she marches out of the store and into the parking lot, where she uses the polish to paint a crimson *XXX* on her forehead.

The clip fades to black and Matthew clicks below it to give the girl a four out of five star rating.

"I'd have only rated her a three, if that. The dare was to pretend to shoplift, not actually do it," I say. "What kind of idiot would record herself breaking the law?"

He laughs. "C'mon. That took balls. And who's gonna complain about her taking the dare further than they asked for? She'd be fun to see in the live rounds."

"Whoa, do not mention that to Sydney. She was dying to try out for this month's game, until she found out it's scheduled for closing night."

"What, starring in the play isn't enough for her?"

I shift my weight from foot to foot. Although I tease Sydney about being a diva, I won't say it behind her back. "High school theater doesn't win you big prizes."

He shrugs and his attention shifts back to the phone. "Hey, check out this clip of a guy letting his dog slurp soup out of his mouth."

"Nasty."

Matthew gives it five stars anyway. As soon as he does, an ad flashes: UPLOAD YOUR OWN VIDEO FOR A CHANCE TO COMPETE IN THE LIVE GAME THIS SATURDAY. IT'S NOT TOO LATE!

He wiggles the phone in front of me. "You should do one, little Vee."

"Hello? I'm doing your makeup on Saturday, remember?"

"I meant do one of these prelim dares, for the hell of it. If by some chance you got picked for the live rounds, someone could cover makeup for you."

Obviously, he thinks there's no way I'll be selected, and even if I were, anyone could slop a little greasepaint on the cast. Suddenly, I feel smaller.

I tug at my skirt. "Why bother? I'd never play for real, anyway." Last month, the first time the game was played, my friends gathered at my house and chipped in to watch the live rounds online. Being a Watcher was exciting enough. Those players in the East Coast grand prize round who spent half an hour with their toes curled over the edge of a roof? No thank you.

Matthew pokes a couple of buttons on the NERVE site. "Here's a list of dares you could try: Eat with your hands at a fancy restaurant, go to an exotic grocery and ask for goat testi—"

"I'm not doing any dare."

He types something into my phone. "I know you won't. Just messing with ya 'cause you're so cute when you blush."

Greta, who does props, runs over from backstage and taps his arm. "You're on in two."

He hands the phone back to me and is already ten feet away when I notice that he's updated my ThisIsMe status from *single* to *promising*. My heart does a little jump.

Although I've got almost half an hour until the closing curtain, I follow him to the wings. He marches under the spotlight and takes his spot downstage left, next to Sydney, where they'll banter, argue, kiss, and sing before the show ends.

For now, Sydney commands the stage, dramatically lit in blond glory. I feel a surge of pride at the stunning vision I created with her natural assets. Of course, I spent more time on Matthew, contouring every plane of his face with tender care. Even twenty feet away, the gleam of the spotlight in his eyes makes my knees go rubbery.

I recite the lines along with the actors for the next half hour until we reach the finale, where the star-crossed lovers reunite. Matthew takes Syd's face in his hands and their lips meet in a kiss that goes on for one, two, three seconds. I bite my own lip, fighting a surge of envy, even though Syd insists that Matthew is way more hype than substance. She always thinks she knows what's best for me.

The cast joins Sydney and Matthew to belt out the final song, and I draw the curtain closed. Since they'll do their bows on the apron, my stage duties are complete, and I head to the dressing room to collect costumes. The girls' area is filled with the scent of hairspray and a huge bouquet of red roses that sits in the middle of the counter. I check the tag. For Syd, of course. A few minutes later, she and the other girls in the cast dance into the room, breathless and giggling.

Instinctively, I hug my best friend. "You were great. And, look what someone sent you."

She gives a little squeal and opens the card. Her eyes widen. "An anonymous fan."

I want to groan at the obvious ploy. "Anonymous for about two minutes until he slinks around looking for credit."

She sniffs at the flowers and smiles, used to this sort of attention. "Did you change your parents' mind about tonight?"

A tightness forms in my chest. "Nah. At least they're letting me out of prison for the closing night party." After five months of following their rules to the letter, I've convinced them that I've earned my freedom. It'll be the first time I've been allowed out with my friends, unless you count working on the play or studying at the library, since the "incident," which was really only an incident in my parents' imagination. Not that they believe my repeated insistence otherwise.

"Then I won't go either," Syd says.

I play punch her arm. "Don't be silly. You've earned a good party. Just don't get so hungover that you end up with heavy bags under your eyes. There's only so much my makeup skills can cover."

She undoes the ribbons on her corset. "You sure? About the party, I mean. I have full faith in your makeup skills."

I help her with the ties in back. "Of course. Tell me all about it, or, better yet, post pics, okay?"

When she and the others have changed out of their

costumes, I collect the clothes, checking for any garment that'll need a quick iron or spot removed for tomorrow's show. Sydney gives me another hug before she takes off with Greta and the others.

A few minutes after they leave, Matthew pokes his head in the room. "How's daring little Vee?"

Even though my belly tingles at the sight of him, I try to maintain my cool as I scan a tweed jacket, checking the cuffs. "I'm good." Who needs a first night party, when I can hang out with him for a bit before curfew? Yes, my status may really be promising after all.

"You and Syd going to Ashley's house?"

"She is. I can't."

"Still grounded? Dang, girl, start studying more." He and most of my friends think my parents' strictness is the result of poor grades. Only Sydney knows the truth.

"At least they're letting me go to the cast party on closing night. With a midnight curfew." Maybe if I float news of my impending freedom by him, he'll help me find ways to take advantage of it on Saturday.

He nods toward the roses. "She figure out who those are from?"

My breathing halts for a moment. "How did you know they were anonymous?"

He winks. "I have my ways. See you tomorrow." With a slow shake of his head, he gives me one last look-over and says, "Mm-mmm, you are way too cute to be working back-stage." With that, he takes off.

That's it? Our chance to be alone and he leaves? My stomach twists. And why did he care about the flowers? I try to avoid jumping to conclusions, but scroll through the possibilities anyway. Maybe a friend of his is crushing on Sydney, and Matthew's doing recon. But something about the tone of his voice sounded uncertain, vulnerable. Could Matthew have brought her the flowers? She is his costar, but still. My only consolation is that if Matthew did buy Sydney the roses, she hadn't bothered to take them home.

I grit my teeth as I pull a little key from my purse to un-lock a small cabinet that holds the secret weapon of costume managers: a spray bottle filled with a mixture of vodka and water. It's a cheap way to freshen up costumes. Ms. Santana insisted that she'd never trusted a student to use the spray without supervision before. I'm happy that at least one adult has faith in me these days, but if Mom and Dad knew, they'd have her job.

Footsteps approach and Tommy Toth, who designed the sets and presides over all the tech stuff, peeks into the room. "Tonight went great, huh?"

I spray inside a heavy beaded dress that's a bit ripe. "Yeah. Super-smooth."

"Everyone else has left. When you're done, I'll walk you to your car." If there were an award for raising polite kids,

Tommy's parents would win it big-time. Even in fifth grade, when he and I were on safety patrol, he'd always offer to carry the Stop signs.

I head out of the room so I can take care of the guys' costumes next door. "That's okay, I'm right outside."

He follows me. "You okay?"

I fold a pair of Matthew's pants that he left hanging over a chair. "Sure. It's just been a busy week."

He stretches his arms upward. "Yeah, between the two of us, we're covering most of the crew duties."

Yep, the backbone. No applause, though. No roses either. I blink my eyes dry and turn to face him. "You did a great job, Tommy. No one else could've designed the sets the way you did." The stage transforms from a war-torn Afghani village to a Tokyo dance club in one minute flat. It's a multicultural play.

He shrugs.

"Don't be so modest. You deserve as much attention as the actors."

"There are benefits to not being center stage."

My eyebrows must go to my hairline. "Name one."

"Privacy."

I laugh, which comes out between a grunt and snort. "That's a benefit?"

He shrugs again. As I finish up with the costumes, my phone buzzes. I pull it out to find a text from my mom, reminding me to be home in forty minutes. Sigh. The leash is a-yanking. When I delete the message, I see that Matthew left the link to the NERVE site up. The game he knew I wouldn't attempt.

I turn to Tommy. "Do you think I'm daring?"

He steps back. "Um, daring? I don't know. But you've got a lot of charisma. Remember that time freshman year when you made up new words to the school song?"

That's the best I'm known for? Offensive lyrics that barely rhymed? With a grimace, I hold my phone out to him. "Would you ever sign up for this game?"

He studies it. "Doubtful. It's awfully risky."

"Not my thing, right?"

"I didn't say that."

Standing next to Tommy, I click through the game site. It lists a number of dares people can do to apply for the live rounds, along with pop-ups promising instant fame, and a video clip of a few of last month's grand prize winners attending a movie premiere. Two of the girls flash the serious bling that they won for their dares. Lucky ducks.

I scan through the list. Most of the dares seem awful, but there's one to go to a coffee shop and dump water on yourself while shouting, "Cold water makes me hot." Sounds kind of stupid, but less dangerous than stealing nail polish, or even pretending to. I check my watch. Gotta-Hava-Java is between here and home. If I was quick enough, I could do it. That would take the "little" out of Matthew's vocabulary, which he includes with my name even when he texts, something he's been doing since we started play rehearsals. Cute, flirty stuff, especially late at night.

I eye Tommy. "You wanna do something out of the ordinary?"

His cheeks get pink. "You're not going to apply for the game, are you?"

"No way. It's pretty late to get picked, anyway. But wouldn't it be fun to try a dare? Just to see what it feels like?"

"Uh, not really." He blinks rapidly as if his contacts are getting ready to call it a night. "You realize it would be posted online for the world to see, and since nobody has to pay to watch the prelim dares, that could be a lot of people?"

"Yeah, that's kind of the point."

He cocks his head. "You sure you're feeling all right?"

I march to the cabinet to lock up the spray bottle. "I'm fine. You don't need to come with me. I just thought it would be fun."

"Maybe it would be." He nods, clearly thinking it over. "Okay. I'll video you."

Oh yeah. I'd totally forgotten that I'd need someone to capture the dare. I grab my purse and head past him, feeling all Lara Croft. "Great. Let's go."

He rushes to keep up with me. "We can take my car." His parents gave him an action-film-worthy Audi for his birthday.

"No, we'll take mine," I say. It's my dare.

There's a dampness in the air that wasn't there earlier in the evening. Even though I'm about to dump water on myself in a coffee shop, I'm not in the mood for rain. Tommy and I hurry to my car, a ten-year-old Subaru with a steering wheel that rattles every time I hit the brakes. But it's mine and it's cozy. We get in and I drive.

I try to hum along to a hip-hop song on the radio, but my voice keeps breaking. "Think anybody at Gotta-Hava-Java will realize I'm doing a dare for NERVE?"

He checks out my dashboard like maybe he'll find something more interesting than the low-end sound system with a little handwritten sticker on the knob that says "PUMP UP THE VOLUME!"

"I don't think their regular clients are in the NERVE demographic."

I think it's funny how easily "demographic" rolls off his tongue, as if he's in advertising. It's the kind of thing my dad says. I suddenly feel queasy, remembering my father's pale face at my hospital bed a few months ago, when he kept shaking his head and saying how my actions had seemed so out of character. Girls like me didn't end up parked in a garage with the motor running. Exactly, I'd told him.

I shake away the thought. "So I'll be making a fool of myself in front of a bunch of folks who have no idea it's for a game. Perfect." Last month, an announcer kept reminding the audience in a whispered voiceover that the players weren't allowed to tell the crowd they were on a dare.

Tommy's raised eyebrows say "Duh," but he's too polite to voice it. Instead, he tells me about a documentary he saw on a samurai-style business school where the students have to sing on busy street corners to get beyond their inhibitions.

"Maybe this'll end up being good for you," he says.

I study him. He's actually better looking than I've ever given him credit for, not that we'd ever be anything more than friends. With his clean-cut features, can-do attitude, and stock-option-wealthy parents, he'll probably end up running for political office before our ten-year reunion.

Then I remember that I haven't even completed the application form. "Do you mind going to the NERVE site and filling out my info?" I ask.

He turns on his phone and starts reading off questions as he types. I give him my address, phone number, e-mail, and birthday (December 24, the almost-est day of the year). For my emergency contact list, which seems like overkill for a two-minute dare, I include Sydney, followed by Liv, Eulie, Tommy, and then Matthew, just for fun.

Five minutes later, after circling the coffee shop twice, I find a spot a block from Gotta-Hava-Java. The air's lost whatever warmth it had during the day, promising an uncomfortable walk back to my car after the dare. Assuming I go through with it, which a tiny part of me is starting to doubt.

I hand Tommy my jacket. "Will you hold this so I have something dry to put on later?"

"Maybe I should hold your purse too, just in case."

What other guy would think about keeping the accessories safe? I shiver. "Good thinking."

Tommy holds my things tenderly, as if he's afraid to mar them, which really wouldn't be a catastrophe, since I buy everything for half price at Vintage Love, where I work.

We enter the coffee shop and my heart races when I see that it's packed. It's one thing to choose a dare from a list on your phone, another to be performing it. Performing, ugh, that's the problem. Like for the school play audition I ran out of, or those World Studies reports I sweated through in front of the class. Why on earth is someone like me playing a game like this?

I inhale, picturing Matthew kissing Sydney on stage, while I watch on the sidelines. Obviously, I'm doing this to prove something. Thank you, Intro to Psych.

Tommy finds a seat at a community table near the center of the shop and sets our things down. He fiddles with his phone. "The NERVE site says I have to capture this on a live feed straight to them so we can't edit the footage. I'll start as soon as you're ready."

"Okay." I creep to the back of the line, fighting the weird sensation that I'm losing control of my legs. It takes all of my concentration to place one leaden foot in front of the other, as if I'm wading across a swimming pool of syrup. Breathe, breathe, breathe. If only the coffee fumes weren't so strong. The ventilation in here sucks. My hair and clothes will reek long after I leave. Will Mom notice?

A couple in front of me argues whether they should get chai tea at night, since it has caffeine, while a group of women in front of them pepper the barista with questions about calorie counts. Their chattering grates at my nerves. I want to yell that folks who are worried about calories shouldn't hang out in places offering dozens of pastry options.

I wave at one of the baristas in an attempt to get his attention. He just smiles and continues pumping espresso. The clock on the wall says 9:37. Crap, twenty-three minutes until curfew and I just realized I'll need to take Tommy back to his car before I can go home. I push my way toward the counter, causing a few angry comments. Once they see what I'm up to, maybe they'll shut up. No one wants to mess with a nut job. At the corner of the counter stands a pitcher of ice water and a stack of plastic cups. I fill one up and move to a spot near Tommy, trying not to spill it despite my trembling arms and legs.

Nine thirty-nine. I take a breath and nod at Tommy, who points his phone and says something I can't make out. A few people around us furrow their eyebrows, shooting me the stink eye. Tommy gives me a little smile and a thumbs-up, which causes a massive wave of gratitude to rise in my chest.

This would be impossible alone. Maybe it still will be. My body won't stop shaking, and I fight the urge to burst into tears. Geez, I'm such a wuss. No wonder I choked at play auditions.

I stare at the clock, suddenly feeling a sense of tunnel vision. Everything around me goes dark. All I see is the clock, pulsing like Edgar Allan Poe's Tell-Tale Heart. This is ridiculous. It's just one cup of water and one line to recite. Syd would pour a whole pitcher while singing her favorite number from *Les Mis*. Of course, I'm not her.

The racing of my heart progresses to pounding, and my head feels light. Every molecule in my body wants to run. Or scream. Or both. I tell myself to breathe. The dare will be over in a minute. Just a few moments more of enduring this terror. I wipe my cheek. As the clock on the wall moves to 9:40, I clear my parched throat.

Can I do this? The question repeats itself even as I raise the cup over my head. Amazingly, my arm still works. In a voice barely above a whisper, I say, "Cold water makes me hot." I pour a few drops on my head.

Tommy squints like maybe he didn't hear me.

I raise my voice, which comes out in a crackle and say, "Cold water makes me hot!" I pour the rest of the cup over my head. The icy shock clears my brain. Oh my God, I did it. And now I'm standing here soaked, wishing harder than I ever have for the ability to disappear.

A nearby woman yelps and jumps away. "What the heck?"

"Sorry," I say as water drips from my nose. I know I should be doing something, but my body is paralyzed. Except for my eyes, which take in a million details at once, and all of them seem to mock me. With conscious effort, I break my immobility spell and wipe my face with the back of my hand while some guy nearby snaps my picture. I give him a dirty look and he snaps another.

Tommy puts the phone down, staring at me with wide eyes. "Uh, Vee, oh boy, your shirt—" He points at my chest with a look of horror. I start to look down but am interrupted by a barista who runs toward me with a mop. He sneers at the puddle around my feet.

"I'll do that," I say, reaching for the mop. Why didn't I think to grab napkins?

He holds it away from me. "Think I'd trust you with it? Please move. And if you aren't buying anything, please leave."

Crap. It's not as if I spit in his blender. "Sorry." I hurry toward the door. The air outside hits my wet shirt like a jump into Lake Washington.

Tommy catches up to me and holds my jacket. "Put this on, now!"

I look at my shirt under the outside light and catch my breath. What I hadn't considered before pouring water on myself was that my blouse was white cotton. And that my bra was a thin silk blend. Me, the costume coordinator, who works part-time at a clothing store, should have realized the effect of dumping water on these fabrics. I may as well be wearing a wet T-shirt. On camera.

Oh my God, what have I done?

two

I grab at Tommy's phone. "Delete the video!"

"I can't. It was a live feed."

I hold my jacket over my chest. "Why didn't you stop when you realized I was exposed?"

He rubs the back of his head. "I was so busy trying to keep you in frame, I didn't notice until I put the camera down. Don't panic, okay? Things come out different on video. Maybe the lighting in there and the limited resolution of the camera worked in your favor." His expression is doubtful, however.

"Is there any way you can check?" Why didn't I wear the pink bra, the one with all the extra lining?

"No, my phone doesn't save a copy of video chats. They take up too much memory."

We get into my car and I struggle into my jacket with

my back to him. Although part of me wants to sit there and figure out a solution, as if there is one, I need to be home in fifteen minutes. I start the engine, turning up the heater full blast, and speed back toward the auditorium.

Tommy works on his phone. "Maybe there's a way to withdraw your entry."

"Yes, do it! Tell them I don't give my approval."

After a couple of minutes, he clears his throat. "It says that all entries are their property. By registering for the game, you released your rights to the video."

I slam the dashboard. "Ugh!"

That's the last of our conversation until we reach the parking lot. Before he gets out he says, "Remember, there are thousands of videos out there, most of them are probably way worse than yours. People will do a lot of crazy things to get picked for the live rounds."

"I hope you're right. Look, I've got to get home in nine minutes, or, well, I just have to."

"I promise I won't say a word." He crosses his heart and closes the door.

I swallow, feeling numb as I race away. How could I be so stupid? Recklessness is not part of my personality. Shy, hardworking, loyal, all of those boring Capricorn traits, that's me.

I speed home, also a new behavior. But I'm not fast enough. It's two minutes after ten when I enter the hallway that connects the garage to the back of the house.

Mom's waiting there like a toll gate. "Where were you?"

"At the play. There was a little problem with the dressing room sink and I got splashed. I tried to dry off as fast as I could. Sorry I'm a tiny bit late." Lying like this makes me want to puke, but if I told her the truth, it wouldn't help anyone.

She hovers with a stern expression. "You promised you'd be home by ten."

"Mom, please. It was an accident." As the words come out of my mouth, I realize my mistake. Calling anything an "accident" is a tough sell to my parents these days, even now, five months later.

Dad approaches from the kitchen. "Everything okay?" What other junior in high school has both parents waiting for her at ten p.m.?

I tighten my jacket around me and smooth back my hair. "Yeah, just a little sink splash. I'm sorry."

Dad's voice is light, but his expression isn't. "Why didn't you call?"

"I thought I'd make it back in time. But I hit one red light too many." Is there any way they can check out the traffic patterns between here and the auditorium to bust this latest lie?

He takes his position next to Mom. I stand a few feet in front of them, wishing I could get out of my damp clothes. She glances at him, he at her.

I cross my arms. "The rest of my friends are at a party right now. I had to spot clean costumes and take care of a broken

31

sink. Don't you think that's punishment enough for being two minutes late?"

Again, they glance at each other, and then Dad sighs. "Okay. We believe you."

Another stab of guilt pierces my chest, but really, I haven't done anything wrong. Well, unless you count exposing myself to who knows how many online viewers.

"Thanks. I should get to bed. It's still a school night." I hold my breath, hoping I haven't played the responsible daughter card too obviously.

"Good night, sweetie," they say in unison, before each gives me a hug. Sometimes I think things would be much easier if I weren't an only child. Is it too late for them to have another? Ew, don't go there.

Upstairs, I get ready for bed, the night's events playing out in my mind. Hopefully, Tommy's right and my video gets lost in the avalanche of other entries. Still, I toss around the entire night and finally give up sleeping at five a.m. With two bonus hours before I have to get ready for school, I should catch up on homework or something productive. But the first thing I do after I get out of bed is grab my phone. No, wait, I can get through the videos faster with a computer. So I sit at my desk and start up my laptop with shaky hands.

It takes a few minutes to get to the NERVE site and figure out their organization scheme for the entries. As I click, ads pop up to remind me that during the first NERVE event, one guy won a trip to Italy to train for a week with a Tour de France bike team, and one of the girls got to interview for a job at MTV. They show photos of the smiling winners. Not bad for one night of terror, I guess.

As I skim through the site, my mood brightens. Over five thousand people have applied from around the country. On Saturday night, tomorrow, NERVE will choose contestants from twelve cities and conduct the live rounds. Last time, they took the best players from the live rounds and flew half to a grand prize round in New York and the other half to a grand prize round in Las Vegas, where the contestants played for all or nothing.

I become almost giddy when I note that the coffeehouse dare is the one that the fewest number of applicants chose to complete. Probably because it seemed easy, which should translate to boring. Perfect. I click open the category and scroll through the video clips until my heart stops in recognition.

A still image shows my face twisted in discomfort and glistening with water. Underneath the picture, a little indicator measures over eighty comments associated with my video. Uh-oh. That's more than double the number for any of the other videos in this category.

I take a deep breath and click on the image to start the clip. There's me with a pained expression on my face, glancing between the clock on the wall and Tommy's camera. I feel like an idiot. And look like one on the video. Why did I think it was a good idea to complete a dare? Because Sydney got flowers and I didn't? How ridiculous. I should be used to that.

Tommy's voice narrates, "Here is the sweetest, most sensible girl I know about to do something way, way outside of her comfort zone. Will she go through with it?"

I hadn't realized Tommy was providing commentary. What's that about? The video me hesitates, as if her answer to Tommy is hell no, she won't go through with it. For a second I hope that last night was just a weird dream. But the girl in the video pours the water on her head and sputters.

Tommy's commentary says, "Oh."

And then the clip shows a very wet girl with very petite breasts in a very revealing shirt. My worst fear.

I click through the comments under the video, feeling a wave of nausea rise in my belly. One comment reads, **Nice raisins!** And that's as kind as it gets. I slam the computer shut and dive back into my bed, pulling the covers over my head.

A hour later, my phone buzzes with a text. I ignore it and the next one that comes in as well. Have my friends seen the video? I burrow myself farther into the covers.

It's seven thirty when my mom calls at my door, "Honey, you okay? You'll be late."

"I'm fine, almost ready," I lie.

"Can I come in?"

"Um, hold on." Quickly I throw on a pair of jeans and a top, and then answer the door stifling a yawn.

Mom peeks at my room over my shoulder, probably searching for a crack pipe. "I made asparagus soup last night. Would you like to take some for lunch?"

"That sounds great. Thanks."

As soon as I close the door, I run to my phone. The messages from Sydney and Liv are about the party last night, mostly saying that they wished I could've come. The final message is from Tommy: "Call me!"

So I do. When he answers, I say, "I've seen it. It's horrible. And what was with your commentary?" I don't really care about the commentary, but it's easier than asking what he thought of my chest.

"I was just trying to make it entertaining, and give you an excuse, you know, in case."

"In case I chickened out?"

"In case you changed your mind. There's no shame in that."

I rub my temple. "Well, thanks, I guess. Anyway, your comments were way nicer than what people wrote in. Did you see how obnoxious some got?"

He clears his throat. "Just ignore them. Things aren't as bad as you think. Some of the clips in the mooning category have three hundred comments."

"Isn't there something I can do to force them to take it down? I mean, technically, isn't it illegal for them to have a video of a minor, showing her, uh, chest?"

"Well, no one seems to mind the butt-shot videos. And all NERVE provides to contact them are application forms and video links, with no way to connect to anyone directly. I can't even track them down through their hosting site; it's like they're based overseas and hop from server to server."

I run a hand across my forehead. "Thanks for trying, Tommy."

"If neither of us tells anyone, chances are no one we know will see it. And once NERVE does the live rounds tomorrow night, everyone will shift their attention anyway."

I want to believe him. His words are logical, his voice soothing. "Okay, what happened at Gotta-Hava-Java stays in Gotta-Hava-Java."

"You got it."

I thank him and hang up. All the way to school, my hands and legs feel shaky, but when I get there, everyone seems normal. For the first time ever, I'm glad my principal has a policy of not using phones in the school building except in the case of emergency. I go through my day acting like everything's fine, and by lunchtime my panic is all but forgotten.

When I pass Tommy at his locker that afternoon, I whisper, "So far, so good."

After school, I rush through my homework, eat an early dinner, which I don't have much appetite for anyway, and promise Mom I'll be home on time. I head out to the theater around five, and, when I get there, the place is buzzing with pre-show excitement. My first instinct is to head to the lighting booth to check in with Tommy, but Sydney runs up to show me a complimentary write-up of the play, which claims that Chinook High School has a few potential stars in the making. A large photo of Sydney slapping Matthew accompanies the text.

Her eyes are bright. "I love that scene."

Matthew joins us, rubbing his cheek as if it's still sore. "I think you love it a little too much."

I examine their faces, looking for any chemistry. There's none in Syd's eye roll before she heads into the girls' dressing room. Matthew's gaze lingers on her, but only for a moment before returning to me.

He taps my nose. "Ready to do my makeup, little Vee?"

"Sure." I grab my cosmetics box and join him in the guys' dressing room, which is empty except for us.

I pull out the cake foundation and grab a glass of water from the sink. Matthew pulls his hair back under a band as I dampen a sponge and get to work. While I hover over him to apply the foundation, he rests a hand on my hip. I swear I feel the heat of his palm through the fabric.

"Missed you at Ashley's last night." His voice is gravelly.

Wow, he's never said anything about missing me before. Maybe my future is more "promising" than I thought.

"Yeah, it sucks I couldn't come. But it was on a school night anyway. Tomorrow's party will be better."

"You sure you can't come out tonight? Even for just a coffee or something?" He squeezes my hip.

Coffee? My chest is tight. There's no way he saw the video, is there?

"I wish I could, but we'll hang out tomorrow, okay?" My fingers fumble as I pull out the contouring cream for the sides of his nose and jawline.

I want to question him about his sudden interest in coffee, but a couple of guys enter and head behind a curtain to change. The room becomes more crowded as I work on Matthew's face, no opportunity for private discussion. When I'm done with him, a line of other actors take turns in the makeup chair, and then I move to the girls' room to fine-tune their faces and hair, since most of them are able to get the basics on for themselves. I have to hurry so I can open the grand drape for the first act. Really, they should get someone else to do that, but the props and special effects team has some tricky preps for the Afghani village scene.

When the curtain is open, I hang out in the wings to ensure that everyone looks the way they're supposed to before I head back to clean up my kit. In the girls' dressing room, Ashley and Ria whisper, stopping short when I enter. We're not besties or anything, but they've never acted skittish around me before.

I gather the used sponges to be sanitized. "Sounds

like everyone had a great time last night. Sorry my parents wouldn't let me come."

Ashley nods. "I understand." She adds some hairspray, although her hair is already shellacked more than a decoupage project. "Um, is everything okay, Vee?"

My shoulders stiffen and I feel a surge of nausea at her question, the same question so many people peppered me with five months ago after my week in the hospital. I immediately go into auto-response: "Everything's great. Why do you ask?"

"Oh, no reason, you just look kind of tired."

Lovely, that's what middle-aged people say to each other as code for *you look old*. "Guess I need to apply some stage makeup to myself." I force a laugh and hurry on to the guys' room.

In there, John and Max give me weird smirks. Is it my imagination? I'm being paranoid, right? Those guys are always smirking. Without making further eye contact, I put everything away, then head out to the fire escape, which fortunately is empty, thanks to Seattle's strict public smoking laws.

I pull out my phone and click to the NERVE site. There are a hundred and fifty comments linked to my video. Do I dare read them? Part of me feels mortified, yet a tiny part feels flattered to get so much attention. Not flattered enough to actually read the comments just yet, so I click over to my favorite shopping site and drag some high-end hair care

39

products onto my wish list, even though what I really need is a good cut.

Shivering, I wish I didn't have to go inside for the intermission curtain. What if I just left it for someone else? But of course, I don't do that. I'm the responsible one, despite what my parents currently believe.

With a deep breath, I enter and scurry to the wings. As soon as the act is over and the drape drawn, I run back toward the fire escape, but Sydney catches up to me. "We need to talk."

Uh-oh. I keep going, but she follows me outside, tugging at my arm. "Matthew just whispered something about you playing NERVE. What's he talking about?"

My lungs deflate. I lean against the rough brick wall. "Okay, don't get mad. It's just that I was bummed about not being able to go to Ashley's party last night. So I did a tiny little prelim dare."

Her body seems to rise off of the ground. "You what?"

"I know. It was stupid. And it kind of went wrong. I had to dump water over my head, but then it made my shirt all see-through and, oh God, it's such a mess." I put my head in my hands.

She makes a pursing sound with her lips. "Stop. It's probably not a total disaster. We'll take care of this. Where's your phone?"

I use my elbow to gesture toward my pocket, not wanting to take my face from my hands. She pulls it out and I hear clicking. Of course she knows exactly where to look online, being a NERVE wannabe. For a second, I feel a moment of satisfaction that I've actually done something that Syd had her eyes on before she was able to. But that feeling is soon squashed when I realize that she never would've been dumb enough for things to end up the way they had.

"So which dare did you do?" she asks.

"Coffeehouse," I say through my fingers.

More clicking. Then, "Oh, I see."

I lower my hands. "Told you."

Her face is serious. "Well, okay, let's stop and think." In addition to being blond and beautiful, Syd maintains an A average.

"No further thinking required. I want to go home."

"Uh-uh, running away is only going to make things look worse. Besides, it's not like the video shows that much. You weren't naked. Maybe we can turn this around. Tons of celebrities got their start with leaked sex tapes."

"Um, my career goals don't include reality TV."

"Okay, but the way those girls got through it was by holding their heads high. So, number one, don't apologize. Just smile when people mention it and shrug, like *aw gee, it could've happened to anyone.*"

I take the phone from her and start scrolling through the comments. Sure enough, there's one from Matthew that says, **Little Vee, I didn't know you had it in you!**

41

Lovely. I close the link to the site and check my messages, finding a few from my friends with *WTF* subject lines and a few from acquaintances with lots of exclamation points and question marks. There's one from a girl I've never heard of with a subject line that says **SLUT**. How did she get my address? I delete it before turning off the phone.

Syd's at the door. "You ready?"

"I guess." I try to keep my head up as we march inside toward the girls' dressing room. In my peripheral vision, faces turn my way.

When we enter the room, Sydney announces, "My best friend had the balls to do a NERVE dare!"

The other girls seem startled at first, but when they glance at me, I smile and shrug, so they burst into giggles and give me high fives. Really? They ask how nervous I was, if the see-through shirt was on purpose, etc. I answer truthfully, with direct eye contact and no slouching. The more I talk about it, the more okay I feel.

Matthew comes in with a lusty grin. "Hey, coffee shop girl! Double whipped cream for me." I let him grab me in a tight embrace, fighting against the embarrassment I feel. In my ear, he whispers, "Told ya, you should be on stage."

When he lets me go, he pulls out his phone and plays the clip for everyone to huddle around and watch. I laugh along with the rest of them although I wish he'd turn it off. Head held high, head held high. Hopefully, this fake confidence in the face of calamity gets easier with practice. After the second showing, Tommy comes through the door with a puzzled expression.

Matthew holds out the phone. "Hey, dude, see Vee's dare?"

"That's Tommy's voice on the video," I say to the room.

Everyone's eyebrows go up and Matthew slaps Tommy's back. "Nice job! Yo, the backstage crew is showing up the cast!"

We all laugh and Matthew plays the video again. Tommy glances at me with a question in his eyes. I just shrug. Thankfully, the overhead lights blink to indicate that intermission will be done in a minute.

As Matthew leaves the room, I pull him aside. "By the way, how did you find my video?"

He shrugs. "They sent it to me." And then he hurries off.

I stand there in the middle of the dressing room, alone and panting as if I've just run a race. Why did NERVE send my video to Matthew of all people? And then it hits me. He was one of my emergency contacts. Weird that they didn't send it to Syd or Tommy.

Although I really want to head back out to the fire escape, I do my best to act normal and take my place in the wings to mouth everyone's lines. The show must go on. And it does, as smoothly as the night before. When it comes to the stage kiss, I imagine that I'm the one Matthew's taking in his arms. And I'm sure he's staring straight at me right before their lips meet. One thousand, two thousand, three thousand, and they part. Maybe tomorrow at the party it'll be my turn.

After the play, my friends Liv and Eulie come backstage to congratulate everyone and to check on me, I'm sure, since they've each sent at least five texts asking about the video that NERVE sent to them during the show. I assure them I was just goofing around and that everything's fine. Being in the honors program, they're both more skeptical than the rest of my friends, but they don't pursue the subject. For now.

"Wanna hang out with us for a bit before you go home?" Liv asks.

"Wish I could, but by the time we get to your house, I'd only have like ten minutes before I have to turn around and go home. You're coming tomorrow though, right?" They created all the posters advertising the show and wrote a glowing preview in the school paper, so that gives them admittance to the closing night party.

Eulie laughs. "Liv's dragging me, but yeah." She crosses her arms over her tall, lean body, dressed in nondescript jeans and a sweater. If there were anyone I'd love to give a makeover to, it would be her. With the right clothes and makeup, she could pass for Syd's sister. Except for the fact that she's as shy as Syd is outgoing. She and Liv leave to congratulate everyone else while I straighten costumes.

Matthew joins me, plopping into the makeup chair and giving me a probing stare. "Feel like missing curfew? I could take some more video of you."

"Hah! If I get home late, I'll never get out of being grounded. But I've still got thirty-five minutes before curfew. We could hang out here for twenty of those minutes."

He checks his phone. "Damn, that hardly gives us time to get some brews."

"We don't really need any, do we?"

He wipes his forehead. "Maybe you don't, little Vee, but I'm thirsty. And twenty minutes, well, that's not enough time, is it?"

"I guess not."

His friends come to the door, scuffling, and calling, "C'mon, dude!"

He gets up and kisses the top of my head. "Can't wait for the party tomorrow. We should hang a Do Not Disturb sign on the dressing room door, huh?"

Whoa, I wonder if his intentions are a little more action-packed than mine, but all I say is, "See ya."

Sydney, who's changed from her corset into a mini-dress that doesn't cover up more than her costume, comes back with Liv and Eulie trailing her. "I think you pulled it off."

"Thanks to you. Have fun." Even though there aren't any cast parties planned, it's still Friday night.

She purses her lips. "I'll be so happy when you're done being grounded."

"Only one more day."

She wags her finger. "Then, don't screw up. No more dares, okay?"

45

"Are you kidding? I've got to be home soon anyway."

She hugs me good-bye and so do Liv and Eulie. Then, like the night before, I'm left alone to finish up. When I'm done, I sit down with my phone to read a couple dozen messages. Most of them are pretty flattering, surprisingly. Whew.

Near the end of my messages, there's one from NERVE. I'm tempted to delete it, but what the heck? Maybe they want to congratulate me on getting so much attention for what should've been a dumb dare.

My heart does a little jump when I read the message.

HEY, VEE!

YOU'VE GOT TONS OF NEW ADMIRERS!

WE'D LIKE TO INVITE YOU FOR A
FURTHER QUALIFYING DARE AND WE'LL
MAKE IT WORTH YOUR WHILE! CHECK
THIS OUT.

I click on a link that shows a still shot from my dare in the coffee shop, only they've altered the image so I'm wearing a pair of lust-worthy shoes that I posted on my ThisIsMe page a few weeks ago. Whoa, there's a three-month waiting list to buy them in brown, and these are the limited edition flamingo ones. NERVE must have some serious connections. How did they know I wanted them? Did someone give them access to my page?

I read the rest of NERVE's message.

> To win the shoes, go back into the
> coffee shop tonight. A guy named
> Ian (picture to follow) will enter
> at 9:40. Demand that he buy you a
> latte. While he's in line, you must
> stand in the middle of the café and
> sing "One Hundred Bottles of Beer
> on the Wall" with your eyes closed
> until he gives you your drink.

What? Why would NERVE want me to go back into the coffee shop where I made such a fool out of myself? Well duh, where better to embarrass me further? Doesn't matter, though; I can't do it. No more dares. I promised Sydney.

But those shoes.

And everything turned out okay, didn't it? Besides, there's no water involved in this dare. Just singing and meeting some guy. I'm so deep in thought, I don't notice Tommy's presence until he's beside me. I show him my phone.

"No way," he says.

I glance at the time on my phone. "If I leave now, I can just make it."

Tommy bounces on the balls of his feet, like he's having spasms. "If you really want to get involved with NERVE, sign up tomorrow night as a Watcher."

"Why should I pay to watch when I can be paid to play? I've had enough watching in my life." Plus, I want those shoes so badly I can smell the leather.

We stand there staring at each other like two cowboys in a Western. Two skinny cowboys who wouldn't know how to shoot a gun or ride a horse if our lives depended on it. But the more I consider doing the dare, the more I think, *Why not?*

Tommy must sense my intentions. He says, "Well, if I can't talk you out of it, I'm coming along as your cameraman and bodyguard."

I stifle a laugh. I guess a computer-whiz bodyguard is better than no bodyguard at all. Kind of. And I do need someone to video this. We make a good team.

"But this time we have to take separate cars so I can get home quicker," I tell him.

As I scurry toward my car with Tommy alongside me, I click open a link and quickly fill out an additional form that has me agree to a scrolling list of terms and conditions. I scan through and check them off before I put my phone away. My neck is damp.

Before I get into my car, I ask Tommy, "Think the baristas will call the police when they see me again?"

He furrows his brow. "Probably not right away."

For some reason, his answer makes me giggle. *Not right away* will just have to be good enough.

three

I park the car at 9:36 and, on the way into the coffee shop, check my phone to find a picture of my dare partner, Ian. Dark hair to his chin, intense eyes as dark as the hair, sharp cheekbones. In a word, hot.

So I have to let cutie buy me some coffee and sing while I wait? The first part I can handle, but singing in public? Going home starts to feel like a better option. No shoes to die for, but no dying of embarrassment either. I remind myself that I actually completed a dare last night. And I've got admirers. Okay, probably drunken geeks with nothing better to do than scroll through a thousand videos to check out cleavage shots in slow-mo, but still.

Inside the shop, no sign of Ian, so I shuffle my feet while Tommy finds a spot to sit center stage. A couple of guys wearing sandals with socks rush inside and seem to scan the room until they see me. Then they find tables nearby, staring my way all the while. To the casual observer, they look like typical Seattle guys, armed with smartphones but no fashion sense. When their phones point my way, I realize they must be Watchers sent by NERVE to capture my dare. Oh, crap. But it makes sense that the gamers would want to see how players respond under the pressure of a live audience. My stomach lurches. That's my response.

I wring my hands and bounce on my toes, staring downward. Every few seconds I risk a glance toward the door. Where is Ian? The dare said 9:40. Does NERVE know about my curfew, the way they knew about the shoes? I'm sure I posted complaints about my prison sentence on ThisIsMe, so if they've seen my page, they know about that plus a whole lot more. Well, whatever, it's not like it's secret.

I stand and wait for what seems like an hour but is actually two minutes, and then Ian walks in. I can tell he recognizes me right away, but he doesn't say anything. Behind him a willowy girl pointing a phone hurries to take up a spot a few yards away. Guess he travels with a bodyguard too.

When he stops in front of me, I cross my arms. The phone pic didn't capture the smooth olive planes of his cheeks, or the lanky gait in those well-worn jeans. But would it kill him to crack a smile?

I say, "Hey, you get to buy me a latte. Hazelnut is my favorite." Is that diva enough?

He purses his lips. "So?"

Huh? This is his dare too, isn't it? Maybe the operational word was *demand*.

I rise onto the fronts of my ballet flats and flip my hair. "What do you mean? I want a latte. Now."

He steps closer so I have to crane my neck to look at his face. "Who do you think I am?"

I'm taken aback. "You're Ian, aren't you?" My voice sounds like something in a cartoon.

"Yeah."

"So, I'm Vee."

His lip curls. "What's Vee short for?"

Okay, now that is secret. "What's it matter?"

He shrugs. "Guess it doesn't." Still no movement toward buying me a latte.

I exhale loudly. "Fine. I guess we both lose. Unless your dare was to be a jerk." I move toward the door.

He grabs at my arm. "What, you giving up already?"

I cock my head. What's his game? "You going to buy it for me or not?"

"What's it worth to you?"

A pair of killer shoes, bozo. "What're you getting at?"

He leans in close. "Part of my dare depends on you."

Hmm. "How so?"

"You have to announce that I'm an amazing lover." His voice is so faint, I can barely make out what he's saying.

"What?"

"You need to tell me that I'm an amazing lover. Out loud."

Is that really part of his dare? Or is he messing with me? Maybe messing with me is his dare. But what if I tell him he's a great lover and he still doesn't get me a latte? Then he'll complete his dare, but I won't complete mine. Whoa, preventing me from completing my dare might even be his dare. God, two dares into the game and my mind's spinning with conspiracies. Does NERVE plan things this way?

I put one hand on my hip and aim at Ian's chest with the other, a pose I've seen Sydney use a thousand times when she wants to make a point. "Get in line for the latte. After you've ordered, I'll tell the whole coffee shop how great you are in bed."

He examines me for a second, maybe dealing with his own trust issues. "Deal."

He gets in line. I feel smug until, with a start, I realize that the worst part of my dare begins now. Inhaling deeply, I close my eyes against the snickers around me. My head goes light again and my heart pounds irregularly. Is this what a panic attack feels like? It's so much worse having to be in the dark. I've always hated the dark. My imagination goes wild with possibilities. What if someone else has been dared to smack me upside the head? Or pull my skirt up? Feeling so vulnerable brings tears to my eyes. Oh hell, I'm crying in front of everyone. What a great show for NERVE. I feel a surge of anger toward the game, which sears through the panicky feelings. Good. Hold on to that anger and sing. I open my mouth and, surprisingly, words come out. Trembly, off-key words, but it's singing.

I get one verse out when it dawns on me that I have another dilemma. With my eyes closed, I won't be able to see Ian order. How will I know when to shout out what a great lover he is? If I do it too soon, will he bail on the latte? I keep singing, digging my fingernails into my palms.

Laughter comes from every direction. Maybe Ian's been dared to pour an espresso over my head. I flinch when I feel the presence of someone a few inches away.

"He just ordered your drink," Tommy whispers as he stuffs a tissue in my hand.

I could hug him. "Thanks," I say between lyrics as I wipe my cheeks. It's only then that I ask myself why I didn't just peek, and how Tommy knew I wouldn't.

A spark of hope ignites in my chest. I've almost completed my dare. Although there's still the matter of helping Ian finish his. Unless I'm the skunk who bails. But, of course, I won't. At heart, I'm a Capricorn.

Squeezing my eyes shut even tighter, I yell, "You're the best hook-up I've ever had, Ian!" Laughter erupts from all sides. With burning cheeks, I go back to the beer song.

When I'm down to sixty-three bottles on the wall, I feel another presence. Ian's voice says, "Here's a latte for the most amazing girlfriend ever." And then he starts singing "Beautiful Girl" in a smooth tenor voice that would've won a starring role in the school play.

I open my eyes and take the hot cup from him as he serenades me. It's almost as embarrassing being sung to in public as it is singing. One of the guys videoing gives us a thumbs-up sign. The girl who came into the shop behind Ian laughs to herself as she films us. Nearby, another two girls type into their phones. Are they rating us? I channel my inner Sydney and give them a pageant wave, even though I'm not seriously applying for the live rounds. I just want those shoes. Which I've earned.

Thankfully, the song finally ends. Okay, dare over. Whew.

I raise the cup to Ian. "Bravo!"

He bows and poses for the Watchers, especially his model-like camerawoman, who's probably his girlfriend. And then, he smiles. Wow. What a difference it makes to his face. His teeth are super-white and straight, and his cheeks dimple so deeply you could stick dimes in them.

Tommy, with a tenseness to his jaw, joins us, eyeing Ian. "It's nine forty-nine."

I turn to Ian. "Gotta run. Thanks for the latte, and the song."

He waves at the girls who're still typing on their phones.

"Sorry I had to act like an ass though. Pissing you off before asking you to yell that lover stuff was part of the dare."

"Good to hear that isn't your true personality."

He stares at me, as if he's trying to figure me out, and something doesn't add up. "You rocked that dare. I'm impressed."

My chest swells. I did rock it, didn't I? "You too."

The barista who mopped up yesterday glares at us. Cue to exit stage.

"Good luck, Ian!" I say as I hurry outside with Tommy.

The cold air rushes past me. But unlike last night, it's refreshing rather than an assault. I did it! I did it! As we jog to our cars laughing, I almost lose a slipper, which is perfectly in character, since I feel just like Cinderella running from the ball.

four

Tommy shakes his head like he can't believe I went through with it. "Congratulations."

I skip along the sidewalk. When's the last time I skipped? First grade? "Thanks for being my wingman, Tommy. I couldn't have done it without you. If you were a girl, I'd lend you my prize shoes."

His smile fades a little. "Uh, thanks?"

"You know what I mean. You're awesome!" I get into my car. "Wish we could celebrate or something, but you know my parents."

"Yeah. See you tomorrow." He hovers for a moment, as if he's waiting for me to say something more, and then, with an embarrassed shrug, he helps me close my door.

On the way home, I turn the radio up loud and sing along

with a country singer about how she takes revenge on the man who's done her wrong. Why are songs like that so fun? When I pull into the garage, I even have a minute to spare. Perfect. I waltz through the back hallway, tempted to shout the words to "Everything's Coming up Roses" from *Gypsy*, but that would invite too many questions from Mom, who's sitting in the living room pretending to read a book.

I give her a hug, hoping I don't smell like coffee. "The show went great."

"Wonderful, honey! Dad and I are looking forward to seeing it tomorrow."

"Third night's a charm. You'll be glad you waited."

I dance my way up the stairs, humming as I get ready for bed. With a *West Side Story* tune in my head, I fall asleep smiling. In my happy buzz, I forget to turn off my phone, so it wakes me at eight a.m. I ignore it, rolling over to continue dreaming of Matthew, but also of hot guys in coffee shops.

The phone buzzes again, and again. Who would want to talk so early? Then my eyes widen. Is this about the dare? I do a quick inventory of last night's events. There should be nothing embarrassing in the latest video. Nothing.

Still, I hop up to check my phone.

The first message is from Sydney.

How could you?

Oh. I forgot I'd promised her no more dares. But wait until

she sees the shoes. Too bad she's two sizes larger than me; sharing them would quickly calm Syd down.

The next messages are from her too. They aren't pretty. But there's nothing about me being exposed or doing anything embarrassing, unless you count my ho-hum singing voice, so why does she care? Then I realize. She wanted to apply for NERVE. To really apply. My dares probably remind her of what she can't do, at least not this month. She has nothing to be jealous of, though. It's not like I plan to play in the live rounds. My dares were just for fun. Well, not fun, exactly— shoes.

I wait until after breakfast to text her back, including the image NERVE sent of me in the shoes. She responds with an actual call. Uh-oh.

When I answer, she shouts, "I don't care about your prize. You said you wouldn't play again. What if something went wrong? Something that I couldn't clean up as easily as your first dare?"

I pull a hand through my hair. "No one's asking you to clean anything up for me. It was just one more dare. You saw, no wet clothes or exposed body parts, and the guy turned out to be okay. Even if he hadn't been, Tommy was with me."

"You don't get it. What if they'd sent other players to harass you or do something really horrible? Remember what they did to that girl who had OCD?"

I shiver. "But that was in the live rounds. Look, no one got harmed. I earned some amazing shoes. Game over." I imagine her shaking her head on the other end.

"Sometimes, Vee, I don't understand you. It's like you're self-destructive or something."

Every muscle in my body goes taut. "Are you implying that I've ever tried to harm myself? You, of all people, should know how tired I was that night, helping *you* learn lines for the Christmas show, remember? For you to suggest that I purposely left the engine running is low, really low."

"I wasn't even talking about that."

"Sure."

There's silence for a long moment.

"Look, I've got stuff to do," I say.

She and I hang up without another word. Lovely, on the night of the closing show, when we should be planning for my first night of freedom, my best friend's ticked at me. How did she know about the dare so fast, anyway? Was she checking the NERVE site first thing in the morning or did they contact her the way they did some of my friends after the first dare?

I get online and find the section of the game site for "Advanced Qualification" clips, which are free to watch, probably to drum up interest for the pay-to-view live rounds. It doesn't take long to find mine. It has over a hundred comments. Really? The dare didn't strike me as all that exciting. I play the video, which begins with Tommy saying how lucky Ian would be to really get someone like me. Very sweet. The video's obviously been edited by NERVE, though, because the next part cuts to Ian, along with a voiceover by a female who describes what she'd like to do to him. In graphic detail. Is this commentary by the girl who came in behind him? Were they together, or did NERVE assign her to be his Watcher?

The video moves to the part where I sing. I wince at how scared I appear. But I do have a certain quality on camera. Something that makes me look really, I hate to admit it, innocent. Maybe it's because I come off as so petite next to Ian. Speaking of camera quality, the guy looks like something out of a movie. Could his bone structure be any more defined?

I read through the comments under the clip. Dozens of girls beg to sign up as in-person Watchers if NERVE chooses Ian for the live rounds, even though it costs triple of paying to watch online. Sure, the in-person Watchers can win prizes if they capture enticing video shots, but the odds of that seem slim.

The rest of the comments break down by gender, with guys writing about how cute and terrified I look, and girls claiming how they would've made a much better partner for Ian. That guy has some serious groupies.

Well, best of luck to him on getting selected tonight. As I send my mental good wishes, a NERVE ad pops up with LOOK WHO'S PLAYING! alongside video clips of the first players they've chosen for the live rounds, in two venues: Washington, D.C., and Tampa. A few minutes later, another pop-up announces LOOK WHO'S WATCHING! with photos of people who've already signed up to be Watchers, either online or in person. Guess even the audience wants its moment of fame.

Now that I've participated in a couple of dares, I'm tempted to watch too, and probably would, if it weren't for the plans I already have for tonight. NERVE will be around next month and the month after. But I want to be with Matthew now.

Time to log off of the computer and get on with my day. In between math homework and sketching ideas for fashion design class, I bake three different desserts to bring tonight. Still, the hours drag.

The second five o'clock hits, I'm in my car. When I arrive at the theater, I'm soon busier than ever with everyone's makeup. They all want to look fabulous for closing night. It's weird when I get to Syd. She's all cheery, joking with the crowd around us, but I'm sure I'm the only one who notices that she barely makes eye contact with me. And when someone mentions how cool it is that I completed another dare, she quickly changes the subject.

Thanks to another fat bouquet, the room is thick with the scent of peonies, but Syd won't reveal the admirer who sent them, despite nagging from the other girls. The second I apply her false eyelashes, she rushes from the room.

Matthew quickly takes my mind off of her, though, resting his hand on my bare knee as I apply his makeup. He wants to play my NERVE videos while I work, but I scold him to stop wiggling.

He holds up another NERVE ad. "They started a live round in Austin. Bet you would've looked great in a cowboy hat and spurs. Feel daring tonight, little Vee?"

"I don't plan to dump any more water on my head, if that's what you're getting at." Which I hope he isn't, because I love this vintage brocade jacket and silk mini. Too bad I had to wear these dumb soft-soled flats for my backstage duties; boots would've been way cuter. Still, I've completed the outfit with a *True Blood* T-shirt, and the Jimmy Carter campaign button I found at an estate sale adds a perfect eclectic touch. Not that guys appreciate well-crafted clothing ensembles. Or Jimmy C.

Once Matthew and the rest of the cast are made up and costumed, I wade through the actors and crew, most of whom pat me on the arm or give me high fives for completing two NERVE dares. Their good cheer reminds me to savor the glory of closing night, where every moment hovers between a bittersweet nostalgia and a giddy sense of accomplishment. Maybe Sydney and I can make up before the party. Especially if I apologize.

For the third night in a row, the play proceeds without a hitch. Guess all those months of practice were worth it, although soon that work will amount to nothing more than memories on video clips.

During Act Three, I stand at the side of the stage, breathing in the scent of old wood and trying not to bump into the dusty velour drape. Peeking around its edge, I spot familiar faces in the audience. Liv and Eulie came for another show. To the far right, I think I catch my mom's profile. Yep, there's Dad next to her, eyes darting around the theater like maybe he thinks I'll tumble from a balcony.

I mouth the familiar lines along with the actors, the last time I'll recite them, except at parties, when the drama geeks show off. Finally, an hour and thirty-two minutes into the show, Matthew and Syd draw together, a melding of lovers that the audience has anticipated for three acts. He takes her face in his hands as she gracefully arches her back. Their lips tremble and slowly come together. A woman seated in the front row sighs. We all do, vicariously savoring that kiss.

One thousand, two thousand, three thousand, four thousand, five thousand . . . What the heck? Endless seconds tick by, but their embrace only tightens with far more intensity than what was called for in the script, lasting eons beyond the length of their previous kisses. A small flame sparks in my chest. Sydney lets Matthew's hands press so tightly onto her body that I bet they leave marks.

I run a finger up and down the frayed curtain rope, tempted to yank it and bring the show to an early close. The theater's so rickety it would be seen as an accident. But, of course, a girl like me would never cause a spectacle like that.

Sydney and Matthew finally release each other with a lingering gaze and move into their duet, which will grow into a full-cast finale. Actors push past me, taking their marks on stage. Sydney's chest swells with the high notes of the song, until all that's left is the echo of melody, followed by hearty applause. Biting my lip, I close the drape.

While the cast members take their bows, I rush outside onto the iron fire escape. At least it isn't raining, which is a springtime miracle in Seattle.

This is not how I foresaw spending closing night. After all the costume coordination, hours applying makeup, afternoons rehearsing lines with Sydney until I knew her role as well as she did, and the three desserts I baked for the party? The one who deserves long lip-locks with Matthew tonight is me.

I slump onto a step that feels like ice through my silk skirt, turn on my phone, and change my ThisIsMe status from *promising* to *open for ideas*. I also post: **Karma does not apply to me.**

I should just leave now. Forget about the stupid party and my first night of not being grounded. My so-called best friend couldn't bear for someone else to take part of her spotlight, could she? It's not like my dares made Syd shine any less brightly. No one else received two bouquets of flowers. Were they from Matthew? Does she feel the same way about him? I mean, that embrace. There's acting and then there's the real thing. My mind spins. Could they be a secret couple? It hardly seems possible that the friend who sprained her wrist defending me in fifth grade from a bully who teased me about my real name would deceive me this way. But that kiss.

The door opens. Is it Sydney coming to apologize?

Tommy blinks rapidly. "What are you doing out here?" He sits on the step above me, smelling like pine trees.

I glance up at him. "Needed some air."

He smiles. "Yeah, air is good."

"Don't you need to be supervising the set crew?"

"Nah, strike-down isn't until tomorrow."

"I should send out another reminder for everyone to get their costumes dry-cleaned. No one better return anything smelly."

"Or what?"

I rest my chin on my hand. "Maybe I'll hang the grimy clothes from their lockers along with a gas mask or something." Yes, the play included gas masks.

His eyes crinkle. "Not what I'd expect from a sweet girl like you."

"Sweet is highly overrated." So is responsible, loyal, and every other adjective you'd find scrawled in my yearbook.

He gives me a quizzical glance.

Through the partially open door, bits of laugher float outside as the cast makes its way to the dressing rooms. I've set out jars of cold cream and tissues so they can clean their faces, but I'd bet a week's pay from my job at Vintage Love that most of them keep their makeup on through the party because they like the dramatic cast of their eyes and the chiseled cheekbones I gave them.

I shiver in the April cold and feel a headache coming on. Watching my best friend publicly throw herself on my guy-of-interest has blown my emotional circuits, leaving me in a numb state.

Or maybe just a stupid one, since the next words out of my mouth are, "So what do all you guys see in Sydney anyway?" Actually, this question qualifies as beyond stupid, not only because it makes me look like an insecure loser, but because the answer is obvious: her ability to make anyone feel important in ten seconds flat, her blond-bombshell hair, and a body she shows off to its fullest with clingy knits and low-rise jeans. Not to mention the corset she wore for the last act of the play, which she'll keep wearing until someone pries it from her, ribbon by ribbon.

He squints. "Uh, not all guys go for her type. Some of us prefer girls a little less, uh, obvious." He blushes.

Does he think petite girls with a fondness for retro clothing are non-obvious or invisible? It's not as though I don't try to add an edge.

The door behind us bangs open hard enough to shake the stairs. My heart does a handspring.

Matthew's face is flushed and he's already rubbed off half of his makeup. Or someone's rubbed it off for him.

"Hey, little Vee. I've been looking all over for you."

"Really?" My voice comes out squeaky.

He laughs. "Reeeeeallly."

Tommy's eyes go into orbit.

I get up and brush at the back of my skirt. "What's up?"

"I was wondering if we could go someplace a little more private."

My heart threatens to stop. "Uh, sure." I resist the urge to pump my fist.

Matthew takes my hand and pulls me inside.

"See you later, Tommy," I say as the door clanks shut behind me.

We wade through clusters of cast members posing with family and friends who've come to shower congratulations. The air is thick with the scent of cologne. For a second, I think I see Dad, but quickly lose sight of the gray buzz cut. Must be someone else's father. Why would Dad come backstage anyway? To say, "Hey sweetheart, great costume coordination"? I mean, this is my night to be free. Surely they'll cut me some slack.

Matthew leads me over to a small closet at the end of the corridor that doubles as a dressing room in a pinch. It's empty. Before I realize what he's doing, he picks me up by the waist and spins me around like a sugarplum fairy.

I laugh, feeling all floaty.

He sets me down and taps my nose. Suddenly, we're back

in our delicious zone, where we've been dancing for the past few weeks. I didn't imagine it. Maybe I misjudged the stage kiss between him and Sydney. They were in character, after all.

My heart thumps rapidly. "You did a great job tonight."

"Thanks to you and the rest of the crew." His arm slides around my shoulders and he leads me to the mirror. "You were like a little angel, flitting around, helping us get into costume. And the food you brought looks amazing."

I sit on the counter as he sinks into the chair. Will he pull me into his lap? The thought makes me tremble.

He takes my hands. "Could I ask for one more little favor?"

"Sure." Wish I'd put on fresh lip gloss.

He points to his cheek. "I accidentally messed up my makeup. Could you redo it? Syd says it makes me look rugged, and I think it'll be cool for the party."

My shoulders droop. He wants a touch-up? To stay in character because Sydney thinks it ups his macho factor? I sit there staring at him.

He points to my makeup box, which he must have brought in here before he found me. Since when has he ever been so prepared? He taps my knees like bongo drums. "Just the basics, you don't need to go into a lot of detail."

I take a breath and stand, trying to calm the rising flush of disappointment. "Sure."

I whip open the box, grab a pencil and some contouring powder. As soon as I start, he takes his hands away from my legs. I sharpen his jawline and nose, and then get to work with the eyeliner. It isn't until I'm halfway done with his eyes that I let the hard questions seep into my brain. Has Matthew ever really liked me? The way I like him? Or am I just a way to get closer to Sydney?

I dig my pencil into his eyebrow, which makes him flinch.

"Sorry," I say. The slash mark gives me an idea. I'm tempted to give his new makeup a subtle shift. There's a fine line between looking ruggedly intense and psychotic. I can make it so the other girls at the cast party feel a shade of anxiety when they gaze into his face. My hand begins to draw the brows a little closer together. But something holds me back. The same thing that never lets me create a scene or get into a confrontation. Holding back tears, I give Matthew the glowering, sexy eyes he wants.

I toss the cotton swabs in the trash. "All done." Is there any possibility we'll return to the flirty magic? I take a seat in front of him, noticing a smudge on his collar that could be lipstick or rouge.

He slides his chair around me so he can examine himself in the mirror. "Great job, Vee! You're the best."

I feel anything but the best as I watch him admire himself. When he gets up, he gives me a playful poke on the shoulder. No thank-you kiss. No fairy lift.

As he heads out of the room, I call out, "Did you send Syd the flowers?"

He stops short with a satisfied expression. "Her ThisIsMe page says roses and peonies are her favorite. They still are, right?"

"Well, if it's on her page, it must be true." I slam the makeup box shut.

"Great. See you at the party." He rushes off.

The last thing I want to do is party. This evening officially sucks. The sooner I get out of here, the better.

I hurry to the props area, where I left my purse. A thick crowd swarms between me and the door to the auditorium, so I decide to head out via the fire escape. As I pass the girls' dressing room, Sydney laughs, a star in the midst of her many admirers and all those stinking peonies. I don't have the energy to push through the crowd or deal with the scene she's sure to cause if I tell her I'm not hanging around for the cast party. Sooner or later she'll figure out that I've left. Probably later.

I rush outside in a race against the flood of tears that threaten to spill over. When I'm on the fire escape, I take a big, hiccupy breath. How could I let Matthew lead me around like a love-sick puppy?

The door creaks open. Aw gee, did he smear off his makeup again?

Tommy peeks out. "I'm not stalking you, promise. But you didn't look so good in there."

I run a finger under my eye. "I'm okay."

He comes outside again. "You want some water or some-thing?" Maybe he thinks we non-obvious girls are fragile.

I force myself to think of Comedy Central shows to keep the tears in check. "I'm fine." As a way to avoid eye contact, I pull out my phone, even though I just checked it a few minutes ago.

My knees go weak when I see my latest text. NERVE is doing a live round in Seattle.

And they want me.

With trembling shoulders, I read the rest of the message. "Oh my God."

"What is it?"

"NERVE chose me! They're doing a live round here."

"That's crazy!"

"I know. I've got ten minutes to give them my answer."

He shakes his head. "You saw how they terrorized the players in the last game. Ever hear of PTSD? My cousin has had it since he got back from Afghanistan. No prizes are worth that."

I rub my hand along my hip. "I agree. But you know a lot of the scary stuff has to be faked, like the special effects in the play. I mean, do you think that guy who played last time was really trapped in a dark elevator with a rat? I'll bet they would've let him out if he wanted. And that rat was someone's pet, guaranteed." I bite my thumbnail. Why did I immediately go into defending NERVE?

"His fear looked real to me."

"It's supposed to. But it's not like they can ask you to do anything overtly dangerous or illegal. They'd get sued."

Tommy groans as if I'm a moron. "If they'll never ask players to do anything shady, why are the owners totally anonymous?"

"They're probably based in the Cayman Islands, for taxes or something."

His voice takes on an urgency. "I don't think you realize what you're up against. It's not like you have to be the girl with the dragon tattoo to dig up personal data on people. They'll use it against you."

"I have nothing to hide." Well, if you don't count my little hospital stay. But even NERVE can't access confidential health records. Besides, I'm tired of being ashamed of something I shouldn't have been ashamed of in the first place.

He nods toward the door. "C'mon, let's just go to the party. You can sing your version of the school song."

I pretend to throw my phone at him. He ducks. From beyond the partially open door, the voices of the cast float out, reciting highlights from the play and laughing. Sydney's and Matthew's voices carry louder than the others, of course. I move past Tommy to kick the door shut.

His voice goes soft. "I know that maybe your feelings got hurt tonight. But that's no reason to turn into some femme fatale."

If only. "It just would be fun to do something totally un-expected."

"You already have. Twice. And look how upset you got when things went wrong the first time."

"But last night wasn't so bad. I won stuff."

"Those dares were preliminary. In the live rounds, thou-sands of folks pay to watch from all over the world. You think they'll be satisfied with you getting your shirt wet?"

"Well, let me see what they're offering, at least." I check my phone. Sure enough, NERVE has dangled the first prize. Whoa, it's a full-day makeover at Salon Dev, including a massage, waxing, makeup consult, the works. Best of all, I'd get a haircut from the owner, who's impossible to see if you aren't a local celeb. As if that weren't enough to have me drooling, NERVE sends an image of me in that cute sundress I checked out on the Custom Clothz site the other night. My image has the correct body proportions this time, and it's not bad, even in an almost-B cup.

Goose bumps rise on my arms and legs, partly because of the amazing prizes, partly because of Tommy's words. This much loot will come with hefty expectations.

I move to the creaky handrail to consider my options. In the alley below, two crows hop onto a nearby Dumpster. Why does Seattle have so many crows? Don't birds like warm weather? The wind picks up, sending the birds on their way and leaving the air around us hushed.

Tonight is my first night of not being grounded since I pulled into my garage last November and fell asleep listening to my favorite song list. Since then, Mom and Dad have seen me as a frail being who tried to do something unthinkable, no matter how many times I've tried to tell them otherwise.

At least Syd believed me. Or so I thought. The story everyone else got was that I'd had a serious case of the flu that sent me to the hospital. For a while, there were rumors going around, but by the time I got back to school, everyone had moved on to the love triangle taking place on the football team.

All anyone cares about is the latest drama. Tonight I have the opportunity to replace my old drama with something new. If only I knew whether that meant something better or worse.

I stare at my phone. "You're a smart guy, Tommy. Probably the smartest one I know. I appreciate your advice."

"So you're turning them down?"

"No way. Game on."

five

Two minutes after I send my acceptance, NERVE responds with a description of the first live dare. As I read the message, my breathing quickens. Instinctively, I shift the phone away from Tommy.

> WELCOME TO THE LIVE ROUNDS, VEE!
> YOU'LL HAVE THE OPPORTUNITY TO WIN
> LOADS OF GREAT PRIZES. AND WE'RE
> PARTNERING YOU WITH SOMEONE YOU'VE
> MET BEFORE—IAN!

That cute guy from the coffee shop will be my partner? Not bad.

> SO, HERE ARE THE COMPONENTS OF YOUR
> FIRST DARE:

DITCH YOUR BOYFRIEND.

The screen flashes with Tommy's picture. Hmmm, maybe their research isn't as thorough as I feared. But boyfriend or not, the idea of heading off without my unofficial partner makes me queasy.

- DOWNLOAD AND RUN THE ATTACHED APP. IT WILL PROVIDE YOU WITH A SPEEDY LINK TO THE GAME.

- MEET IAN AT PACIFICA BOWLING LANES IN TWENTY-FIVE MINUTES.

- GO INSIDE AND ASK TEN GUYS THERE FOR A CONDOM.

- LEAVE WITH IAN, SINGING THE FIRST VERSE OF THE SONG BELOW.

On the slim chance I'm Amish or live off the grid, they include the lyrics of a song about getting laid, which plays twenty times a day on the radio. Okay, most songs on the radio are about getting laid, but this one is the most explicit.

Tommy leans against the wall. "So, what is it?"

"Um, I'll be doing a dare with Ian."

"He's your partner?" His voice cracks on the last word.

"I'm sorry. They really should've teamed me up with you. Too bad you didn't apply."

76

His eyes shift away and he swallows. "What's your dare?"

"I don't know if I'm allowed to say."

"Technically, I'm not part of the crowd or a Watcher. Besides, no one'll know."

I tell him.

His expression remains neutral, but there's a hardness in his eyes. "Well, at least let me go with you. It would be crazy to meet him alone."

"I kind of have to." I show him my phone.

His jaw tightens the way it did when Ms. Santana, the drama coach, tried to slash his budget for set construction. "You're too smart for this."

"It's not like I'm taking off with the guy. The bowling alley's a public place."

He takes out his own phone. "I'm signing up as a Watcher."

"You don't need to spend money to keep tabs on me."

He shrugs. "I would've signed up anyway. Cast parties don't interest me much."

"You sure? Matthew's planning to add an extra ingredient to the punch." Ms. Santana isn't known for her chaperoning skills, and I think Tommy could have some fun if he loosened up.

He sighs. "Just be careful. Promise?"

"As long as you promise to only sign up as an online Watcher, not an in-person one, otherwise you'll get me disqualified."

He nods. "It's a deal. Remember, you can quit whenever you want."

"Of course. The minute anything sounds sketchy, I'm out."

There's no time to determine whether it's hope or doubt flickering across his face. I hustle to my car and check the driving directions NERVE sent along with the dare. I also start downloading the app they gave me. It's too bad Tommy can't join me to discuss strategy. But the dare seems straightforward enough. Of course, so did the water-dumping one. A tremor goes up my spine with the memory of that cold fabric plastered to my chest.

I try to take my mind off of the upcoming mission by tuning in to a hip-hop playlist. But it only makes my heart pump faster. Twenty minutes later, I pull into a parking lot full of SUVs and mini-vans. Ian's next to the front door, shuffling his feet. Heh. It's only fair that he had to wait for me this time.

I check the lot for Watchers. Shouldn't we have a few to record us? Maybe they're on their way. No reason to hold off getting out of the car to greet my partner, though. When I reach him, I notice a sign on the door that says: "WELCOME PURITY PROMISERS!"

"This dare just got a lot harder," I say.

He shrugs as if he expected this. "Just remember, the dare says we've got to ask. It doesn't say anything about waiting for an answer."

Why didn't I figure out that angle? I'll need to step up my game if I want to win anything tonight. "Good thinking."

He taps my Jimmy Carter button. "I met him once at a Habitat for Humanity project."

Wow, a guy who notices accessories and helps the homeless. See, Tommy had nothing to worry about. "So, how long should we wait for the Watchers?"

"Why wait? We can film this ourselves. The NERVE app includes a video chat link to use."

I check my phone, which now has a little NERVE app, front and center in my faves section. As instructed, I run the program, which displays my darc, along with a video chat button and a little status bar that reads: TASK NOT BEGUN.

I say, "The camera on my phone is a piece of crap."

"No worries. You can just open the link to catch some audio as a backup. We'll use my phone for the main video. How about I film you first, before we get them too riled up, and then you do me?"

I thank him, glad for his consideration, but twinging at the thought of what riling people up entails.

A pink-cheeked girl and her boyfriend stroll past us on their way inside. They giggle and hold hands, their shy glances suggesting they haven't had their first kiss yet, which makes me feel worldly in comparison, although I haven't gone much beyond the kissing stage myself.

My shoulders tense. "I feel like a jerk. These kids'll think we're teasing them. They don't deserve that."

Ian takes a deep breath, staring inside. Then he types into his phone. After a minute of reading, he says, "The studies they've done on abstinence programs show that the most successful ones are those that don't disparage safe sex practices. So these guys should be aware of condoms. If they aren't, we'll be doing them a favor."

I shake my head. "Great rationalization."

"Look, it's just a dumb dare. Maybe they'll find it funny. We'll ask gently, okay?"

People our age should be able to deal with a couple of goof-balls asking for a condom. It's not like we'll be hurting anyone. Who knows, maybe some of them have heard of NERVE and will laugh along with us. One big happy joke.

"Ready?" he asks.

I nod before I can convince myself otherwise.

As we enter the fluorescent-lit alley, waves of shouting and giggling hit us, along with the aroma of French fries and the wood polish they use on the lanes. The place is filled with dozens of teenagers chaperoned by a handful of adults. Banners on the wall proclaim: "Save your best for marriage!" and "Mr. Right Now is NOT Mr. Right."

My heart throbs like a bass guitar; no, make that a banjo. Ian takes my hand, which does nothing to calm me, even though his skin feels warm and smooth. In the far corner of the snack bar, half a dozen video games blink and whir. Five husky guys stand around booming displays, aiming joy sticks shaped like rifles. I can get half of my quota if I ask each of them, and no one else will be able to hear what's going on, hopefully. I jerk my head in their direction. Ian leads the way.

When we reach them, Ian starts the video chat to NERVE. The guy nearest me, a huge blond with a buzz cut, raises his eyebrow.

I clear my throat. "Excuse me. Do you have a condom to spare?"

He puts his hands on his hips and sticks out his chest. "What?"

I say, louder, "I'm looking for a condom. Got one?"

"That isn't funny."

One down. I step over to a curly-haired guy at his side. "Do you have a condom I could borrow?" As if it's something you'd ever return after using. Yuck and double yuck.

The curly guy scowls. "Get lost."

"Not until I've asked your friend here." I lean toward a short guy biting his lip. "Gotta condom?" Before he can say anything, I ask the guys holding the joy stick rifles. They both point them my way, and the sound of a bowling ball slamming into pins pierces the air like a shot. I jump. Ian places a hand on the small of my back, which I swear sends a pulse of electricity through me despite my anxiety.

"Thanks anyway." I pant as we dart toward another cluster of kids.

A group of three guys and two girls sit around a table drinking sodas. Without waiting to formulate a plan, I tap the shoulder of the first person I reach. When he turns toward me, I catch my breath. It's a guy named Jack, who my friend Eulie has crushed on for months. Guess his presence here explains why she's never gotten anywhere with him. I think he also hangs out with Tommy in the video club. Please God, let him realize that I'm playing NERVE. Somehow, though, I suspect God won't be taking my side in this little escapade.

I rub my hands against my skirt. "Um, hi, Jack. So I was wondering if you could give me a, um, condom?"

His face turns crimson. "Why would you ask such a question?"

I fight the urge to cry. "I'm so sorry." Apologizing isn't against the rules, is it?

He squints as if examining me, shaking his head.

Ian grabs my arm and drags me to another table. "Don't stop to think about it. You're almost done."

He's right. I ask two more guys in rapid succession, not waiting for an answer. One of them stands and gets in my face. "This isn't funny. I think you should leave."

I feel like an ass as we move to the girls next to them. These kids haven't done anything to deserve our harassment. With shaky hands, I take the phone from Ian. "Go easy on them."

Ian addresses a girl with layers of blue eye makeup. "I don't suppose you have a condom on you? Not that you'd use it or anything."

"Get out of here, asshole!" she snarls. Is *asshole* on her approved vocabulary list?

"How about you?" he asks the other girl. When she screams no, we scurry from the table.

Eight down for me, two for Ian.

We approach another mixed gender group. Jack still watches me from his table, his brow wrinkled. I turn away from his gaze and blurt my request to two more guys, one of whom is the boy I saw walking in with his girlfriend earlier. She clutches his hand and wears a horrified expression. Have I ruined their date? I shout a quick apology and take the camera from Ian. That's ten. Why don't I feel elated? All I want to do is shout how sorry I am and run out the door. But, I can't. Not until Ian's met his quota. I aim the camera at him while he asks a tiny brunette. She squeals like an injured puppy, which summons the guys from the video game.

The big blond guy glares. "We've had enough of you two. Now get out!"

"We'll be going soon," I say. "Just a few more minutes."

Ian asks girls number four and five as the crowd circles us. The blond guy's face looks like he can't get enough air. Guess all that purity-promising doesn't include any stress-reduction exercises.

One of the adults, who's been eyeing us from the corner of the room, joins the fray. His hair is slicked back and his jacket's worth more than half of my wardrobe. Is he their leader or something?

The man puts an arm around Ian and says in a jovial voice, "What's going on here, kids?"

Ian jumps out of his grasp as if he's been scalded. "We're, uh, conducting an interview. And I'm happy to say that so far, your group is passing with flying colors."

The man scrunches his forehead. "Interview?"

Ian pushes through the crowd to another table with three girls. His olive cheeks have acquired a crimson edge. I follow as best I can with the camera, not sure if it's picking up his latest request, but the shriek from the tall redhead he just spoke to should be proof enough for the NERVE folks. He quickly causes similar yelps from the girl's two friends. Eight down.

The blond guy says something to the man with the expensive jacket, who just nods and smiles. What are they plotting?

Ian glances at me, shiny-faced and breathing rapidly. He runs toward a table near the door. The crowd follows, shouting very non-pure sentiments. I flash the camera their way and the blond guy makes a grab for it. His fingers just miss it as I tuck it down my bra. I stick out my chest, daring him to reach past the vampire fang decal on my T-shirt, praying he doesn't call my bluff.

He reaches forward and stops a few inches from my chest.

His neck is covered in red splotches that weren't there before. "Outta here, you whore!"

Well, I've never been called that before, but I'm not about to debate my love life with this guy. I hustle to catch up with Ian. He's asked another girl, but I didn't get it on video. Will it be enough for me to vouch for him? I yank out the phone and catch his next request.

"Ask one more girl," I yell.

"But that's ten," he says.

"One wasn't on camera."

He groans.

A female chaperone joins the crowd, waving her finger in Ian's face. "You should be ashamed of yourself!"

"I am, but could you spare me a prophylactic?" he says with a sweet smile.

The blond guy yells in Ian's face, "Show some respect, asshole!" He looks like he's about to blow.

I tuck the phone back into my shirt and wave my fist. "Hey, remember, thou shalt not murder!"

In answer, the blond spits in my direction. I scream as it lands on the tip of my shoe. The man laughs and pats the younger guy's back.

"You pigs!" I spit back.

The blond guy grabs my arms, squeezing them at the elbows. His breath is like gasoline, definitely an advantage to his purity maintenance.

Ian pulls at the guy's shoulder. "Dude, we're going now. Leave her alone."

The guy pushes forward. "You had the chance to leave your way. Now you'll do it our way." He drags me toward the door as the man with the slicked-back hair and a few other boys grab Ian. The crowd around us yells.

Jack tugs at the blond guy and shouts, "Just let them go. I think it's for a game."

Finally, someone's figured it out, but the blond guy shoulders Jack aside and keeps his grip on me. My arms feel like they're in a vise.

I take a deep breath and although the thought of what I'm about to do makes me want to curl up into a ball, I start singing the getting laid song. Jack stares at me in horror. Maybe Tommy or Eulie can convince him I'm really not so bad. If I survive.

Ian chimes in and we sing it at full blast as they push us out the door. A crowd has gathered outside too. Will we be able to reach the car without getting beat up? Someone shoves me hard from the back. I fall with a scream onto the asphalt, landing sharply on my hip. Ian tumbles next to me. We turn back toward the door and sing in shaky unison as it slams shut.

The urges to cry and laugh are equally strong. Instead, I keep singing to myself as if the song is a mantra that'll keep the hostility around us at bay.

Ian stands. "The dare's over. We did it."

He helps me to my feet with a gentle but firm grip on my forearms. Once I'm stable, I brush at my skirt. No rips, but a huge bruise will bloom on my hip tomorrow. Ian rubs his elbow, staring at me, probably because I haven't stopped singing.

He places his hands on my shoulders. "I said the dare's done. Take a deep breath."

I try to, but it comes out as a hiccup. "Sorry I didn't get us doing the song on video." I pull the phone from my bra and wipe it on my shirt before handing it to him.

He laughs and nods toward the parking lot. "You didn't need to."

In all the commotion, I hadn't noticed that the crowd outside is much friendlier than the crowd inside. As we face their direction, they applaud. Most of them point phones at us. They're in-person Watchers, all with direct links to NERVE.

Ian takes my hand and we bow. As the applause increases, so do my spirits. Even the pain in my hip fades. Suddenly, the dare doesn't seem as awful as it did a minute ago, the rush of having survived potent. I want to dance, to run around and holler.

A dozen Watchers, ranging from our age on up a few decades, approach to high-five us. I had no idea so many different types of people were into this game.

"We saw it from the windows. NERVE said we couldn't

go inside for this one," a petite woman wearing horn-rimmed glasses says. "Looked like those folks wanted to string you guys up."

I say in a loud voice, "Must be all that pent-up energy."

The crowd laughs, although what I said wasn't that funny. Still, their good cheer buoys me.

I make an exaggerated pointing motion toward my phone. "I hope you guys got good video of us getting thrown out." The more evidence the better.

Ian's still breathing hard, but smiling for the cameras, giving them every angle they ask for as if he's on the red carpet. I want to hug him for having my back in there. My heart beats like an athlete's, and the more the crowd cheers, the more pumped I get. This must be what fuels celebrities.

At Ian's prompting, we do a victory dance for our admirers, singing a few lines from "our" song. The people nearest us start singing too, and then those behind them join in until we're all howling and dancing. What a rush. I can't believe I'm having this much fun with a hundred strangers, especially when I consider there are another hundred strangers inside the building who want to beat me up.

In the midst of the din, I hear what sounds like a little kid yelling, although there aren't any kids around. Weird. I also notice my phone vibrating. I check it. NERVE has sent their congratulations. Ian and I hold our phones in the air.

The crowd chants, "Another dare! Another dare!"

Am I up for that? This one was awfully intense. Players can quit at any time, but no one left the game voluntarily last month, as far as I know.

The ruckus of the crowd fades in anticipation. Their stares send a thousand tiny prickles to my skin, yet we're connected somehow, like a creature with a hundred lungs that breathe in unison. I've got goose bumps, but laugh along with the crowd.

What do my friends think? Some must be watching. I pull out my phone again, only to find an empty display. No texts? From anyone? I try texting Tommy and a few other friends, but get an error message. So I try calling. Everything is blocked. Even access to my ThisIsMe page. Despite the crowd around me, I suddenly feel alone.

The sound of a kid's voice comes at me again, in a mocking chant. I finally realize that it's my phone. NERVE must've re-set the ring tone. And their message comes through without a problem. Lovely, their app provides a "speedy link," but blocks everyone else out. I should've guessed.

I read the message, which is basically a status report. Our audience is bigger than most of the ones they got on the East Coast and Deep South a few hours ago, so there'll be a premium with the next dare. All those people watching us? I look down at my chest to see if my shirt has ripped or gotten wet again. Nope, very modest.

Ian checks his phone too. "Looks like we're all kinds of popular."

Popular? Huh. Who's among our Watchers? Matthew? What does he think about little Vee now?

"Wonder what kind of prize they'll offer next," Ian says.

It has to be at least as tempting as the shoes and the spa day. Maybe a trip to New York? A girl can dream.

The crowd renews their chant, sending waves of warmth through me. Overhead, the neon casts a pastel glow on everyone.

Ian smiles. "You want to sit in my car while we wait for the next dare? It's right over there." He points to a gray Volvo two cars down. A sensible car, owned by a guy who helps build homes for the needy.

I nod. It'll be nice to get a little quiet time to focus. We wave at the crowd and get into his car. There's a delicious moment of silence as we close the doors.

"So, partner, we've completed a live round dare!" he says.

Hard to believe that we're still almost strangers. I examine his well-defined features. "So what does NERVE know about you that I don't?" Holy crap, am I flirting?

"Hmmm. A whole hell of a lot, I'm sure. Let's see. I'm a junior at Jackson Academy, eat way too many pretzels, and love long walks on the beach. How about you, Vee?" Saying my name causes his perfect front teeth to press into his perfect lower lip in a way that turns my legs rubbery.

"Junior at Kennedy, theater-crew geek, and I dream of making the world a better place." I give him the same pageant wave I gave the crowd earlier.

"What made you try out for NERVE?"

"Nothing special. Just wanted to do something out of the ordinary. How about you?"

He leans in close. "The prizes, of course."

Yeah, the prizes. "What did you win?"

"So far, some cash for the prelim dare, and a bus ticket for the last dare."

Is he messing with me? But why lie about a prize? I say, "A bus ticket? That seems kind of, I don't know . . ." The word I'm thinking of is *random*.

"It's perfect. I could use it to travel anywhere in the continental U.S. Anytime."

"Why not just drive?"

"Because then I'd have to steal this car from my parents." His face takes on a hard edge for a brief moment before he turns back to me. He smiles slowly. "We were lucky to escape that gang of vicious virgins." Two more *V* words—I want to lick my lips with the pleasure of watching him say them, even if I think his taste in prizes is unusual.

Before I can devise a way to make him say *victory* or *vivisection*, our phones go off in unison, singing *nah-nah-nee-boo-boo, nah-nah-nee-boo-boo,* in little kid voices that sound like something out of a slasher movie. It's the NERVE ring tone. And our next dare.

SIX

HOW WOULD YOU LIKE TO WIN THIS?

I click the link that shows the next prize—a premium phone loaded with all of the apps I could want plus a high-def camera, lightning-fast Internet access, and two years of unlimited service. Wow.

> YOUR NEXT DARE: GO TO THE AREA OUTLINED IN THE MAP BELOW. WALK ALONG THE STREETS INDICATED UNTIL YOU CONVINCE SOMEONE TO PAY YOU A HUNDRED DOLLARS FOR SEXUAL SERVICES. NO, YOU DON'T HAVE TO ACTUALLY PERFORM ANY TRICKS, JUST FIND SOMEONE WILLING TO PAY.

My stomach churns. I've got to act like a hooker? In that part of town? Yikes. They should provide me with a weapon and bulletproof vest. When my mom used to work in an office building a block away, she'd complain to Dad about the nasty stuff she'd find in the parking garage. He'd make jokes about how her company should advertise that as a perk and offer its employees extra coffee breaks along with "If the van's a-rockin'" bumper stickers. I've missed their joking around. Our house used to have a more buoyant energy, which evaporated, thanks to me.

I try to peek at Ian's phone, but he's holding it close to his chest. His face flashes in different colors under the bowling alley's neon lights, one second in gentle lavender, the next in harsh red.

The crowd outside also checks their phones for where the good times will be heading.

One woman, with tumbling red curls that remind me of the soprano in *Phantom of the Opera*, taps on Ian's window and shouts, "What's your dare?" She points at me. "Must be a good one, 'cause the little lady looks like she's going to upchuck."

Ian lets down his window and gives her an apologetic shrug. "Sorry. You'll have to wait until NERVE tells you." He shouldn't have to tell her the rules. Didn't she watch last month? Or maybe the in-person Watchers earn prizes if they get the players to break the rules, just like they can if they capture great footage. Geez, there I go with the conspiracy theories again.

We wave to our supporters—fans?—as Ian puts the window back up. One guy tries to block him, thrusting a phone forward. His flash causes me to see spots for a moment, but Ian manages to get the window closed and gives the folks outside a peace sign.

I fan myself with my hand. "Whew. They're like paparazzi."

"So what's your dare?"

"You first."

He leans his head back onto the seat. "I have to be charming in a pretty non-charming part of town. Charming enough to convince one of the working girls to offer me a freebie," he says. "Okay, now spill."

"If, hypothetically, I were to do another dare, I'd have to get someone to offer me a hundred bucks for my services."

He looks me up and down with a lazy gaze. "That would be a bargain."

"Thanks. I think." Then I frown. "But is it a bargain in that part of town? I mean, I can't believe someone would sell herself for any amount of money, yet if I'm asking for more than the going rate, this could be a really hard dare."

He laughs as he pulls out his phone. "The harder the better, as far as potential clients go."

I groan.

After a minute of looking up info on his phone, he says,

"Typical rate for a call girl is between one and three hundred. But for a street walker, we're talking twenty to fifty. So you'll be asking for something over the going price, but you don't look like a meth addict, so that'll help."

"Gee, thanks, partner." My stomach does a heavy flop. Then I remember the prize. A great phone without Mom and Dad complaining about the bill would be heaven. But am I up to putting myself on the streets to win it?

Ian tells me he'd win a set of deluxe camping gear. This guy definitely has a travel theme going with his prizes. His eyes sparkle brighter than the neon outside, and brighter still when NERVE sends us the bonus offer: For every thousand additional online Watchers who sign up, we'll each earn two hundred bucks. Whoa. How many folks will pay to watch us survive hookersville?

I say, "Our dares would be difficult to document without scaring the prostitutes and johns away."

"We'll just have to be discreet. So will our Watchers."

A few dozen of them, mostly in their late teens and early twenties, surround the car, hovering like zombies.

My phone teases me again. It would be worth quitting just to get my old ring tone back. When I see who's calling, I can't believe that NERVE let this call through. I answer before they change their minds.

Tommy says, "Are you okay? Looks like you got pushed pretty hard on the last one."

Wow, NERVE posted our video really fast, almost real time. They must not have edited our footage much. But why allow me to speak with Tommy? Is our call being broadcast? Maybe they want to see where I stand; that must be it.

"My hip stings a little, but I'll be fine."

"I can come get you now. I'm not far." Of course he isn't.

I take a deep breath. "Wait, Tommy, don't. We just got our next dares. I'm still deciding." From the corner of my eye, I catch Ian grinning.

Tommy's breathing comes out in gulps. "You're not seriously considering another dare?"

"It's for a great phone plus maybe some money. That may not mean much to someone with a trust fund and new car, but for me it's a big deal."

"You've already been injured. It's not worth getting killed for."

"Don't be overdramatic. They don't give you dares that'll risk your life. Just make it seriously uncomfortable."

"So what's the dare?"

"You signed up to be a Watcher, so I can't say." Is there any way to keep him nearby as my security blanket? If only we had a secret code so I could tell him our destination ahead of time without NERVE finding out.

Secret messaging reminds me of when Syd and I were in seventh grade and prepping for her audition for *The Miracle Worker*. We memorized both the Annie Sullivan and Helen

Keller roles, even going so far as learning to sign the alphabet, which turned out to be a handy skill for communicating during classes. I wish I could call Syd and let her know what I'm up to even more than I wish I could tell Tommy. Why did she have to go after Matthew?

Tommy's voice interrupts my train of thought. "Don't go, Vee. I heard rumors that one of the girls who won last time—" The call ends in a sheet of static. When I try calling back, it won't go through. Crappy phone.

Ian taps his steering wheel. "If you hypothetically keep playing, do you want to ride with me?" He snaps on his seat belt, which comforts me. Do psychotic killers buckle up? Besides, riding to that part of town alone in my own car strikes me as way riskier than riding with him. And with all these Watchers around, what's he going to do anyway?

"Sure," I say, answering not only the question of transportation, but also of my participation in the next dare. I can hardly believe that I've completed a live one, and here I am about to attempt another. Me, Vee, the behind-the-scenes girl.

Ian starts the car and we both give the Watchers a thumbs-up to let them know we're still playing. They cheer and head to their cars while I inform NERVE of my decision. What'll the game come up with next? Behind us, a bunch of horns honk, and someone's car stereo is cranked so high I can feel the bass.

Ian wrinkles his forehead. "Even though it would be cool to get someone besides us to document the next dare, these guys might cause more harm than good."

A guy outside moons his friends to loud guffaws. I see Ian's point, but ditching the Watchers means losing their goodwill. Last month, a player in the L.A. rounds kept flipping the bird at his in-person Watchers and they sabotaged his next dare, knocking him out of the game.

I say, "We can ask them to behave if they get too rowdy. Besides, NERVE'll be telling them where our next dare is sooner or later."

Ian has to swerve to avoid a girl doing cartwheels alongside us. "They're dangerous."

He races out of the lot and makes a few quick turns to separate us from the majority of the pack. A couple of cars screech behind us, but a dash through a light turning red loses them too. Who knew such a sensible-looking car could handle so well?

I understand his actions, but I feel as if I'm crossing a bridge where a cable has been cut. Did NERVE put him up to it, the way I had to ditch Tommy? If so, what else will the game ask him to do without telling me first?

I fiddle with my seat belt. "I'm not sure that losing our Watchers is such a great idea."

"Don't worry, it's only temporary." When he's made a few more turns to make sure no one's following, he turns on the stereo and says, "We'll give them some juicy footage to make up for it, I promise."

"There're a lot of people we'll need to make things up to after tonight," I say.

"Yeah. Sounds like your boyfriend's pissed." Is he saying that to determine whether I have a boyfriend?

"I'm sure your girlfriend wasn't happy about getting ditched either."

The corners of his mouth rise a bit. "I don't have a girl-friend." Hmm, good news is that he's available, bad news is that maybe he can't stick with a single girl.

"Well, Tommy isn't my boyfriend. And he doesn't under-stand why someone would put themselves out there for cool prizes."

"People born with buckets of money never do."

"How would you know, academy boy with a crazy-expensive phone?"

His face is hard. "I earned this phone. And the academy."

"Really? How? I want your job." Not that I mind working at Vintage Love. It's just the pay that sucks.

He shakes his head with a tight smile and turns up the volume on the player. The car vibrates. Okay, he doesn't owe me an explanation. It's not like I'm revealing my life history either.

I nod toward the car speaker. "Who is this?"

His jaw goes slack. "You've never heard the Rolling Stones? Mick Jagger? They're classic."

"I've heard of them, just not this song before."

"Then tonight's your lucky night."

Is he right? Is this my lucky night? Less than two hours ago, my best friend moved in on the guy I'd liked for the past month. Yet now I've won an amazing pair of shoes and a makeover. Plus, I'm riding with a smoking-hot guy. Granted, we're headed toward the skankiest part of town, where I'll pretend to be a hooker. And maybe get beat up. Or worse— everyone knows that prostitutes' lives aren't like *Pretty Woman* or *Gypsy*. But I'll just be pretending. So, all in all, my luck is probably breaking even.

We park a couple of blocks away from the area on NERVE's map, and I dab on some lip gloss while I consider my costume options. My outfit and ballet flats are hardly prostitute material, but maybe I can go for a slutty schoolgirl look. I pull down my T-shirt to let my bra straps peek out, hike up my skirt, and put my hair into pigtails with a couple of elastic bands I find at the bottom of my handbag. If only I had a lollipop.

Before we get out of the car, we decide that my purse will be safer in the glove compartment than on me, which makes my stomach twist even more about hanging out in this part of town. But at least I'll have my phone. No way I'm leaving that.

Outside the car, Ian points to my campaign button. "You might want to take that off. I don't think it's wise for people in the, uh, entertainment industry to take political sides."

"I doubt most of the guys out here even know who Jimmy Carter is, but you've got a point." I remove the button and stick it in my pocket.

Okay, time to get into character. Syd says it always starts with your posture. Trying to channel any diva genes I might possess, I strike a pose. "Hello, Seattle, new flesh for sale!"

Ian spends a long moment looking me over from head to toe. "Bet you get propositioned in ten minutes. Creepy guys strolling for prostitutes probably love gorgeous brunette, blue-eyed girls who look like they're in middle school."

"Um, thanks." The *gorgeous* and *middle school* kind of cancel each other out, but I think he meant it as a compliment.

I rub my hands along my thighs. "Wish I brought some more makeup, though."

He gives me a lingering gaze that sends shivers down my shoulder blades. "You know that prostitutes were some of the first women to wear lipstick?"

"Makes sense. They'd want to look pretty to attract clients."

"Sure, they used it to attract clients, but it wasn't so much about looking good as about advertising that they offered special services, of the oral variety."

"Oh." I squint at him. "First the abstinence research, then hooker pricing, now ancient prostitutes. I'm learning a lot of sex stuff from you tonight."

He pulls out his phone. "We can talk about non-sex stuff

too. Like, did you know there are cultures where they think having your picture taken steals part of your soul?"

"I thought that was an urban legend people tossed around when they were having bad hair days."

He aims the phone at me. "Suit yourself."

I give him my best supermodel pout while he takes my picture. How many photos of me does that make so far tonight?

He runs a hand through his hair. "Guess we'd better get started. It won't be easy convincing a busy lady to offer me a freebie."

With those dark eyes and knowing smile, I bet he's used to receiving tons of offers. "You'll be great."

We move briskly, which suits me fine, partly because it's chilly, partly because I hope to ease the jitters in my chest. Still, I have to work to keep up with his long strides.

When we reach the main avenue, he slows to a stroll. "Why don't you walk ahead of me? I'll keep the video chat open to NERVE. Stay under the streetlights as much as you can."

That's all the plan we come up with for now. With a wink and a wave, I'm on my own, sashaying my hips in an attempt at a boldness I don't feel, especially with the icy air numbing my butt cheeks. The sidewalks swirl with people from all parts of society—frat boys carrying bottles of beer, couples arm in arm, grizzly guys in five layers of clothing who ask passersby for "food" money.

The college boys laugh and burp. Charming. As they

stumble by me, I cross my arms over my chest and look away. Working retail has taught me how to distinguish a potential client from a looky-loo.

"Hey, baby, how much?" one them calls out.

"More than you could afford," I snap, getting into what I hope is a streetwalker groove. Although I've helped Sydney rehearse parts from Liesl in *The Sound of Music* to a ninja princess in a *Crouching Tiger* tribute, she's never played a hooker, so I don't have much to draw upon.

I strut away as the college guy's friends taunt him. Fortunately, he doesn't follow me in an attempt to prove his manhood.

I'm so focused on the boys that I don't notice I'm in the path of two girls, one light-skinned, wearing Day-Glo colors, the other dark-skinned, wearing metallic. Both look my age, except for eyes that appear more tired than my mom's. Their skimpy camisoles reveal mounds of jiggling flesh to the icy night air, causing me to shiver in sympathy.

The one in Day-Glo snarls, her gold tooth flashing. "What're you doing here?"

"Just walking." I pull my jacket tightly around myself, covering what was supposed to pass for cleavage, but now seems like wishful thinking.

The girl in metallic points a finger at me. Her nails must be an inch long, painted in a dark shade. "That's all you best be doing." She and her friend move in closer.

I try not to imagine the damage their claws could do, but it's hard not to envision jungle cats disemboweling their prey. This dare sucks. Even more than the last one. But I'm not totally alone; Ian has to do a difficult one too. That's when I get an idea.

I will myself not to take a step backward, the way the rangers teach you to do at Yellowstone if a bear sniffs around your campsite. When the girls are almost within striking distance, I say, "There's a musician who's supposed to be here after his concert tonight. Maybe you've seen him?" I try to smile, girlfriend to girlfriend.

The lighter-skinned girl licks her lips. "Musician?"

I bounce in my flats, all groupie-like. "Yeah. His name is Ian, uh, Jagger. His dad is in the Rolling Stones? They're an old rock band? So it's like father, like son. Cool, huh? Anyway, Ian's band had a show in Seattle tonight. I saw on his fan page that he'll be looking for company afterward and he mentioned a bar near here. You know The Flash?" That's the name of the club where arrests occur every weekend, right? I have to take a few breaths after this speech to avoid hyperventilating.

The girl scowls. "Why would he go to a lame-ass place like that?"

I scan the street and do a theatrical double take when I spot Ian about twenty feet away. "Oh my God!" I rush up to him with the girls jingling close behind.

I grab his arm. "Ian Jagger! I love, love, love your songs!" My panting doesn't need to be faked.

Ian hides his surprise with a big smile. "Thanks, sweetheart."

The girls, reeking of perfume and cigarettes, push me aside. How do they expect to attract business smelling like that?

"Hey Ian," the darker-skinned girl says, "I'm Tiffany. You really famous?"

Ian shrugs and smirks in perfect rock star style.

The other girl announces that her name is Ambrosia. "Damn straight he's famous. I recognize his face from the magazines."

This is going better than I thought it would. Does Ian realize what a huge favor I'm doing him? And how much he'll owe me in return?

He gives an *aw shucks* smile that brings out those killer dimples. "We're only in town for the night. Don't suppose you know where I could go for a little fun?"

"Oh, I could show you some fun, baby," Tiffany says.

Ian passes me his phone. "Hey, princess, can you get a shot of me and these lovely ladies? My label likes to see what I'm up to in different cities."

I take the phone and point it. "Sure, but I can show you more fun than these girls, and I won't charge anything."

Tiffany balls her fists as she takes a step toward me, "Who said anything about charging, bitch?"

Bingo. "Sorry, I just assumed . . ."

Ambrosia, hands on hips, stomps forward too. "Don't assume nothing, slut."

Ian steps in between the girls and me. "Hey, forget about her. So you both wanna hook up with me? No strings attached?"

Tiffany says, "Sure. You gonna post our pictures on your fan site?"

He smiles my way. "Your faces will be all over the Web. I promise. That's why I gave the scrawny-ass girl the camera."

They both give scrawny-ass me a triumphant look down their noses and ask Ian where he's staying and whether they can order room service.

That's when a huge white guy wearing a fedora approaches us. A fedora? Is he kidding?

His hands are shoved deeply in the pockets of a trench coat, which really should have a leopard collar if he wants to complete the look. "Tiff, Am, this guy giving you any trouble?"

Tiffany and Ambrosia almost trip over themselves scurrying to the guy. Each girl takes one of his arms and whispers in his ear.

He frowns at whatever they're telling him. "I've never heard of no Ian Jagger."

I hold the camera at my chest, hoping the guy doesn't notice me. His eyes narrow in Ian's direction. He pushes the girls aside and approaches him. "I said I never heard of you."

Ian shrugs. "We play mostly emo."

"Homo? You play homo music?"

"No, emo. It's kinda punk, kind of angsty."

He keeps approaching, hands still in pockets, stopping a couple of feet in front of Ian. "You play like a punk, huh? Where'd you play tonight?"

Ian swallows. "At a small venue. You probably never heard of it."

"I asked, where'd you play, Ian punk homo Jagger?"

The guy moves a step closer to Ian so they're only inches apart. Ian swallows. I keep the video going even though I think we've got what we needed. It's like I can't get enough. Tiffany and Ambrosia huddle behind their pimp, exchanging wide-eyed glances that make them seem years younger.

The pimp says, "Seems like you were interested in spending time with my girls." His voice has gotten lower.

Ian smiles. "We were just chatting. They're awfully pretty."

The pimp pulls one hand out of a pocket to rub his stubbly chin. "That they are. Tell you what, I'm fun to chat with too. Why don't we walk a little, and chat?"

"That sounds cool, but I should get going. My band mates are probably wondering what happened to me."

The pimp whispers, "I ain't asking."

Ian glances at me with a helpless expression. The camera is slippery in my hands. I'm tempted to tuck it into my pocket before this guy takes it from me, but don't want to lose this footage.

"Stay here," Ian says to me.

For the first time the pimp flicks his eyes my way. "She with you? Cute. She can come too." He nudges Ian's elbow.

I don't know whether to follow or run the other way. He can't chase us both at once, but he could send Tiffany and Ambrosia after me. I dart my head around looking for someone to call out to.

At that moment, a cluster of twenty-somethings appear from around the corner. One of them points at us, and the rest pull out their phones.

The Watchers have arrived.

All around us, people shoot video of Ian and me.

As the crowd approaches, the pimp's forehead furrows. "What the hell?"

Ian waves toward the Watchers. "Looks like I've been spotted by more fans. I should spend some time with them, you know?" He heads into the densest part of the swarm.

I back into the group, recognizing a number of them from the bowling alley. Surprisingly, no one seems angry about us ditching them. And I don't mind all their cameras in my face this time. We move down the street amidst cheering and questions.

"You'll see everything when NERVE broadcasts it," Ian says to the crowd. He takes the phone from me, and, with a laugh, films our Watchers as they film us.

The pimp and the girls stare after us with puzzled

expressions. Tiffany's crying, like she missed out on some-thing big.

I feel like crying too, in relief. The good cheer of the Watchers envelops me like a shield. A big, rowdy, beautiful shield. With them, I am somebody. I am safe.

Seven

I jostle next to Ian. "Okay, now you can take a bus ride to Kentucky or Kansas or anywhere U.S.A. and go camping."

He laughs. "That was great what you did with those girls, even if it almost got us mugged. Lucky I've still got my phone."

The Watchers surround us, high-fiving Ian.

He accepts their congrats. "I promise you guys the video will rock, thanks to my amazing partner! Now, you need to give her a little space so she can do what she needs. Otherwise, show's over."

They seem disappointed, but agreeable, staying on their side of the street when we cross over and move to the next block, out of Tiffany and Ambrosia's business territory, I hope. Now I have the lovely prospect of finding business of my own.

Ian strolls to a place advertising "Live Ladies Lusting Lavishly." Guess that even with a million porn sites on the Net, some guys still want that face-to-face, nasty cubicle experience. Which is good for us, since it provides a brightly lit patch of sidewalk that extends almost thirty feet.

The line of guys eye me, but no one approaches, even when Ian waves them over. We decide that maybe they want to talk man to man or some such BS. I stroll near the curb, facing traffic, one hand on my hip, the other dangling at my side. As each car passes, its lights temporarily blinding me, I give a pressed-lip smile as if I'm about to say "prune" and stick out my chest. I'm wearing twice the amount of clothing as Tiffany and Amber combined, but I've never felt more naked. From across the street, hints of laughter travel through the night air. The Watchers had better behave or I'll never complete this dare.

When I've covered a block, I turn around to walk slowly back toward Ian. He's chatting up the guys in line, pointing my way. My very own pimp. The potential customers, or so they think, stare at me, smacking their lips, but shaking their heads. What's their problem? Maybe from a distance they think I'm a skinny tweaker who's wearing long sleeves to hide her needle marks. Or maybe the clothes and shoes tell them I'm not really in business. Guess I'll have to convince them. Ugh. Even though my stomach feels like it's tightening into a knot that'll never be untied, I head toward the guys. Thankfully, the Watchers have the good sense to quiet down.

The closer I get to the peep show parlor, the more I detect a sour odor, like cabbage soup. With an inward groan, I realize it's coming from the men. Did Ian have to pick the stinkiest pervs on the street?

Ian motions to me. "Come here, Roxie."

Roxie? Is that even a name? "Uh, sure, Stone."

He grabs me by the wrist like he owns me. "These fellows don't believe you'll be worth the money."

I chew on my lip. "They might be right. This is my first night out, and I'm pretty nervous."

A flabby-faced guy leers at me. "You never done this before? Well, that explains the strange clothes."

Strange? I'm insulted, and then flattered. Who'd want to fit in here?

"It's all I could afford," I say, sniffing. "Party clothes are awful expensive." I stare down at my poor non-hookery flats. In the distance, a siren wails.

The guy scratches his armpit. "I'll give you fifty, but that's all I got, and it's more than what the girls around here normally ask for."

I raise my head and make doe eyes at Ian. "I'm not sure I can do this, even though Mama needs that operation really bad. Let me get some air, okay?" This last bit is actually true. If I don't get away from this smell, I'll faint.

"Sure, sis." Ian pats the top of my head and goes back to negotiating with the guys, like a good brother should. I make another trek along the curb.

A few couples pass me by, all with the same expressions, a half smile and quickly averted eyes from the guys, a huff of contempt and a longer stare from the girls. Don't they realize that I'm one of them? Shoot, the last girl who frowned my way was wearing the same T-shirt as me.

I can't take this personally. It's role playing that has nothing, nothing to do with real life. I force a smile at the next couple to walk by and am shocked when they return it. Then the guy runs to my side and puts his arm around me.

"Hey," I say, trying to squirm away from him.

The girl takes our picture while the guy tugs at one of my pigtails and whispers, "You're doing great, Vee."

I slap him away. "Hands off, you creep."

Ian races to us and threatens to beat the crap out of the guy, but he and his girlfriend just laugh and hurry off the way they came. When Ian starts to run after them, I pull him back.

I take a deep breath. "Forget about them. We need to focus on the dare."

He seems torn, but, after a few seconds of considering it, listens to me. "If you see any more stalkery Watchers, holler, okay?"

I agree and get back to work. Within minutes, a car slows

down and pulls to the side of the street, right next to me. Inside is a middle-aged guy with thick eyebrows.

He grins. "You seem kind of young to be out here by yourself. Look at you shivering."

"I'm old enough. Just cold."

"My car has heated seats. I could give you a ride."

I stand there, waiting for him to continue. Please, someone, be capturing this on video. I'd try it with my lousy camera if I didn't think it would scare this guy off.

He taps the steering wheel in time to a disco song. "So, you want to come in?"

"Um, you're cute, but . . ."

Ian passes by, his arms folded across his chest so he can hold the camera raised without it looking like he's filming. He takes up a position at the rear of the car. Hopefully anyone passing will think he's a pimp looking out for his girl.

The guy in the car doesn't seem to notice Ian. He rubs his cheek. "You need food money? Maybe I can help."

"Yeah, I'm hungry." I draw out the *hungry*.

He grins. "How much do you eat?"

I want to hurl then and there, but manage to get out, "A lot."

He laughs. "Small girl, big appetite. Like twenty bucks' worth?"

I open my eyes wide. "Um, like five times that."

His smile disappears. "Greedy little thing, aren't you?"

I rub my hand along my waist. "No. Just someone who's willing to work hard."

He raises a caterpillar-y eyebrow. I don't want to imagine what's flashing through his brain. "You're awfully adorable, but I can't go that high. It's against my policy."

As if guys trolling for underage hookers have policies. "That's too bad. Hope you have a nice night." I strut forward.

He puts the car in reverse, causing Ian to scramble back. "You think you're hot shit, huh?"

I can see that this won't go well. "No."

He yells, "Bitch!" and hits the engine, blowing exhaust until he stops up the street, next to a girl in five-inch studded boots.

My knees feel rubbery. First the hookers and now this guy. I can't remember being called "bitch" twice in the same night before, or even the same month. My bottom lip quivers.

Ian comes up to me and squeezes my shoulder. "Don't let him get to you. Just a prick who didn't get what he wanted. We'll get this done. You'll see. In the meantime, we're getting some great video." He heads off to take up a position nearby.

I swallow in frustration and watch the girl in studded boots chat with eyebrow guy, lots of nodding and smiles. With so many hookers willing to work for less than a hundred, how am I ever going to find a client? Obviously, NERVE calibrated this dare for difficulty. What did I expect for a new phone with icing on top?

After a couple of minutes, the girl trudges around the back of the car to get to the passenger door. As soon as the guy can't see her, her face goes blank. What's she thinking? That this isn't her real life, just like I've been telling myself it isn't mine?

Suddenly, I feel tired, wishing I could go home, take a hot bath, and go to bed. I check my phone as I walk. No new messages. NERVE must still be blocking them. Don't they realize I need moral support?

I'm about to ask Ian for some change to use a pay phone so I can connect with a friendly voice, assuming I can find a phone that's in working order and not covered in something disgusting. But another car slows down, its Mercedes symbol stopping just behind me. The window lowers next to a clean-cut guy in his thirties with neat sideburns and boyish features, the kind of man who shouldn't require the services of a streetwalker. Whatever revs your Harley, I guess. He rests an arm so it sticks out the window, showing off a huge watch worth more than my car.

"Hey," he says, revealing glow-in-the-dark teeth.

I take up a spot just out of arm's reach, and jut out my sore hip. "Hey, yourself."

"You don't need to be out here, you know."

I wait for him to add how I should come in and take advantage of his car's toasty seats.

Instead, he says, "Whatever problems you have that make

you feel this is your only choice, are problems you can solve another way. Especially if you let someone help you."

"Someone like you?"

He smiles. "I was thinking of someone a little more powerful."

Whoa. "You mean a three-way?" If he offers a hundred for an orgy, will that satisfy the dare?

His lips pull back in a mask of disgust for a brief moment before he recovers his smile. "I was referring to a higher power. My wife and I run a ministry to help girls like you."

I fight to stay in character. "Girls like me? You don't know me."

"I know you need someplace where you can feel safe. If you're open to enjoying a home-cooked meal and having the opportunity to chat with other young women who've been in your shoes, you can get off the streets right this minute."

I glance toward Ian as he passes us with his camera raised. "That's really nice, but I'm okay."

The guy in the car tracks Ian with his eyes, leaning out to stare at him when he takes up his normal filming position in what should be the guy's blind spot. There must be a higher power taking care of this guy if he's been staring down real pimps on a regular basis.

He speaks to Ian. "Are you the one responsible for this young lady's welfare?"

Ian shrugs. "We're friends."

The guy holds out a hand. "Good to hear. Because I want to take her someplace safe, where she can be helped. I'm sure you won't mind, friend."

I wave. "Uh, hello? I mind. Look, thanks for your concern, but I'm fine. This isn't what it seems. We're just hanging out."

He shakes his head without a hair shifting out of place. "Sad to say, many young women out here are harmed most severely by men who claim to be looking out for them, their so-called friends."

I point across the street. "If you really want to help someone, there are a couple of girls named Ambrosia and Tiffany who could use it. But their friend seems kind of dangerous, so be careful, okay?"

I march away, pulling at Ian's arm until we're on the next block. The guy stares after us, but finally drives off.

Ian shakes his head. "All kinds of crazies out here."

"He didn't seem crazy, and I hope I haven't sent him into harm's way." I rub my temples, unsure of whether I've done something noble or idiotic.

Ian takes my shoulders. "You aren't responsible for anyone out here except yourself, and, if you want, me."

Too bad the girl in the studded boots went off with the eyebrow guy. She looked like she could use a little hope. Once again, I'm thankful that for me this is just a game. Which reminds me.

"Guess it's time to get back to the dare," I say.

He winks. "Yeah, we can save the world after we win our prizes." He saunters off, leaving me alone once again. I gaze across the street at the Watchers, wishing I'd get a glimpse of Tommy, even though he said he'd sign up to view the game online only. Is he still looking out for me, or did he go home in disgust?

I amble back and forth while Ian tries to hustle guys on foot. A few more cars stop alongside me, but it's always the same story—I'm asking too much. As the fourth car in ten minutes roars away, I can't help feeling rejected, even though they're the losers who have to pay to get laid.

Another round of haggling goes by before a Ford Taurus pulls up. I sigh and wait for the negotiation to begin.

A soft-faced guy opens the window. "You alone?"

I bite my lip. "For now."

"Me too. Loneliness sucks, huh?"

I nod. Is hooker talk always so inane?

He taps the edge of his door. "What would it take for us to change our alone statuses?"

"A hundred dollars."

He raises his eyebrows. "My, oh my. What would I get for that much?" He hasn't called me a greedy bitch or driven off yet. A good sign.

I run a finger down the middle of my chest. "What would you want?"

He gives a low chuckle as his gaze slides over me. "A lot."

I glance around, catching Ian's eye as he passes us with his phone out. I turn to the guy in the car, smiling as Ian takes up his filming position.

I bat my eyelashes. "So is it a deal? You'll pay a hundred?"

"Anything I want?" His lips are plump and shiny, like he licks them a lot.

"Mm-hmm."

A hairy hand emerges from the window to stroke my skirt. I fight the urge to vomit.

He presses a button to unlock the passenger door. "Then it's a deal. Why don't you get in already?" He leans away to clear a box from the seat. As his body shifts, I see something flash in his breast pocket. Oh geez, was that a badge?

"Look, sir, I was just kidding. Sorry for any confusion." I hurry toward Ian and yell, "Run!"

Behind us a door slams.

"Get back here! Freeze!"

The crowd across the street erupts into whoops. We sprint in their direction, dodging cars. The frat boys double over in laughter and the others nearby hold out phones. But none of our fans are going to protect us this time. Ian and I head south and keep running. I doubt any of the Watchers are dumb enough to chase after us. Not with a cop waving his gun as he jogs across the street.

Ian and I turn the second corner. My feet are killing me. Ballet flats have lousy arch support.

I pant. "I'm not sure I can keep up this pace all the way to the car."

Three doors down is an alcove that Ian pulls me into. I instinctively hold my breath, afraid of what smells lurk in such an obvious place for winos to spend the night. Although it's musty, the odor I fear most is absent. We huddle in the shadows, Ian against the wall, me in his arms. Half a minute later, footsteps approach, and the cop huffs by, cussing to himself. Behind him are two boys in athletic jackets, giggling and filming him. Okay, someone was dumb enough to follow.

Ian's heart pounds hard against my cheek. Neither of us moves a muscle.

"Come here!" The cop yells to the boys.

By their footsteps, I hear that they're following orders; even the laughter stops. He demands their phones, probably hoping to delete whatever footage they got before it ends up online. Too little, too late, dude.

As they march past the alcove, one of the boy's eyes get wide like he spots us, but instead of ratting us out to save himself, he hangs his head. The cop also glances our way, squinting, but keeps going. I don't dare breathe until their footsteps are far in the distance. When I do, I notice Ian's scent—like mountains on a late summer hike. I take another long breath of him.

"I think we did it," he whispers.

"Amazing." I look up into his face, although I can barely make out his features.

He strokes my jawline with a finger. "Ian Jagger, huh?"

"Don't you want to be a rock star?"

"Out there, you were the rock star." He pulls me in closer, as if that's possible.

Is he going to kiss me? I barely know this guy. But we've faced all kinds of danger together already. That has to count for something. And he seems to have my back. That counts for something more. Okay, maybe his attention is just part of the game. But that tingle along my spine sure feels real.

He moves his finger from my jaw to my lips, gently tracing their outline. We stand there breathing each other's air, feeling each other's pulse.

A light goes on inside the building, causing me to jerk away from our clinch. The thick glass door next to us reveals a tiny foyer with a shabby sofa and a row of mailboxes. A white-haired man limps down a stairway, leaning on an ornately carved railing.

"Recess over," I say, with all the disappointment of a second grader heading back to class.

We tiptoe down the steps, peek both ways to make sure the cop's gone, and trot to the car with our fingers loosely laced. It isn't until we get inside the car that we discuss my dare.

"Think it'll count?" I ask.

"Hell, yeah. An offer's an offer, whether it's from a cop or not."

I hope he's right. As we wait to hear from NERVE, we sit there grinning at each other. Hard to believe that earlier this evening I was sulking behind a dusty curtain while I watched my best friend backstab me. And now? Prizes, fun, and maybe cash. But most importantly, a smokin'-hot guy who's eyeing me like candy.

I love this game.

eight

Ian starts the engine and turns on the heat. Outside, it's begun to rain. Do the girls on the street carry umbrellas, or does rain not even factor into their complaint list? Maybe the drizzle helps wash away the stench of their clients. I rest my cheek against the seat, content not to be running or shivering or negotiating with horny older men.

Ian adopts the same position as me, so that we're face-to-face, less than a foot apart. "So how far do you want to take this?"

Is he talking about the game or something more? Even though the evening has been exciting so far, it's not like I'm eager to subject myself to whatever the NERVE dare-makers, which I suspect are really a roomful of greasy guys eating cheeseburgers, come up with next.

But the words that come out of my mouth are, "I don't have to be home until midnight."

He brushes a lock of hair from my forehead. "We could have so much fun in the next fifty minutes."

My insides melt into latte foam. Fifty delicious minutes. Or wait, is he talking about the game?

"Fun is good," I say, hoping he'll elaborate upon what he's thinking.

Keeping his eyes on mine, he slips off his jacket and shifts closer. Heat emanates from his body, drawing me in. I run a hand along his shoulder, amazed by how solid he feels, and more amazed that I reached out to touch him without a second thought. Maybe the game is altering my risk-taking DNA somehow. The drumming of rain on the car roof gives me a tingly, under-the-covers sensation. Settled inside this cozy space with Ian is good. Really good.

So, naturally, this is the moment our phones blast with trumpet music. My head almost hits the ceiling. Never thought I'd miss that creepy kid ring tone. I open my phone, not because I care what it says, but to stop the noise. The message from NERVE is packed with exclamation points.

"Holy shit," Ian says as I read.

My thought exactly. Not only have I earned my new phone, but the audience grew by seven thousand Watchers, which tacks on fourteen hundred dollars of bonus money. I feel faint.

In addition to my winnings, NERVE allowed incoming messages to go through. A dozen each from Liv and Eulie, first with condolences (IT'S MATTHEW'S LOSS), then with amazement (IS THAT REALLY YOU?), then with congratulations (OMG! OMG! OMG!).

I can't wait to hash over every detail of my night with them, the way I normally would do with Sydney.

Still, it's weird there aren't any texts from her or Tommy, even WTF ones.

As a test, I select Tommy's number and press it. His voice comes through harshly. "Are you okay? Why didn't you call me back sooner?"

Crap. I should've just texted him. "NERVE blocked my phone as part of the game. You're the first person I'm calling. You'll never guess how much bonus money I've won."

His exhalation fills my ear with static. "Better be a ton after what they made you do. Seriously, you know how many people get shot in that part of town? And if you get arrested, you'll have a criminal record."

The rain outside intensifies, with a rumble of thunder. The hip I fell on outside the bowling alley starts to ache again. "I didn't actually do anything wrong. It was all just pretend."

"You trolled for johns, negotiated a deal, and resisted arrest. Good luck proving you were only kidding."

I laugh. "Congrats on earning your Law and Order degree." A nagging stitch in my side tells me he's right though.

"Hey, you've won some stuff and had your fun, so you're quitting while you're ahead, right?"

A ripple of lightning flashes everything around me blue for a second. "Yeah. It's getting late anyway."

"Good. I'm glad you're going home before things get even more dangerous. I don't trust that Ian guy."

That Ian guy strokes my fingers like a mini harp. Every hair on my arm rises in pleasure. His caresses work like some kind of magic acupressure, calming the pain in my leg.

Oh yeah, I'm still on the phone. "Ian's been great. I'll see you tomorrow morning to help strike down the set, okay? Thanks for being my wingman on the prelim dares. I owe you. Bye, Tommy, you're the best." I clap my phone shut before he can nag me any more.

Ian frowns. "I thought I was the best. You two-timing me already?" His mouth curls upward.

Mmm. He's feeling we have enough of a connection where "two-timing" is even worth mentioning? He bites his lip in a way that makes me want to bite it too. If he's playing me, he's good. And why would he want to play me anyway? We're on the same side.

My phone rings with a rock song I recognize from a cop show. Seems like I can't get away from the Rolling Stones tonight. Weird that Ian's phone is silent.

When I read the next message, my face scrunches up.

His eyes widen. "What is it?"

I try to make sense of what I'm reading. "This dare's, um, different."

"How?"

The warmth of the car dissipates. Telling Ian about this dare means explaining some stuff about myself. Behind-the-scenes second banana to Sydney kind of stuff. Once he sees the real me, this fairy tale will end.

I swallow. "It has to do with my real life."

His harp playing moves from my fingers up my arm. Sweet music. "As opposed to this, your fake life?"

"Not fake, just more like surreal, you know?"

His gaze is steady. "The dares are a game, but everything between them isn't. Not for me, anyway."

"For me either. What I mean is that this time NERVE wants me to mess with people who aren't strangers. And for some reason, the dare doesn't mention you."

He shrugs. "I'm sure they'll come up with something for me. So what do they want you to do?"

I stare out the windshield. "To go to the auditorium where we had a school play tonight. I did the makeup and costumes. Anyway, I need to go to the cast party and confront a friend about something, and then I have to add a negative critique on her performance." The last bit just seems silly and cruel. But what I really can't get my head around is how NERVE knew I was mad at Sydney. Who told them? Liv and Eulie? Did they think they were helping me?

He slides his hand down my arm. "Doesn't sound too bad compared to what else you've faced tonight. Those hookers could've scratched your eyes out. Your friend wouldn't do that, right?"

I consider it for a moment. "Nah. She's more about drama than violence." I exhale loudly. "But this dare feels harder. It's one thing doing obnoxious stuff in front of strangers. These are my friends." Which in theory should actually be easier, but nothing about this dare feels easy.

His hand is smooth and warm against mine. "I get it."

Does he? It's hard to imagine him flustered or tongue-tied in front of his friends. Although he did seem nervous when that pimp wanted to take him for a walk. Who wouldn't?

"You going to tell me what the confrontation is about?" he asks.

I sigh. "A guy. But it's ancient history." Surprising how fast my feelings for Matthew have faded.

He raises an eyebrow. "Will this confrontation be leading to a catfight? Please say yes. I'll pay you myself."

I hit his arm. "Don't get your hopes up. This guy's not worth it. I told you, ancient history." Nothing like one hot guy to get your mind off of another.

"How ancient?"

I check my phone. "About three hours."

We both laugh.

His own phone buzzes. He reads with a puzzled expression.

"My dare's in two parts, but they only sent the first one, where I get to be basically a prop for your dare."

"What do you have to do?"

"Flirt with the hottest girl there."

My heart sinks. Another coup for Sydney. How did NERVE know the best way to ruin my night? Confronting Syd while Ian flirts with her would be my own custom-tailored hell. I grimace. Then I realize that it's only hell if I decide to go through with it.

"Well, the dare doesn't matter anyway," I say. "I'm quitting."

He sits upright. "Why? It wouldn't be dangerous. You'll get to see your friends. And I'll be gushing over you the whole time."

"No, you'll be too busy flirting with the hottest girl there." And she'll be lapping it up.

He places a hand on each side of my face. "The hottest girl there will be you, no question."

I study those succulent lips. "You haven't met my divali-cious best friend, Sydney, star of the play and every other event at my school." There, now he'll begin to see the truth. My admission is the first crack in this dream façade we've constructed, more temporary than any of the sets Tommy built for the play.

His gaze grows intense. "I've met you. And I promise, you're way more enticing than any drama queen. Flirting with you will be the easiest dare ever."

"Ha. You make it almost sound tempting."

"You should know all about being tempting." He pulls one of the elastic bands from my hair, and then the other as he leans forward, slowly. An electric buzz shimmers across my skin as our lips meet. His mouth feels as luscious as it looks. I could drown in this guy. So I do. All sense of time is lost as we press into each other. He tastes like berries, the kind you can't get enough of. My body aches in all the right spots. I can barely catch my breath when we part.

His voice is husky. "C'mon, Vee. This dare will be all about you. I'll do whatever it takes to make you shine in front of your friends. Drama girl will be forgotten by the time we're done there."

As if Sydney's someone you could ever forget. She's always been larger than life, back to the first day of kindergarten, when she arrived wearing a tiara and peacock feathers. All the kids wanted to play with her, but she chose me as her confidante, the quiet girl who color-coordinated her outfits with her pencils and erasers. I wore a lot of yellow and pink in those days.

But that year and every one since then, I continued to feel special that she singled me out, and valued my opinion. Not that she doesn't value her own opinion more. She always claims to be an excellent judge of character and that she knew from day one we'd be friends for life. I've accepted her friendship gratefully, not caring that everyone sees me as her sidekick. She may be emotive and bossy, but she's always been loyal. Until tonight. How could she have turned on me?

I study Ian's perfect cheekbones. He responds by running a finger along my temple that sends a yummy tremble through my core. Who knew that such a light touch could feel so good? What a rush it would be to show up at the theater with someone who seems to be so into me. For once, I'd be the one with the prize. The image is too delicious to ignore.

I calculate. We could make it to the auditorium in twenty minutes and be out in another ten. With luck, I'd make it home by curfew. And if not, maybe Mom and Dad will have fallen asleep watching a late-night news show.

Ian smiles. "If I complete the first part of my dare, the prize is a gift card to Gotta-Hava-Java. You wouldn't want me to miss out on that, would you?"

"I'm sure the barista would welcome you with open arms."

"Welcome us. You'd be my date."

A date. The future. Sounds so magic. His mention of a prize makes me realize that as soon as I'd spotted Syd's name in my message from NERVE, I'd skipped over the link to what I'd win. Taking a breath, I open my phone and check.

My jaw plummets. "Oh wow, if I do this dare, I'll get a shopping spree at my favorite clothing store. With a three-thousand-dollar limit." That would buy a whole new wardrobe. Still vintage, of course, but way less frugal, and way more flashy—no, not flashy, noticeable. And why not? I'm the girl who's completed two live dares tonight. People will see me differently when I return to school on Monday.

He shifts closer. "There's no downside, baby."

God, I'd do the dare just to keep hearing him call me "baby."

"But I've never confronted Sydney before. Not like this." I wring my hands, unsure of how to continue. "Most of our arguments are no big deal, since she usually gets her way. When we get really mad at each other, she goes all reality show, crying and stomping, and I get quiet. But we always make up. And we've never fought over a guy." I don't add that there isn't a point. Sydney snags whatever guy she wants, regardless of what anyone else thinks.

"She sounds spoiled. And whatever guy you were fighting over sounds brain-dead."

I laugh. Would Matthew be jealous if I walked in with Ian? It would serve him right for leading me on the past few weeks. Sydney would understand my desire to teach him a lesson. And she should respect me for calling her out on going after someone I was interested in, even if this is a dramatic way of doing so. Then again, who better to appreciate drama than her? Maybe tonight will be a turning point in our friendship. One that makes things a tiny bit more equal.

With visions of patriots demanding justice, I say, "Okay. Let's do it."

He guns the engine. "Vee, Vee, Vee," he sings, narrowing his eyes, "is so very . . ."

"Very what?"

He gazes at me, boring into my soul, it feels. "Very very. That's what you are. Very, very, verrrrrrry." Those *V*s. Those lips.

"You're very very yourself."

At the stoplight, he pulls me toward him, giving me a reminder of how very very he is. A car behind us honks when the light turns.

Quicker than I would've thought, we're at the parking lot. There are at least a dozen cars, but not Tommy's. He must have been watching and worrying about me from home. Hopefully, if he's still watching, he'll understand. How was I supposed to know that NERVE would throw me a dare like this? Come to think of it, what's the appeal of this dare to the audience? It's not like random Watchers can crash the party. Ms. Santana may not be much of a chaperone, but she'd kick strangers out in a heartbeat. Maybe NERVE has put together a whole long fairy tale about how much I like Matthew, but now I like Ian too. The audience will think they're witnessing a love triangle. Awkward, since Ian'll be the one videoing it, but if that's how NERVE wants to spend their money, fine with me.

Well, maybe not so fine. Now that we're here, I'm having second thoughts about Ian seeing Sydney. When has a guy ever paid more attention to me than her? What if he can't help himself?

He turns off the engine. "The rain's eased up. We should run in before it pours again."

No time to weigh the options. The more I think, the more likely I am to chicken out. And I'm sick of that. I bite my bottom lip so it's plump and red, the poor girl's makeup. Pulling our jackets over our heads, we exit the car and jog through the drizzle.

"Showtime, beautiful," Ian says, grabbing my hand.

I force a smile and take a deep breath. And another.

Yeah, showtime.

nine

We enter the main auditorium door and wipe our damp faces with our sleeves before heading farther inside. Dance music blares alongside yelps of laughter. As we enter the main hall, Sydney, still dressed in a corset snug enough to asphyxiate most mortals, flits around the stage with the male cast members, gay and straight, following in her wake. They dart behind a scrim that Tommy designed and I helped paint. Depending upon how the gauzy drop was lit during the play, the view from the audience shifted between an arctic meadow and the stark tableau of an interrogation chamber. Right now it's in meadow mode, with Sydney featured as its most colorful butterfly.

I wrap my jacket around me like a cocoon and watch Ian watching the actors. Is his gaze lingering on Sydney?

When she catches my eye, she jumps down from the stage. "Veeeeeee! We've been rooting for you!" Despite four-inch heels, she dashes up the center aisle and almost knocks me down with a hug so tight I feel the bamboo slats in her costume.

Huh? If she was mad after my dare last night, she should be furious now. Maybe this is just a public show of support for her best friend. Which is hard to believe after the public betrayal with Matthew.

She pulls away, her eyes on Ian. He puts one arm around me and extends the other, introducing himself.

She laughs and holds up her phone. "Of course I know who you are. We all do. Did you see the grand prize rounds in Chicago? One guy just swam in fish guts."

She motions to Jake, a guy almost as small as me, who holds up a tablet. Someone sloshes around in the video, and I swear I can smell rancid fish. As soon as the clip is over, an ad floats across the screen. It's an image of a girl who's also swimming in something gloppy, only it's green and she's gasping. A pop-up replaces her photo with one of another girl wearing pigtails and a vampire shirt, shying away from two girls in shiny hot pants. Oh my God.

I point to the screen. "I don't believe they're using pictures of me to promote the game."

Sydney howls at my reaction. "Believe it. So why are you guys here? Is the game over? Did you decide not to risk everything you've won on a grand prize round? They just started one in Colorado."

Ian moves his arm lower and squeezes my waist, a move not lost on Syd. "We're kind of in a wait-and-see mode. Your makeup looks fantastic, by the way."

She strokes her cheek. "Yeah, Vee's very talented."

He presses his face momentarily to my hair. "Yes, very."

She cocks her head as if maybe she didn't hear him correctly.

Part of me wants to savor the moment; part of me wants to get this over with. Now. Ready or not, I open my mouth. "Um, Syd, there's something we need to discuss." I wish I could tell her that this is part of a dare.

Her brow furrows. "Like why you decided to keep playing NERVE? I think I understand." She winks at Ian. What's with her? Does she think we'll put in a good word when she applies for the game next month?

He ignores her and pulls out his phone like he's checking for messages. He glances at me and gives me an air kiss, never shifting his gaze to Syd for a second. I think I'm in love.

Sydney stands there with a blank look. Has a guy ever ignored her before?

"So, Syd—" I say.

From the back of the theater, a door slams.

Tommy marches through the main entrance. His eyes shoot me like lasers.

A wave of guilt threatens to swallow me. I give him a weak wave. What's he doing here?

He raises a serious-looking camera in front of his face. It has a microphone boom attached to the front like a rhino's horn. Oh geez, he must be our official Watcher.

I turn toward Ian, but he stares at his phone with a stunned expression. Then he swallows and says, "Just tell her what you need to. Fast."

I clear my throat and say to Syd, "I agreed to play in the live rounds because I was mad at you."

She puts a hand to her chest. "Me?"

I can't help feeling a little sorry for her. My behavior and Ian's must be causing her to question reality as she knows it.

Tommy stops next to us so that Sydney and I are in frame, beneath the microphone boom. A red light on his camera pulsates like an angry heartbeat.

Sydney squints. "What are you doing, Tommy?"

He raises a finger to his lips.

I grab Syd's arm. "Let's go back to a dressing room."

She resists. "What's this about? Why were you mad?" Her voice has risen a few decibels.

Does she really not know? "I'll tell you when we have some privacy."

Tommy grunts. "If you wanted privacy, your boyfriend wouldn't be broadcasting this."

Sydney's forehead tightens. She grabs at Ian's phone.

"You're filming us too? Is this is a dare? You're doing this for another dare?"

Ian pockets his phone, but instead of answering Syd, he glares at everyone in the room, as if daring them to stop me.

I try to finish this awful mission. "Look, Syd. I just need to say something really quick, then we'll be gone." I tell myself this isn't an invasion of her privacy. Not that she's ever cared much about privacy. Her ThisIsMe page is filled with bikini shots.

I say in a low voice, "I was mad because you came on to someone that you knew I was interested in."

"Louder," Tommy says. "Your audience can't hear you."

Sydney crosses her arms in front of her chest, which only gives her more cleavage. Now that she knows she's on stage, there's no telling where things will go, except that she'll end up looking good for her audience. Wait a minute, it's my audience.

The faster I get through the dare, the more likely I am to survive. Or at least not faint. I'm already seeing spots. "You know I liked one of your costars." I glance at Ian, hoping he noticed I used the past tense, but he doesn't seem to notice me. His face is filled with pain.

I continue anyway. "But you threw yourself at him during the last act tonight. The script said kiss, not maul."

Syd's eyes go wide. "Are you talking about Matthew?" Her well-trained voice carries across the theater.

"What about me?" Matthew says, jumping down from the stage. When he joins us, I notice three different shades of lipstick on his cheeks and the aroma of at least that many perfumes. The guy's a freakin' petri dish.

I put my hand up toward him. "Nothing about you, Matthew."

Someone has turned off the music. Ms. Santana? Where is she, anyway? And where are Liv and Eulie? They'd stick up for me, I'm sure. Everyone else stares at us, and a few point their phones. Even Jake, the one kid who sometimes helps me with costume design, holds up his tablet to film the scene. I should be used to this kind of attention tonight, but the camera glares burn like hot pokers on my skin.

I turn toward the crowd. "Okay, back to partying, you guys. This'll all be posted soon enough."

No one moves.

I rub my palms against each other. "Anyway, that's all I wanted to say, Sydney. I'm leaving now. Oh, and you over-emoted during the interrogation scene." That should satisfy the dare. And now that I've done it, I'm not super-mad at her anymore. Who cares about Matthew?

She grabs my arm. "I'll show you emoting. You just accused me of betraying you. I didn't think you were still seriously into Matthew, not after all my warnings." Her cheeks have gone scarlet, which would look hideous on anyone else, but highlights her amazing bone structure. "You've accused me of some dumb-ass stuff before, but I would never stab you in the back. Didn't you notice how hard Matthew grabbed me on stage? I couldn't get away. See this bruise?" She points to her arm.

Matthew wouldn't let her go? His grasp was awfully tight. And just because he might be the one who gave her flowers doesn't mean she reciprocated. Oh boy, have I messed up. I back away. "Uh, sorry. Look, we'll talk about this tomorrow, okay?"

She lunges forward. "No, we should talk now. That's what the cameras are for, after all." Her hands are on her hips and she towers a good seven inches over me, thanks to those stupid stilettos I chose for her costume.

The theater has gone silent. When I glance around, faces and phones observe me with the glare of a jury. Hell. I've screwed up big-time. Sydney stands there, statuesque, radiant, indignant. As usual, she prevails.

"I'm waiting for an explanation, Vee." She taps her foot.

Everyone else seems to have assumed the same stance. I swear they're tapping their feet too. The theater thrums with accusation. Once again, I'm the wannabe, only now my second-rate status is there for thousands to witness, no longer hidden behind the curtain.

Time seems to stop. How can I reverse it to the delicious moments in Ian's car, before he witnessed this utter humiliation? Too bad Tommy's ticked off at me too. If anyone could invent a time machine, it would be him.

As a last resort, I shake my right hand at my side to get Sydney's attention. When she looks at it, I use sign language to say, *Sorry. Really. Let me go, okay?*

She watches my hand, her eyes softening. Will she give me a break? She's got to understand why I thought what I thought, why I did what I did. Who knows me better? And always wants to protect me?

I hold my breath and sign, *Please.*

Her head snaps up. "You owe me an apology. Now."

I just apologized in sign language. Does she want to publicly humiliate me? Of course she does. Payback. How did things end up so backward? A hotness fills my chest. "I have to leave."

Her eyes fix on mine. "Again? After you've betrayed me and provided your expert critique on my acting?" She shakes her head. "You should've cleared things up right after the play. Off camera. You didn't even stay long enough to say hi to your parents."

My breath catches. "My parents?"

She tsk-tsks. "Yeah. They were incredibly proud. Until they found out that you left without telling any of us where you were off to. Nice job, Vee."

I can imagine my parents' faces. It had taken a lot for them to let me out of their sight tonight. And I was eager to show them they had nothing to worry about. How could I let them down? And how could Syd bring them into it? This is the worst dare. If I hadn't signed up for NERVE, I would've been here for my parents, shown them that everything truly was back to normal. But I've blown it all for a phone and a new pair of shoes. Tears of frustration and rage begin to spill down my cheeks.

Ian steps forward. "You assholes happy now?" Without warning, he springs toward Jake and grabs his tablet. "Turn this thing off before I pound you."

I reach for Ian's arm. "Jake's okay."

Ian shrugs me away and breathes into Jake's face. "Get out of here, runt."

Jake scurries backward, looking like he'll burst into tears. He stumbles into chairs on his way to join the rest of the cast on stage.

Ian grabs my hand. "C'mon."

I don't want to join him when he's acting like this. But staying here, where everyone's eyeing me like a criminal, seems even worse.

As we march past Tommy, he puts down his camera. Deep smudges have formed under his eyes. "Another fine performance."

I glare at him. "I hope they're rewarding you well for your little film production, Tommy."

He grunts as he fiddles with a cord. "I got what I wanted."

Something prompts me to pause and say, "Look, for the record, when I spoke with you, I honestly thought I was done with the game, but they offered me this one, and it was too juicy to resist."

His face bunches up. "If this is what you call juicy, you aren't the girl I thought you were."

I'm not the girl I thought I was either. I don't know what I am. Except for the person following Ian out of the theater with her head hanging.

Sydney rushes up to us when we've reached the lobby. Has she had a change of heart?

But she breathlessly announces, "Even though I'm supremely pissed at you, I don't think you should go with him. Quit the game now. That hooker dare was seriously dangerous. And look how twisted this dare is. You really want to leave with this jerk, after the way he treated Jake?"

She glares at Ian, who turns away, looking totally uncomfortable. All the rage he'd shown moments ago has evaporated. Is he some kind of Jekyll and Hyde?

I say, "I just want to go home."

She speaks to Ian. "Could you give us a minute? Without beating anyone up?"

He exhales loudly and then heads outside.

She shakes her head. "I know he's hot, but seriously, Vee, do I have to explain why you shouldn't go with him?"

A tiredness overwhelms me. "What do you think I am? Some brainless bimbo who can't look out for herself?"

She stabs the air with a perfectly manicured finger. "I'm

telling you this as your friend, even though you haven't acted like one in the past few minutes. That guy is bad news."

I sigh. "How do you know?"

She wrinkles her nose. "You saw how he just threatened Jake. And even before that, there was something too, too, uh, perfect about him."

A tenseness takes hold of my neck. "You mean too perfect for me?"

"That's not what I mean at all." But it is, I can see it in her expression.

"Good night, Syd." I run outside to think. Maybe I should call a taxi.

Ian's huddled under the awning, which isn't doing much against the wind and rain. His expression is sad, not angry, but I still don't want to get into a car with him.

I keep my distance and call out, "What the hell was that in there?"

He slaps the wall. "My dare. Those assholes wanted me to act like something I despise. Sorry."

Aw, crap, of course. The game wouldn't let either of us off easy. I go over and nudge him toward the car. As we trot toward it, Sydney opens the door to shout something behind us that gets swallowed by the breeze. Once we're in the car, Ian turns on the engine and the heat.

His jaw is still tense. "Think that Jake kid'll be okay?"

"Yeah, it's not like you actually hit him."

"But I humiliated him. And I scared him. Believe me, sometimes getting hit is way better than that."

"Yeah. That dare sucked. My friends all hate me now."

He takes my hand. "Maybe one small good thing is that you stood your ground with Sydney. And you were pretty cute with your fists clenched."

"Ugh. I wish there was some way to go to the NERVE site and delete everything." I check my phone. It's ten to midnight. Even if we race to the bowling alley for my car, I'll never make it home in time. Well, being grounded again can't exactly hurt my social life. I've messed up something fierce.

"We should go," I say.

He nods, looking as defeated as I feel. But before he can pull out of the parking space, our phones chime with soft harps and tinkling bells. I don't have the energy to answer mine. This game has ruined my life and now it wants to soothe my feelings by sounding like twinkly music from heaven? As soon as I'm up to it, I'll text NERVE with a big "I quit" message. For now, I bury my head in my hands. Any minute, a big ugly cry will take over my face like a tsunami, leaving pools of mascara in its wake.

But the car doesn't move. And after a minute, Ian whistles. "You aren't going to believe this."

ten

"Just take me home, please." Hoping to prevent a meltdown, at least until I get home, I force myself to think about a time when I didn't completely suck—like when my design for a reusable prom dress won a silver ribbon in the Fashion High contest. Sydney beamed with pride that day and made me promise to design her wedding dress when the time came. However, this line of thinking only reminds me that even in my element, I'm second place—never, ever the star. And that Syd's been the loyal one, not me. Now Ian's seen me for what I am: a nothing-special wannabe who orbits in Sydney's mega-wattage. Not that she or anyone else will want to be my friend after tonight.

Ian leans in so closely, I feel his breath on my ear. Those perfect lips whisper, "Seriously, check this out."

I uncover my eyes to find his phone in front of me, playing

a montage of the dares we've endured tonight, along with a banner that says: LOOK WHO WE WANT FOR THE GRAND PRIZE DARES!

Ian's eyes are bright. "They're in Seattle. If I complete them, I'll win my own car and a huge credit for gas, enough to go anywhere."

"Where do you want to visit so bad?"

He swallows. "It's about the ability to leave. The freedom."

"What do they want you to do for the car? Bungee jump without a cord?"

He laughs. "That's my girl."

His girl? And how can he find anything about me amusing? "I'm serious. The dares must be impossible."

He shrugs. "We'll find out soon enough. Check your phone and see what your grand prize would be."

"Who cares?"

He smiles slowly. "You do."

I close my eyes. He's right. Despite my newfound hatred for the game, I'm curious. All night, NERVE has dangled the things I want most. What do they think will entice me after the disaster of a dare with Sydney? A fake passport along with foreign language CDs and matching currency?

"I'll check what they're offering if you start driving to the bowling alley. I'm already going to be late."

He drives while I check my phone. When I read the message, all my blood rushes downward.

My voice is faint. "Oh my God. They can't be serious."

"You know they can. You saw the video of that winner who got to fly with the Blue Angels."

I swallow. There's no trace of the lump in my throat that was there a minute ago, because my despair has been obliterated by shock. "A full ride to fashion school."

"Sweet."

Another text comes in. My voice trembles as I read it aloud:

YOU'VE SHOWN YOU MAKE A GREAT TEAM.
READY TO GO FOR ALL OR NOTHING?
HERE'S THE DARE:

- GO TO CLUB POPPY AND ENTER THE VIP
  SUITE BY 12:30. (MAP TO FOLLOW.)

- PARTICIPATE IN A FIVE-MINUTE
  INTERVIEW.

- REMAIN IN THE VIP SUITE FOR THREE
  HOURS AND COMPLETE THE GRAND PRIZE
  DARES THAT'LL BE GIVEN TO YOU THERE.

Ian and I stare at each other. Outside, the rain has turned to drizzle, leaving jewels of moonlight on the side windows. Maybe the worst of the storm is behind us.

I shake my head. "I think that's a private dance club. At least they aren't suggesting we go to an abandoned slaughterhouse in the boonies."

He grins. "You sound like you're contemplating it. The grand prize round, not a slaughterhouse."

"I'd catch hell from my parents."

He laughs. "You've faced an angry mob of virgins, pretended to be a hooker, escaped from a policeman, and pissed off your best friend. Now you're worried about violating curfew?"

"My mom's scarier than any of those guys."

"What's the worst she can do?"

I stare at the ceiling. "The worst? Ground me for the rest of junior year, for starters. I'm not exaggerating. I've already been grounded since November."

He rubs his chin. "Wouldn't tuition for fashion school soften her anger? All you'd have to do is remind her of the fun she and your dad could have with the college fund you'll no longer need. Maybe a vacation to Fiji?" He takes my hand nonchalantly, as if we're an old couple. But his skin against mine feels electric, new.

"It's more complicated than that. Things have been pretty weird between me and my parents for a while." Geez, why don't I tell him what brand of tampons I use while I'm at it?

He takes a long breath. "Maybe you need this dare. To change things up."

My skin burns, sensitive, like maybe he's seeing too much. "If I don't get home soon, they'll be worried."

"Call them with an excuse. Your car's old. It broke down and I'm helping you fix it."

"Like they'd buy that. And even if they did, they'd come track me down. My phone's camera may suck, but I'm sure the GPS is state of the art."

"Okay, so you've got to decide which is better. Going home now, late for curfew, with credit for new clothes and a phone, or getting home in a few hours with all that plus tuition money? If you end up grounded, use the downtime to work on your portfolio or whatever you need to get accepted into the most expensive program you can. And don't forget the extra benefits. When your friends see how kick-ass you are in the grand prize round, they'll forget about that little scene with Sydney, probably find it hilarious."

Hilarious. Sure. Obviously, he's telling me this because he thinks he still needs me as his partner and he wants the new car. I feel a little pressured, but who could blame him for trying? Anyway, even without his nudging, the thought of attending fashion school flashes shiny in my brain, like a beacon. Especially since so much of my college fund was raided to pay for hospital bills. Sure, I'd be risking the prizes I've already won, but none of those prizes will do much to relieve the tension in my family or open the path for a fresh start.

I wrap my arms around myself. "What do you think'll happen in the VIP lounge? With thousands of Watchers, they can't hurt us, right?" Safety in publicity, my new mantra. How many TV shows have relied upon that concept to keep their players from killing each other?

He taps the steering wheel. "They could set things up so that someone else might want to beat the crap out of us. Like those Purity Promisers. But I doubt it would get out of hand. They want to keep attracting players."

At a stoplight, I stare out of the window at a man walking his dog. When he glances upward, our eyes meet. With a tiny jolt, he shifts direction, tugs at the leash, and crosses the street, as if he thinks I'll jump out and attack him. Is my face that much of a mess? No one's ever been afraid of me before. Ever.

Gentle piano notes float from my phone.

WE'VE REVIEWED THE LATEST VIDEOS FROM IAN AND TOMMY. LOOKS LIKE THAT LAST DARE WAS MORE COSTLY TO YOU THAN WE THOUGHT. HOW ABOUT A CHANCE TO PUT THINGS RIGHT? IF YOU COMPLETE THE GRAND PRIZE DARES, WE'LL ADD AN INTERVIEW WITH A HOLLYWOOD AGENT FOR SYDNEY. OUR SMALL WAY OF EASING THE HARD FEELINGS BETWEEN TWO GREAT FRIENDS.

Sydney would love that! It could be her big start, and better than anything I could ever get her on my own. It's as if NERVE knows both of us intimately. Why should that surprise me?

Another text flashes:

ARE YOU IN OR OUT? YOUR AUDIENCE IS
WAITING.

Our audience. How big is it? The cast and crew of the play are probably still watching, even though they've seen the worst, up close. Or have they? I need advice from someone I trust, someone who doesn't have a new car at stake. I try phoning Eulie, then Liv, but both calls are blocked.

A text comes up:

YOU NEED TO MAKE THIS DECISION ON
YOUR OWN.

"I can't call anyone." I run a hand through my limp hair. "Not even my parents to make up an excuse if I want to stay out longer."

He glances between me and the road ahead. "Guess you'll have to beg for forgiveness after the fact. That is, if you decide to go for it. It's all up to you, Vee."

All up to me.

I stare at his profile as I think aloud. "Three hours in a cushy suite at a dance club, with thousands of people watching our every move. To pay for fashion school. And you'd get a new car."

"Freedom for both of us."

"Yeah, freedom, and maybe something else. I've been a huge disappointment to a lot of people."

"I doubt that. You're too compassionate. Look how you

were worried about offending the purity kids. And how you wanted to rescue the hookers, even after they threatened to jump you. You've got heart, Vee. And presence. I don't know why you hide it when you're around your friends. But I've had a chance to witness it, and it's sexy as hell."

His words are like balm. Whatever his motivation is. I'm not sure how much I can trust him yet. Certainly not with my life, but probably with certain parts of my body.

He grabs my hand as he drives and kisses my fingers. "So now you need to decide about this dare. I'll understand if you choose to quit. Really."

I take a deep breath. Without doing anything further, I could go home with $1400 plus some amazing prizes. And Ian would still have his golden bus ticket if he has to quit the game because of my decision.

But if I break curfew by a few hours and put up with whatever crap is waiting for us in the grand prize dares, I could seriously change my life. Instead of returning to school as an idiot who fought with her best friend on camera, I'll be someone who risked it all to win big. Everyone will know that the mild-mannered brunette who looks like she sings in the Pentecostal choir is not who they assumed she was.

I'm someone with presence. Thousands of viewers' worth. And more if I do the next dares. Tonight's shown me how to think bigger. Or at least differently. I pretended to be a hooker, for goodness' sake. If I can do that, what else is possible? Trying out for the next play? Asking for a raise at work? Making Tommy not hate me? I could apologize to Sydney for including her in the dare tonight, yet refuse to put up with her demands in the future. And maybe I'll finally get Mom and Dad to believe that I didn't try to asphyxiate myself in the garage. Anything is possible. Anything.

Even another dare.

"I'm in," I whisper.

"Yes!" He pulls the car to the side of the road and leans over to kiss me lightly on the lips and then harder. His hands are on my hair, my arms, my waist. When he pulls away, my mouth is raw.

He says, "You won't regret this—I've got your back. You know that, right?"

"Mm-hmm." With Ian at my side, I'm unstoppable. We're unstoppable. Holding my breath, I send a message to NERVE.

Ian starts the engine and turns the car around. We clasp hands so tightly I feel his pulse, strong and sure. At every stop, our mouths meet frantically. NERVE got one thing right—we are a team now.

On the way, I try texting and calling Mom and Dad with an excuse, but of course NERVE blocks my calls. Not much I can do about it unless we pass a pay phone. I need to focus on the prize. Fashion school, family, future.

It takes twenty minutes to reach Club Poppy, a five-story

building with a flashing dance club on the first floor. Throbbing music leaks into our car as Ian finds a spot marked "VIP" near the side.

I exit the car to meet a damp wind that whips at my legs and a light that flickers above. Although there's a crowd at the front entrance, the path to the side of the building, marked "VIP Lounge," is unoccupied. At least it's covered by an awning to shield us from the drizzle. We hurry along the path and meet a hulking doorman who demands that we give him our names as he compares our faces to images on his phone.

Finally, with a nod and a smirk, he opens the door. "Take the elevator up."

Inside, we're safe from the wind, but I still feel a chill, even snuggled against Ian. Our footsteps ring hollow on the marble floor of an entry area that smells vaguely of cloves. There's a faint pounding of bass and drums coming from the club. I'm surprised it isn't louder, but I guess VIP guests get soundproof walls that let them pick and choose what they hear.

In front of us is a small elevator with a sign above it that reads "Welcome, VIPs," in case we forgot that we used the VIP parking spot and VIP entrance. We enter the elevator, meeting our reflections in a full-length mirror. I don't look like the sunny retro girl I did earlier. Bluish smudges mar the skin under my eyes. Ian's face is drawn too, his jaw tighter. How much will this night age us?

"Don't be scared," he whispers. His breath is warm and tickles my neck.

We go up several floors before the elevator opens to a plush entry area done in shades of red and glowing warmly with mood lighting. To our left is a larger elevator door that's marked "Housekeeping." The only other door, directly in front of us, is of ornately carved wood and surprisingly does not include a sign to remind us of our VIP status. It looks like something out of a castle, the kind with dungeons. Suddenly, I'm tempted to turn around and run home.

My body must show my inclination, because Ian presses his cheek to mine. "We can do this, Vee. Only three hours. I'll protect you." He kisses my temple and squeezes my arm.

A warm, liquid feeling floods my chest. Three hours for three years of fashion school. More importantly, the chance to put things right. With a major first step along my career path taken care of, Mom and Dad will have to believe that I'm looking to the future. And they should. Plus, Sydney'll flip over getting to meet an agent, possibly jump-starting her own dreams. We'll figure out our friendship—we've got too many years of confidences and too many good times to throw it away. Yes, these prizes could make a huge difference. I can win them for my family. For my best friend. For myself.

Three hours. Less than two hundred minutes. I've watched movies longer than that. With a nod, I straighten my shoulders.

Together, we push on the heavy door.

eleven

We enter a small room, with the same dim lighting as out by the elevators. The only furnishings are a gleaming concierge desk and three armchairs with tiny end tables that hold something you never see in public—ashtrays. Beyond the counter is a single long corridor, where a light shines from an opening about thirty feet down. To our right, in the foyer, are two doors that have lighted signs above them reading "Ian" and "Vee."

My phone buzzes.

Enter the booth for your interview.

"Time to start earning our prizes," Ian says. He kisses me and ducks into his booth. The door swings shut behind him before I can make out more than a simple table and pale green walls.

I enter the "Vee" booth. It smells of cedar and has racks along the side that indicate that in real life this is a coat closet. But tonight it's decorated like a cozy dressing room, with a gleaming vanity table in cherry wood and a red leather chair in front of a well-lit mirror. I sit. On the table, someone's left an envelope with my name printed in calligraphy. Inside is a card of heavy paper, scented with lilac and filled with flowery handwriting. How old-school. The note tells me to freshen up and that there are plenty of supplies available in the drawers. I open one to find stacks of tiny cellophane packets, each stamped with the logo of a cosmetics brand that I only treat myself to at Christmastime, and filled with single servings of lip gloss, eye shadow, mascara, you name it. The next drawer down contains a bottle of water and a small insulated pouch filled with cold compresses. I take a long swig of water and press one of the compresses to my puffy eyes. The combo instantly refreshes me.

Tinkly notes float out from a tiny pink speaker on the table, and a woman's voice says, "You have three minutes before we begin the interview."

I examine my reflection objectively, the way I do with every actor I work on. Ashy skin, tired eyes, raggedy hair. No wonder NERVE wants me to freshen up. But what role am I playing? Daredevil vixen? Innocent victim? Maybe if I paint on some war wounds I'll attract more sympathizers. Oh, screw it. I'm going as myself, no more, no less.

As I search through the packets for the right colors, a certain comfort settles in. This is what I know how to do. I go with gray eye shadow, basic black mascara and liner. Some powder to even up my skin tone, and lip gloss to polish things up. I find a fancy brush that's supposed to smooth out my hair with some kind of ionization process. Its ads on TV have always left me skeptical, but after a few strokes, my hair appears silky.

I stare at my image. It's odd, seeing my own face instead of someone else's as the finished creation. The tiny amount of makeup has done a miraculous job of hiding the ordeals I've been through tonight. I sit back, satisfied. However, my image suddenly melts away, and the mirror transforms into a blank screen. Whoa. Up pops the face of a woman, which pierces my thoughts with childhood games of Bloody Mary. But instead of a grotesque ghost, this woman is maybe ten years older than me, with dark hair, blue eyes, and a ruffled shirt. She looks puzzlingly familiar until I realize that she could easily be what I look like in the future.

"Hey, Vee," she says, "I'm Gayle."

I realize that when I watched the game before, the announcers were just voices and shadowy figures in the background. Will the audience see Gayle? Is she the brains behind NERVE? Wait until I tell Tommy that the game has an identifiable human face, not just some anonymous businessmen with an account in the Caymans.

I smooth my top. "Hi. I didn't think I'd get to speak with an actual person."

Gayle brushes her hair back behind her ear in a girlish manner. "We thought it would make the interview a little easier."

Since when did NERVE care about easy? I glance around the room. "Where are the cameras? This is being filmed, right?"

She smiles, showing off dimples. "It's embedded in the screen. I think there's one near where you see my right eye. And, yes, your Watchers will get to see you."

I squint. Sure enough, the screen's pixels appear a little less uniform in the area around her eye. Lovely, the audience witnessed me making faces in the mirror as I applied makeup.

She crosses her legs. "So, what have you thought of the game so far?"

Where do I begin? With how it's alternated between offering a thrilling ride and ruining my life? "It's been harder than I thought, but in ways I didn't expect."

"Like the dare with Sydney?"

Guess we're diving right into things. "Uh-huh."

"Is there anything you'd like to say to her?"

My heart quickens. "Is she still watching?" I ask, fully expecting that this person from NERVE would know the answer.

"I can't say if Sydney's in our audience. But if she were?"

I stare down at the vanity while I consider what to say, and then I stare straight into Gayle's right eye. "I'd tell her that I'm sorry for ambushing her and that when this is over we need to have a long talk. By the way, you guys blurred her face on the broadcast, right? 'Cause she didn't sign a release form." Not that it matters. Everyone who counts will know exactly who I was arguing with.

Gayle's calm demeanor remains in place. "We don't want to waste our time on boring technical details, do we?"

Actually, there are a few technical details I wouldn't mind discussing, like when they'll stop blocking my calls or how they found out I was mad at Sydney in the first place. But I know this woman won't provide those kinds of answers, so I just sit there with a bland expression.

She uncrosses her legs and leans forward with her forearms on her thighs. "Let's talk about Ian. What do you think about him?" Her tone has become intimate, as if we're at a slumber party. I remind myself that there are more than nine thousand viewers. Probably way more.

I feel my cheeks going pink. "He's a great guy."

"Our audience thinks he's drool-worthy, don't you?"

I shrug. "I've got eyes."

She laughs. "I'll take that as a 'yes.' Think you'll hook up after tonight?"

What does she expect me to say? "We haven't talked about

it." Unless he was serious about taking me to Gotta-Hava-Java. Was he?

"Have you kissed?"

I sit up. "Um, that's kind of private, don't you think?"

She smirks. "Honey, we're way beyond privacy, don't *you* think?"

I'm not sure how to respond, so I wait for her to continue.

"So, Vee, why did you sign up for NERVE? Some folks might say it's not part of your profile to do something like this."

Her smug expression makes me stiffen. How can anyone claim to know what I would or wouldn't normally do? Anyway, after all that drama with Matthew and Sydney, it should be obvious why I'm playing. What else does she want me to admit? That I was sick of feeling invisible?

I lean forward and whisper, "Sometimes it's fun to do something outside of your profile."

She claps. "Brava, Vee. We're all proud of you. Where did you find the guts?"

Guts or idiocy? "Um, I don't know. I'm just focusing on one dare at a time."

"So modest. That's why your audience loves you. Anything you'd like to tell them?"

I smooth my skirt against my thigh. This is my first time to address all of the Watchers directly. What do you say to thousands of people? Sydney would know. "Thanks, everybody.

Especially you guys who joined us on the hooker dare. You saved our butts."

"That they did. I'll bet you're excited to get your butt started on the next dare."

Not at all. Just eager to win the prize. "I think I'm more nervous than anything else."

She laughs again. "Nerves are the name of the game, right? But so is fun. You've had a lot of new experiences tonight. I'm sure this will only add to them. Before you enter the game room, though, I want to go over a couple of key points."

I nod.

She holds up her index finger. "First, you're playing as a team with six other players. If one of you doesn't complete a grand prize dare, you'll all lose all your prizes. But don't worry; there will also be a few icebreaker dares that are just for fun and optional."

"Okay."

"The other point to remember is that if you do anything that violates the integrity of a dare, NERVE may issue a consequence to make future dares more difficult."

"Violate the integrity of a dare? What does that mean?"

She waves a hand dismissively. "Basically, performing the dare, but cheating somehow. Don't worry, we'll know it when we see it."

Hey, I'm the girl entrusted with a spray-bottle of vodka, so integrity doesn't sound like a problem. "Fine."

Her eyes are bright. "Wonderful! Good luck, Vee. Oh, and our product sponsors would love for you to help yourself to as many of the toiletries as you'd like. You may want to freshen up again later."

The screen blips off and the mirror reappears. My face is flushed and my eyes are shiny. Are they still filming me? Dumb question. The audience must think I look dazed. And why would I need to freshen up again? Will I be dumping more water on my head? Well, water or not, these are some quality items. Too bad my purse is still in Ian's glove compartment. I fill up a small makeup bag with packets.

"Thank you, product sponsors," I say to the mirror.

Out in the foyer, Ian waits with freshly combed hair and points to the room down the corridor. "We should head over there."

Something about that interview left me feeling queasy, despite the goody bag of cosmetics I scored. The interviewer's fake friendliness did nothing to calm me; just the opposite. Probably what it was designed to do.

I shrug. "I guess."

Ian takes me into his arms. "You having second thoughts?"

Not about him holding me, I'm not. I sigh. "It's kind of late to back out now."

"The exit's right here."

"You'd lose the car. I'd lose fashion school plus all those other great prizes."

"Well, we'd still have won something major," he says with a soft glance at my face.

That should sound cheesy, but coming from him it doesn't. Or maybe I'm just too far gone in crushville.

He kisses the top of my head as I nestle it into the spot between his neck and shoulder. Even after the running and fighting, he smells like sandalwood soap. I inhale deeply. The dare's only for three hours. And look who I've got for a partner.

"Let's play," I say.

We walk arm in arm past the concierge desk. As soon as we're in the corridor, laughter spurts from the lit room, which is down the hall to our right. I imagine a game of quarters or spin the bottle going on. Nah, too easy. NERVE probably invited those hookers Tiffany and Ambrosia to beat me up. In a muddy pit. With knives.

A few voices come from the doorway ahead, but nothing loud enough to make out. The left side of the corridor leading to the room is lined with armchairs, as if misbehaving club-goers are sent here for time-outs. The right side of the hallway is covered in an ornate wall-hanging that looks like it's made of silk. I stop for a moment to admire the embroidered but-terflies and flowers in gemstone colors. It's fabric fit for an empress's gown, and a hundred times more detailed than the meadow scene Tommy designed for our play's scrim.

Ian nudges me forward to the open door, which stands at the midpoint of the corridor. The only other door I spot is at the far end of the hall, and it's closed. When we're just about to reach the open room, where all the action seems to be, Ian pauses and whispers, "Maybe it's better we don't let whoever's inside know we're, uh, so together. Makes us more of a target."

Target? We're all supposed to be on the same team, right? But with NERVE, you never know, so I agree with Ian's advice, and miss his warmth when he steps away from me. The chattering from inside halts the moment we pass through the doorway into a room that's about twenty feet by twenty feet. So this is a game room? The left half is bare save for candy-apple-red carpeting. The right side is filled with several love seats, two on either side of a long coffee table made of glass. Instead of resting on a base, it's suspended by silver cables. Sitting around the table are three girls and two guys, all in their teens.

"Hey," Ian says as he heads to the empty love seat on the far side of the table.

I give them a small smile and take the spot next to him, tucking my makeup bag at my side. The seat bounces as if it contains mattress springs. I try to still it down, but it's like being on a boat. With each bounce, the cushion sighs and pushes me back up. The other kids sit there bobbing too. Why would people pay extra to hang out in a weird room like this? Or did NERVE decorate it especially for tonight?

"So you decided to join us," says a red-haired guy across from me. He has the overdeveloped biceps and jowly cheeks of someone on steroids. One of those bulky arms winds around a deeply tanned girl with exaggerated curves and a hundred jangling bracelets. She rubs a bare foot along his shin. Beneath a glass coffee table, there are no secrets.

In the love seat next to theirs sit two more girls, one white, one Asian, each with at least five piercings. I recognize the white girl as the one who stole all that nail polish in the preliminary dare video. She's huddled close enough to the Asian girl to suggest they're "together" too. However, there's no playing footsie with those safety boots. On our side of the table, a dark-skinned guy with super-short hair and tiny framed glasses sits with his arms crossed. Somehow he's balanced himself in the middle of his love seat so it stays still. He's cute in a Tommy sort of way, clean-cut with a trace of geek, but there's no girl, or boy, with him.

Ian leans forward, holding on to the seat cushion for balance. "So, think they'll send any Watchers to hang out with us?"

The guy with the glasses blinks. "The Watchers are there." He points toward a camera mounted in the corner of the ceiling.

I examine my surroundings. Four cameras perch like hawks in the corners of the room. Between the cameras, black screens cover the top three feet of the walls. The surface beneath the panels is covered in richly textured wallpaper of gray with red geometric patterns. The only wall that appears slightly different is the one next to the door, which has the same pattern but is more shiny than matte, as if it's covered in paint rather than paper. Either way, it looks expensive, and ugly.

Ian reaches a hand to glasses-guy. "I'm Ian."

The guy shakes Ian's hand. "I'm Samuel."

No one else pipes up with an introduction. Maybe the dare is to feel socially awkward. I wring my hands together.

The white girl with the heavy boots, whose piercings are mostly safety pins and bolts, barks out a laugh. She wiggles her fingers next to her face. "You scared, Thelma?"

I scowl at her. But if the worst I have to endure for the next three hours are Scooby-Doo insults, I can deal.

Ian nods toward the red-haired guy and his braceleted girlfriend. "What's the best dare you guys got tonight?"

The girl giggles. "Definitely the porno store one. We had to pick up the merchandise and tell everyone what we thought about it." She cha-chas her eyebrows at the red-haired guy.

Ian laughs along with her. I kind of smile. Yesterday a dare like that would've seemed impossible. Now I think they got off easy.

The Asian girl, who wears a pink Mohawk, scrunches her forehead. "Damn, wish we'd gotten that one."

Her friend rubs her shoulder. "We can go tomorrow, cupcake."

I try to settle into my seat by keeping my butt very still, but the tiniest movement causes a ripple. If this is the VIP lounge, what kind of digs do the riffraff in the dance club downstairs get?

Ian glances around the table. "Did any of you guys meet each other before the live rounds?"

Bracelet-girl smiles at her guy. "Nope. Tonight's been a blast. NERVE blows away those hookup sites at making hot connections."

How much research has she done? I have to admit NERVE did well with Ian and me. All they had to go on was the application data, and whatever info they snagged from my ThisIsMe page. Did they contact Liv and Eulie too? When this is over, I'm going to interrogate my friends to figure out who said what.

Ian turns to Samuel. "How about you? Did they give you a partner?"

He shrugs. "Yeah. But she was allergic to lime Jell-O."

Before anyone can ask for more details, Samuel's phone buzzes in a normal ring tone way. No fair. After reading it, he gets up to close the door. When it shuts with a loud click, my gut tenses.

"Why'd you do that?" Bracelets asks.

Samuel smiles. "Cause NERVE offered me a fifty-dollar bonus."

Bracelets's red-haired boyfriend slams a hand on the table, causing the glass plank to swing away from him. Ian stops the table's motion before it hits our knees. Can't any of this furniture sit still?

Red-hair faces one of the cameras and holds out his arms. "Hey you guys, I woulda closed the door for thirty."

I halfway expect the cameras to nod. Instead, the lights overhead dim. We glance at each other questioningly. One by one, we pull out our phones, waiting to see who'll earn the next fifty dollars. My display remains blank.

Beeping sounds fill the room, causing a fresh round of chair bobbles as we sit up. The black panels on the walls flash scrolling lights that blink on and off like a pinball machine.

The lights are replaced with the image of Gayle, the woman who just interviewed me, and a guy in his thirties with a shaved head, indie band T-shirt, and the kind of donut earrings that leave permanent damage.

Together, our masters of ceremony shout, "Welcome to the grand prize dares!"

The screens alternate between their image and the word WELCOME! along with graphics of fireworks and a staccato song that I recognize as the theme from last month's game. The camera shot eventually settles on the hosts, who stand on a small stage, surrounded by folks with the semi-delirious expressions I've come to associate with Watchers. The male emcee introduces Gayle and then himself, Guy.

He wags a finger at the room of players. "To reiterate the rules: You're playing as a team now, so if one of you quits, no one wins any prizes."

The girl with the safety pins makes a fist and glares around

172

the table, stopping at me. "If anybody wusses out, I'm coming after you."

I suddenly feel the need to go to the bathroom.

The camera goes to Gayle. "We'll get things started with a few icebreaker dares. So let's relax and have some fun."

I want to ask the others what they've been offered for their grand prizes, but figure it would be like asking someone's weight or bra size, so I say under my breath to Ian, "I wonder how big the audience is now."

Guy smirks from the overhead screens. "Good question, Vee. You have a ton of new admirers. Care to guess how many? Oh, let's make a game of it, shall we? Whoever guesses closest wins a hundred dollars."

We throw out estimates from twenty thousand (my guess) to half a million (red-haired guy's guess). Guy and Gayle grin at each other before Guy announces that someone named Ty wins, which turns out to be the red-haired guy. But our hosts won't tell us what the exact number is. Still, since the second-highest guess was a hundred thousand, it means a lot of people are tuned in.

That should make me feel all kinds of famous, but all I can wonder is how much the audience is paying to watch seven teenagers in a VIP lounge with unstable furniture. And what are they expecting to see?

twelve

Gayle claps her hands in fake excitement. "Okay, your next icebreaker comes from the audience."

Her image is replaced by flashing letters that say LOOK WHO'S WATCHING! along with the rat-a-tat theme music. The screen comes up with a group of kids huddled in a small space that looks like a dorm room. A long-haired girl with glassy eyes reads aloud from her phone, "Time for some quick intros to start things out friendly. For fifty bonus dollars each, go around the room to state your first name and what city you're from." She pumps her fist. "Go, Wolver—" The image cuts out.

Fifty bucks to tell the other players my name? Too easy. There's probably some trick behind this, but I can't figure it out. Intros could even work in our favor. Didn't I read somewhere that it's more difficult to be mean to someone once you see them as a fellow human being? Not that these guys are planning to attack us. Who knows, maybe I could even become friends with some of them. Not chummy enough to do any kind of pervy dare together, of course. More like being able to laugh about this afterward at a NERVE reunion party, the way players from last month did in those epilogue videos.

We go around the table. Asian, pink Mohawk girl is Jen. Her friend who threatened me about wussing out is Micki. They're from Reno and make some cracks about joining the mile-high club on the charter plane NERVE flew them into Seattle on. Bracelet girl with the bronzer addiction is Daniella; she and her partner, Ty, are from Boise, and were also flown in immediately after their last dare. We already met Samuel, who lives in Portland.

When I introduce myself, Micki rolls her eyes. "What kind of name is V? Your parents couldn't spring for more than one letter?" She laughs along with Jen, Ty, and Daniella.

I raise an eyebrow. "Your parents named you after a mouse?" So much for budding friendships.

I can tell the rusty hamster wheel in her brain is trying to devise a comeback, but before it can, the panels light up with our emcees' beaming faces. Gayle tells Ty to open a door on the far wall behind him, and then to open the red cabinet (and only the red cabinet) inside.

Ty remains seated. "How much will you pay me?"

Guy smiles. "You and your friends may have whatever you find inside the red cabinet, first come, first served."

Ty jumps up and examines the patterned wall farthest from the furniture. There's no obvious door. He raises his shoulders to the camera. "Is this a trick?"

Probably more of an IQ test. On the wall, one of the spirals lights up like an elevator button. When Ty pushes it, a pocket door slides open. I swivel my head to check out the wall behind me. How many hidden doors are there? From the number of spirals, it could be quite a few.

Daniella rises to huddle behind Ty. With a wink at the camera, she gives his butt a squeeze. Samuel turns our way and rolls his eyes, causing me to have some hope for him. At least I dare to imagine that if it comes down to a fistfight, he'll stay out of the way. Wait a minute, why am I even going there?

The space that the door reveals is lined from top to bottom with cabinet drawers, each a different color. Ty pulls the handle on the red one at the top, which pops open like a refrigerator. I sit up tall, trying to scan what's inside, groaning inwardly when I see the bottles of beer. If they want us to get drunk, that can't be good. Of course, Ty and Daniella whoop it up as if they've discovered buried treasure. Micki and Jen hop over to join in. Ty opens a few bottles and passes them out. The other players clink them with loud "Cheers!"

A message scrolls across the panels: FOR EACH BEER

I glance at Ian. "What do you think?" I whisper.

"We should be social," he says. "But we need to maintain control."

I nod. "One beer each, max."

We head toward the cabinet, and as we scoot past Samuel, Ian offers to get one for him too. But he decides to join us, probably not wanting to be the odd man out. At the cabinet, Ian opens a beer and passes it to me. I examine the bottle for signs of tampering.

"There was a tiny hiss when I popped the top off," he says.

I sniff. Smells like beer. And I'm parched. But, technically, I'd be breaking the law. Not that I'd care in real life, but who wants to be broadcast doing so? I whisper my concern to Ian.

He laughs. "How would anyone prove this isn't apple juice? It's whatever we tell them it is."

Of course. I take a small sip. Ice cold and bitter. Definitely not apple juice. The label's mostly in German, but I make out that the alcohol content is six percent. Figures they'd give us something strong. So much for keeping the game legal. If NERVE doesn't care about underage drinking, what else will they ask us to do?

Ty and the other girls cluster in a corner, swigging like they're at a party, launching into stories of alcohol-induced puking. I'm sure the audience is hanging on their every word.

Ian nudges me toward them. Although I think they're

obnoxious, I get Ian's strategy. We don't need cliques forming, especially if they don't include us. Even Samuel seems to get the idea, and stands at the edge of the group, looking at his feet.

I examine my fellow players, noting that NERVE has tried to cover as many bases as possible in terms of ethnicity, sexual orientation, body type, and who knows what other categories. All designed to appeal to a huge range of demographics, as Tommy would say.

Would any of us hang out with each other if we went to the same school? Besides Ian and me, of course. My school's social groups aren't as cemented as they are in some places, but most people know where they fit. Besides Sydney, Liv, and Eulie, I'm most chatty with girls who know their *Vogue* from their *W*, who seem to respect my vintage-meets-budget-conscious look. I'm comfortable with my friends, yet I've always envied how Sydney moves between crowds as though she has a free pass. In the back of my mind, I wonder how friendly people would be if I weren't her sidekick. Maybe after the fiasco of the last dare, I'll have to find out.

Micki belches and holds her bottle up to the camera. "German beer rocks."

Samuel clears his throat. "We probably shouldn't drink too much. We might need some coordination for the next dares. Just saying."

Micki laughs. "Thanks nerdboy, but the game is called

NERVE, not CANDY ASS." Her next gulp is a little smaller, though.

Ian raises his bottle. "I propose a toast. To grand prizes and buckets of bonus money!"

Everyone cheers and clinks bottles as though we're one big happy family. Maybe this won't be so bad, even with nasty Micki. The beer goes down smoother with each sip, and a pleasant buzz fills my head. I check my phone, flashing it toward Ian. Two hours and thirty-eight minutes to go. I get a crazy urge to sing the hundred bottles of beer song, but don't want to give these guys ideas.

Ian takes my hand, which adds to the warm feeling building up in my chest. "We can do this," he whispers.

I squeeze his fingers. No use pretending we're just buddies.

Ian tries to include Samuel in a conversation about video games. I don't have much to add, but I try to keep a non-threatening, beer-happy smile on my face. Not that I'd pose much of a threat even if I grew fangs.

Metallic techno music starts playing, and the other couples dance to it, swinging their bottles. Their second beer each—I've been counting.

The music morphs into a beeping that means the black panels are going into action. LOOK WHO'S WATCHING! A screenshot comes up of two really cute guys nestled next to each other on a red velvet couch.

One of them waves. "Hey, players, Houston here! NERVE

will add a hundred dollars to each of your bonuses if y'all dance." He and the other guy get up and start jumping and fist-pumping along with a crowd of folks behind them.

I don't mind dancing. Love it, in fact. But something about being paid to do so makes my shoulders stiffen. NERVE acts like we're trained monkeys who'll jump every time a banana is dangled in front of us. Okay, that's kind of the point of the game, but still.

The music in our room is the same stuff that's playing in Houston, and apparently at a bunch of other Watcher gatherings, because each wall panel displays a different shot of people dancing, as if we're all at one huge club. Next to me, Ian sways his shoulders and hips, moving as smoothly as a straight guy can. Even Samuel's arms swish back and forth. Everyone stares at me. Micki's eyebrows squeeze in toward each other as she says something to Jen. Ian smiles and takes my free hand, pulling me into a spin. I hesitate for a moment. Do I want to be the one who's seen turning down easy money for myself? What's a dance anyway? Especially if it keeps the social vibe flowing. I start moving in synch with Ian, surprised when an energy awakens in my spine.

I let the music envelop me, and I laugh when it seems that some of the Watchers are waving directly at me from their screens. The tunes get louder and louder and I dance more and more freely, not really caring about the cameras. Was the beer drugged? I set my empty bottle down next to the wall and continue moving. Everyone thrashes, laughing when we bump into each other. Even Micki's scowl disappears. After three or so songs, the music slows and I melt into Ian's chest. The lights dim to a candle glow and the screen images fade until they're just a blur, giving the room a sexy feeling. Nice. If the dares go on like this, I can handle them. In the meantime, I nuzzle into Ian.

Of course, NERVE can't let things remain so cozy. The music clicks off and the familiar beeps alert us. It isn't until I stop dancing that I realize how warm I've become. I lift the hair from the back of my neck and Ian blows on my damp skin, raising goose bumps.

Guy and Gayle reappear overhead. With a grin, she says, "Well, some of our audience members claim that Samuel's moves weren't exactly what they'd call dancing. But since this wasn't one of the mandatory dares, we're not going to give him any consequences."

She laughs and continues, "Time for the last icebreaker! On the wall behind the table are four doors, each leading to a private lounge. Enter them in any combination of players you choose for a game of 'Seven Minutes in Heaven.' I'm sure we don't need to explain the rules." She winks. "The team or player who provides the most entertaining show for the audience earns five hundred dollars. Runner-up wins a hundred. Everyone else just gets some time in heaven. Enjoy!"

Ian nudges me. "Should we?"

He's kidding, right? As fun as it would be to fool around with him, the closest I'm getting to being a prostitute tonight is the pretend stuff we did earlier. The Watchers got to see us dance, didn't they?

I flap my hair up and down. "Let's save it for later."

He takes my hand and kisses it. "Cool."

The music resumes with a techno track. Very romantic. Ty and Daniella get started before they even enter a room. I seriously don't want to see where he's putting his hands.

But I am curious what the private lounges look like, so I go to the other side of the room and tap on one of the spirals. A door swings open to show a space large enough for a small bed and tiny nightstand, nothing more. Well, except for whatever products live in the nightstand's single drawer. A dim light shines from overhead, next to a mirror on the ceiling. I move aside so Ian can take a peek. He laughs and says at least we could take a nap. Hah. As if I could lie next to him and get any sleep.

Micki and Jen gnaw at each other and moan as they stumble toward the next cubicle. Before they enter it, Jen calls out to Samuel, "Wanna join us?"

It seems like he's seriously considering it, despite Micki's threatening glare over Jen's shoulder. Finally, caution seems to win out over lust, because he shakes his head. The girls shrug and shut the door.

Ian, Samuel, and I settle back into our bouncy love seats.

Samuel pulls out his phone, poking at it like he's playing a game. The conversation with Ian must've given him the idea that this is a socially acceptable thing to do at a "party." Well, at least it's more palatable than what's going on a few feet away from us. I lean my head against Ian's shoulder and close my eyes to try for a catnap while my fellow players create real-time porn.

The panels startle us with beeping and up springs a row of what look like mug shots for each player, with captions underneath that read WATCHER APPROVAL RATING. Aw, geez, mine's the lowest at twenty-two percent. Samuel has a twenty-four rating, and Ian's groupies must be voting, because he's at sixty-seven. Micki and Ty lead the board with scores in the nineties, and Jen and Daniella fall somewhere in the middle. It shouldn't bother me what the pervs watching us think, but my cheeks burn with the feeling of rejection.

Ian tells me to ignore it, easy for him to say. After a few minutes, the doors behind us pop open, but when I take a quick peek, I quickly turn back toward the coffee table, trying to erase the image of Ty's belly from my brain. The others return to their seats, adjusting their shirts and wiping their mouths with the backs of their hands. They laugh and point to their ratings before the screens go blank again.

Guy announces, "After a close vote by your Watchers, the best use of seven minutes goes to Jen and Micki. Well done, ladies!"

Bet it's the first and last time that Micki's referred to as a lady.

Gayle's head bounces next to Guy's on the screen. "Okay, gang, the icebreaker dares are over. Now we get to the best part, the grand prize dares, which you all have to complete to win your prizes."

She raises an eyebrow. "Ready for the first one?"

A few players actually say "Yeah," as if Gayle or NERVE cares.

She and Guy lean forward and say in unison, "All you have to do is make a phone call."

thirteen

A phone call? It hardly seems possible that our first task for such big prizes is a prank call.

Guy shrugs. "It's easy. We'll give you the prompt and you make the calls. Each one will only last a few minutes. Who'd like to go first?"

For a moment, no one volunteers, but then Daniella raises her hand. "Why not? I love chatting on the phone."

Gayle's smile is wide. "Great! An extra fifty dollars for taking the plunge, Daniella! Your call will be to your ex, Marco. Tell him how all those times he accused you of cheating with his brother, he was right."

Daniella's tan loses some of its luster. "How did you— Wait, but, even if I did, Marco and I are over now."

Gayle's expression grows stern. "Make the call or forfeit the grand prizes for everyone."

Ty squeezes Daniella around the shoulder. It doesn't look like a romantic gesture. Her eyes dart around the room, looking for what, a way out? When it's clear that NERVE isn't going to surprise her by changing the dare or popping open one of the closet doors so she can hide under the stained covers, she pulls out her phone. The rest of us bob and sway on the crazy furniture, becoming part of the audience, at least for a few minutes. Even though I feel bad for Daniella, part of me is curious about how the call will play out. God, what's wrong with me?

Daniella turns away from the rest of us, but somehow NERVE has linked her phone to the sound system, probably through that sneaky app they made us download, so the sound of the phone ringing on Marco's end comes through clearly over the room's speakers, as does a close-up of Daniella's face. After two rings, a guy answers.

"Um, hey, this is Dani."

There's the sound of music on the other end of the phone line. "What's up?"

Is it possible he's not watching the game? Daniella and Ty must be celebrities in Boise tonight and he isn't tuned in? Did NERVE know that before coming up with this dare?

Daniella uses a baby-doll voice. "I just wanted to say that when we were together, I was with Nate too. You were right."

The call seems to go static-y and then explodes with, "I knew it, you skank!"

Daniella holds the phone as far from her body as possible, which does nothing to quiet the insults and swearing on the other end. Crying, she shouts to the camera, "Okay, I did it." She ends the call and glances up at Ty, who's scowling as though she'd cheated on him.

A soft-focus image of Gayle appears above. Her voice is gentle. "See, that wasn't so hard, was it?" She then calls on the rest of the players, making each person phone various exes and friends with messages designed to make the callers and the callees squirm. Ian has to contact an old girlfriend and tell her how breaking up with her was the dumbest thing he's ever done, and how he'd love to get back together. The girl's voice is so full of expectation at his words, it gives me a knot in my stomach.

After the call, Ian wipes the sweat from his forehead. "I hope someone tells her the truth before I have to. What an effed-up dare."

How did NERVE find people to call who weren't watching the game? Did they arrange for them to be otherwise occupied with free concert tickets or something? I'm beginning to believe their power is unlimited.

Too soon, it's my turn. I have to call Tommy and tell him that I know he has a crush on me, and list three reasons why we'll never get together. My breathing calms. Tommy does not have a crush on me and he knows what I'm playing. In fact, I'll bet he's still watching, so I could tell him whatever I want and he'll know it's all for show. Whew. Maybe NERVE has limits after all, or maybe because I did my prelim dares so late, they didn't have time to get all their evil plans in order. Whatever the reason, I'll take it.

Tommy answers on the first ring.

I say, "Hey. Sorry about before."

A loud beeping comes from the overhead panels. STICK TO THE SCRIPT.

What? I can't apologize before getting into the conversation? Is that what they meant by integrity of the dare?

I go on with the call, although I wasn't able to hear Tommy's response. "Anyway, I know you kind of like me. But there's no way we can get together, because, uh, um, because we're too much alike. You know, always working behind the scenes and all. Plus, you're, uh, pretty intense." He is, isn't he? All those hours and hours he spent redoing the set. "And, I could never really measure up to your standards anyway." Whoa, where did that come from? I should've scripted this better. But that's it. Three reasons.

He's silent for only a moment. "Wow, I knew you were selfish, but this proves it."

Wait a minute, why's he saying that? He knows this is a dare. Oh, I get it, he's just playing along.

He says, "The real reason you could never get together

with someone like me is because you hate yourself too much to be with someone who's into you for the right reasons. You'd rather go for a guy who belittles you and makes you look desperate in front of your friends. I thought you were different, smarter than the rest of the tribe. But now I see you just weren't given a chance to grow into your true miserable self."

He hangs up before I do.

I feel like I've been punched in the gut. Once again, I've been humiliated for the world to see. So much for him being my wingman. I want to crumple into myself.

Ian reaches for my hand. "He's jealous and hurt. What did you expect?"

I don't know what I expected. But NERVE got what they wanted, from all of us. Bastards. Only a single grand prize dare, with two hours left to play, and we're like a roomful of shell-shocked soldiers.

Guy shows up on-screen, wearing a jacket and tie, but no smile. "Okay, now that we've contacted our friends, time to call our families."

Everything goes a little fuzzy. There's no way my parents, who can barely work the remote control for the TV, are watching NERVE. My mind races with possibilities of how the game could torment them.

Guy clears his throat. "All of you will have the same script for the next call, but you'll each speak to another player's closest family member. The message is simple. Say that your fellow player has been in a serious accident, and then hang up. That's it."

Oh God, oh God, oh God. The thought of my parents' faces on hearing that kind of news makes my eyes burn.

"I can't do that to them," I whisper.

Ian takes me in his arms. "Yeah, it sucks. And trust me, my dad's not the kind of person you want to give bad news to. But think of how happy your parents will be when you come home with fashion school all paid for. Besides, you've got a lot of friends watching. One of them will call your folks and tell them the truth. I know my friends will." He turns to the closest camera. "Right?"

He says this with a smile, but there's a pulling at his eyes, like he's afraid of something. Still, he has a point. Even if Syd's mad at me, she wouldn't let my parents believe that I was hurt. Not for a minute. She'll be on the phone as soon as she sees this. So will Liv and Eulie. That means my parents will only suffer for a matter of seconds in exchange for all that tuition money. Plus, a call from one of my friends will also explain why I missed curfew, so this could be a win-win dare, even if I still end up grounded, which is pretty much a given.

I take a deep breath. "Okay."

Since I was the last to go on the prior dare, I'm the first to make the call on this one. I've been assigned to call Jen's dad, whose phone number is displayed on the panels. Despite her tough-girl persona, she glances at me with worried eyes.

I nod her way, wishing I could tell her I'll go easy on him, but it's not like there's a kind way to tell someone that their kid's been in an accident. Hopefully, her outside friends are looking out for her.

The sound of me punching in the number is played over the loudspeakers like a death march. As soon as Jen's dad answers, I give him the message and then hang up in the middle of his "What?" Maybe the abrupt end to the call will clue him in to the fact that this is a prank. A demented, psychopathic prank. Please, Jen's friends, put him out of his misery quickly.

The rest of the calls go the same way. My fingernails have dug ruts into my palms by the time Ty makes the call to my house.

When my mom answers the phone, Ty's voice takes on a strained quality as if he's been crying. "I'm sorry to inform you that Vee's been in a really serious accident." Smirking, he stays on the line long enough for her wail of pain to come through in a straight shot to my chest.

Thinking only of her anguish, I call out, "I'm okay, Mom!"

As soon as I yell, Ty hangs up the phone. Did Mom hear me? I close my eyes in a silent prayer. Oh, Syd, no matter how much you hate me now, please look out for my mom the way you always have for me.

A beeping from the wall panels brings me back into the game. Several shots flash up of different groups of Watchers booing. And then Gayle fills the screens. With a disappointed sigh, she says, "Oh, Vee, and you thought karma didn't apply to you."

Huh? And then I remember what I posted on my ThisIs-Me page earlier.

Large, crimson-colored letters scroll slowly under Gayle's shaking head: VEE HAS VIOLATED THE INTEGRITY OF THE LAST DARE. WE WILL DISPENSE A CONSEQUENCE AT A TIME OF OUR CHOOSING.

So that's what they meant by integrity? I wait for them to give me a hint of what my punishment will be, but the panel goes blank. They want me to stew over it, of course. Maybe they'll put me in one of those time-out chairs we passed in the corridor. Or maybe I'll get shoved into one of the make-out closets with Ian. But I know I won't get so lucky.

I grit my teeth. Was Gayle right about karma? Do I deserve any of this? I think about that apple-cheeked girl in the Purity Promisers and her sweet boyfriend. Ian and I ruined their date. And who knows whether that guy who wanted to save hookers survived the pimp I steered him toward. Geez, he could be in a hospital now. At least what I'd done to Sydney hadn't caused physical harm. But I didn't stop Ian from bullying Jake. And I signed up for this twisted grand prize round, which has traumatized my parents. On the whole, I've earned way more bad points than good tonight.

Karma probably wants to kick my ass.

fourteen

Micki chants, "Someone's getting a whuppin'."

I slump onto the stupid love seat, letting it fling my body around. "Shut your piehole." I'm sure that's the first time I've ever used that term. Look how the game is improving my vocabulary.

She bolts up. "What'd you say to me, bitch? First you try to ruin everything and then you call me names?" She begins making her way around the table. "Is the game putting you up to this, trying to get us to screw up our dares? Like those Watchers did in Atlanta? If you're a fuckin' plant—"

Whoa. What? Does she really think I work for NERVE? I estimate the distance between me and the door. She's closer. Great, I'll get beaten up for the next round of entertainment.

But Ian stands between us and says, "Calm down."

She thrusts her tree-trunk chest out toward his. "Don't tell me to calm down, pretty boy."

He's a head taller than her and doesn't back away. "Are you serious?"

Jen calls from across the table, "Get back over here, baby. We don't wanna scare off any players. You'll lose out on that Harley."

Micki stabs her finger toward me. "I better not find out you're trying to sabotage us, or I will beat your puny ass into the ground." What's with this girl and why is everyone pointing out my skinny butt tonight? At least she returns to her side of the table.

Even though the wise thing to do would be to keep quiet, I say, "You really think I'd team up with the rotten people behind this game? How do we know you aren't a plant sent in here to keep things stupid and violent?"

"You wanna see violent?"

Jen tugs on her girlfriend's shirt and says something into her ear. Whatever it is, it gets Micki to sit down.

Ian takes his spot next to me, his head fitting into my neck, and whispers, "I think the phone call dares tore her up more than she's letting on." Micki's first grand prize dare had been to tell a girl that she'd crushed on her for years and would do anything to get together. The girl sounded kind of grossed out by the admission, and Micki's face had bloomed pink. On the next dare, she tried to act like she didn't care when Ian called her grandma, who's in a nursing home, but her neck pulsed like it was about to explode.

"What do you think my consequence will be?" I ask Ian.

"All I know is that it'll make the dares harder."

I groan. "Because what we've been doing isn't hard enough?"

NERVE leaves us alone for a minute, probably time for a commercial break, or maybe there's still another grand prize round going on. Naturally, the players across the table use the time to grab another beer. While they're burping away, I lean against Ian and dream about what it would be like to be with him outside of the game. He whispers how great I'm doing and a few other suggestive tidbits made all the more enticing by his hot breath against my ear. Who needs dares to make things exciting when every touch is electric?

But my fantasy is short-lived. Gayle appears on-screen to inform us that the setup for the next round of dares is complete. She licks her lips. "Everybody ready?"

No one bothers acting enthusiastic except Ty. We all know it'll suck. I check my phone. An hour and forty minutes to go.

Gayle clasps her hands in front of herself like she's about to sing a solo. "The next round has been custom designed for each of you. On the long wall opposite the door are four exits that lead to special rooms. We'll conduct this round in two groups. When we call your name, head to the open door."

The first door pops open from the wall. Does it lead to another of those pervy closets? Or maybe a diving board off of the roof? I'd hate to meet the people who make up this club's typical clientele.

Guy shows up on the screen next to Gayle and calls Ian's name. Ian hugs me quickly and marches to the front of the door. If he's nervous about going first, he doesn't show it.

Gayle says, "Once the door closes, it'll go on a timer, not to be opened again for fifteen minutes, unless there's a fire alarm."

An interesting way of locking us into our dares, making the trap totally our own doing. Ian shrugs and closes the door behind himself, probably eager to get whatever it is over with. I share that feeling, while at the same time dreading a dare where NERVE wants to lock doors. But I'm not one of the names that Guy announces for the first phase. Samuel, Micki, and Ty enter the next rooms, leaving Daniella, Jen, and me behind.

While our partners are off being tortured or caged with rats, the other girls and I get together near the refreshment cabinet to share some chocolate that was tucked into the fridge with the beers. Why not? It strikes me that we're the weaker half in each of our couples. The better to terrorize us during the second phase?

Jen nibbles on a piece of chocolate and wipes the side of her mouth. "Micki's not as much of a hard-ass as you think. The game's just getting to her."

"Or maybe it's showing her real side," I say, not willing to cut Jen's partner any slack. "Anyway, thanks for getting her to back down earlier. It's crazy for her to think I'm working with the game."

She raises her eyebrows. "Is it?"

My mouth drops open. "Yes, totally."

She hits my arm. "Just messing with you. If anyone's a plant, it's Samuel. He's just too quiet."

Daniella shivers. "I'm scared of the dark. You don't think they'll make us sit by ourselves in a room without any lights, do you?"

I straighten my skirt. "Now that they know your fear, they might." It's not like I'm trying to be bitchy, but someone needs to give her a clue that any weakness she shares will be used against her.

Her shoulders do a quivery thing.

I smile at her. "But nothing bad will happen. If they turn out the lights, try to take a nap and get some energy for the next dare." Easy for me to say.

Her eyes are wide. "No way. The minute I close my eyes, they'll send in spiders or something. Remember that girl Abigail last time? Her biggest fear was of snakes and look what they did to her."

I recall watching the terror on that player's face a month ago. I'd told myself that there was no way the snakes were venomous. If she'd just relax, she'd be all right. But she didn't relax, and I watched her squirm. For entertainment.

Jen grabs some more chocolate. "That girl wanted to be

in movies. You think all those screams were for real? The game was just a big audition for her. Even afterward, she kept showing up all over ThisIsMe. Did you hear what she did last week, jumping from a cliff at a waterfall, in front of someone who just happened to film it? Total attention whore."

I grab a can of soda. "That's pretty far to go for a movie role. And I heard she went off the grid since that last video."

Jen laughs. "All a big publicity stunt."

We discuss the other dares from last month, ranking the ones that were the most exciting, and comparing gossip on things we'd seen online about what the former players were up to. Not that anyone will care after tonight. The only cast that counts is the freshest.

Hmmm. I'm thinking of myself as a cast member? Interesting.

I decide that at least Jen and Daniella aren't so bad. If only they'd hooked up with decent partners. But if they had, I doubt they'd be in the grand prize round, since their partners seem to be the bigger personalities. Is Ian responsible for us being here? Or did I make such a fool of myself that people wanted to see more?

The first door pops open with a little trumpet blare from NERVE. Ian stumbles out, his eyes bloodshot and his legs wobbly. What on earth? I run over to help him to our seat.

I'm surprised to feel the tremor running down his back. "What did they do to you in there?"

He shakes his head. "Reminded me of stuff I don't want to remember. And things I don't want to talk about. Sorry."

Here, I'd thought we were partners. "I understand. Do you want anything from the cabinet?"

He rocks back and forth with his head in his hands. "Nah, thanks."

What could have shaken him up like this? The next door opens and Ty saunters out. He does a fist-pump and demands a beer from Daniella. But his eyes twitch in a weird way as if he's trying not to cry. Guess even psychopaths can get psyched out.

Micki exits her door with glassy eyes and yells, "Any of you make one wrong comment and I don't care about scaring you out of the game, understand?"

Finally, Samuel enters the room. Marching with his head pointed down, he takes his seat and stares at his knuckles. I can't tell how much his dare affected him, since that's a posture he's taken a few times tonight.

Guy's on the screen, clapping. "Okay, next group, up, up, up. First room goes to Daniella."

Trembling, she trudges to the door and then turns around to give us all a little wave before entering her dare. I'm next. If only I could stay with Ian for a few minutes. I hate leaving him behind when he's so vulnerable. But what can I do? I give him a hug, more to reassure him than myself, I believe, and head to my doorway.

The air coming from it is chilled, like it's straight from outside. I enter a passage with lights along the floor pointing ahead at a steep, downward slant. Once inside, I close the door behind myself. *Click.* I could swear I hear a faint ticking from the timer, or maybe it's a bomb. I follow the lights down a hall that heads at least one floor below the game room. At the bottom of the ramp, the corridor turns to the right, where there are two doors. The indicator lights skip the first door and lead me to the second. I push against it into a room lit by a red dome on the ceiling. It illuminates a small space filled by a leather seat that faces the wall opposite the door.

Gayle's voice seems to come from multiple points in the room. "Sit down and get comfy, Vee."

I slide into the leather seat, and the door behind me thuds shut. What is this, some kind of amusement ride? Slowly, a panel moves toward my lap, tiny lights on it beginning to glow as the red dome on the ceiling fades. I'm in near darkness, which makes my heart pick up speed. Did they give me Daniella's dare by mistake? Maybe she's been thrust onto a stage wearing soaked clothes while Matthew laughs and Sydney accuses her of being a rotten friend.

The panel in front of me takes shape as my eyes adjust. I reach out to find a steering wheel and knobs on the display next to it. It's a dashboard. What is this, a driving simulation?

"Buckle up, Vee," says Gayle, still without an image to go with her voice.

I don't realize that the words are an actual request until she repeats the command in a firmer tone.

"Fine, fine." I touch the seat at my sides until I find one end of the belt at my right hip and the other at my left shoulder. I pull it across my chest and snap it shut. Maybe this building includes a roller coaster or something. Totally possible, since there were three floors between the dance club and the VIP lounge. Well, I've done rides in the dark before. They weren't my favorite, but I survived.

In front of me, little details sharpen, like the dashboard's air vents and sound system. Do they actually work? The rest of the details reveal themselves, forming a cohesive picture. I squint at the dials and find myself catching my breath when I notice the little PUMP UP THE VOLUME! sticker on the radio knob. It's a mock-up of my car.

Frowning, I turn on the radio. It plays an indie song I have on my player, one I listen to a lot. Who fed NERVE the details of my playlists? Has Syd teamed up with them to get back at me?

From underneath the dashboard, there's the sound of an engine starting, and my seat vibrates with the gentle rumble of a real car. It's kind of pleasant, actually. Soothing. So soothing I lean my head back against the seat and close my eyes, even though I know it'll probably prompt NERVE to send in the spiders. Let them.

I love the song that's playing and sing along. The next

tune is even better. This is as comfy as my own car. Their set designer paid attention to the details, just like Tommy did for our play. There's even the faint smell of exhaust fumes.

Fumes? Inside a closed room?

My body jolts forward. No way! I jab at the button on the seat belt, but it won't open. The more I yank at it, the tighter it seems to get. And the music becomes louder.

With a chill I realize that the soundtrack playing is the same one that played that night in my garage, which had also started out peacefully. How could they know? Or did they poll all my friends on my music tastes and take a lucky guess?

The smell seems stronger and my head feels fuzzy. This can't be real. Someone's probably having a cigarette on the other side of the wall and blowing it in through a vent to scare the hell out of me. Which is working.

I pull out my phone to call for help, but there's no signal. Maybe these walls are made of steel. Like a prison. That thought only sends another tremor through my chest. I keep yanking at the strap, and then realize I must have an audience. Of course.

I lift my head up a few inches, to where I'd expect a camera to be pointing. "Gayle, Guy, let me go!" I'm way past worrying whether this violates the integrity of the dare.

Is that Gayle's laughter floating over the speakers?

I yell, "Whoever's watching the dare, call 911, now! They're pumping in exhaust fumes and I feel dizzy. This isn't a joke. Call the police and have them come to the VIP lounge at Club Poppy. Please!"

Will anyone listen? Or will they assume that someone else will save me, like how they warn you about in CPR class?

"Sydney, Liv, and Eulie, all of you call the cops now! I'm begging you. NERVE is a totally twisted game." Will they see me? NERVE must have some kind of time delay to ensure that the Watchers only see what they're supposed to. With Daniella's and Jen's dares going on simultaneously, the game could be switching the feed from room to room. But they wouldn't actually harm me, would they? There has to be a limit to what they can do. There has to.

But my head feels lighter and lighter. I use all of my strength to tug against the belt. It's on so tight. Even if this is a huge hoax, every muscle in my body squirms to escape. I bend sideways, trying to slip under the upper strap that goes across my chest. My arm and shoulder slide beneath it, but there isn't enough room for my head to duck under it. I twist as far as I can to the right so that my body is almost lying on the seat, then press myself into the cushion and limbo my torso beneath the strap. It sends a sharp pain up my neck, but I'm able to free myself from the top part of the seat belt.

Using the steering wheel for leverage, I shimmy my lower body upward to get out of the lap belt as well. After a few minutes, I'm panting, but free.

Or am I? I jump out of the bucket seat and hold my arms

out until I hit the wall behind the "car." It's cold and smooth, like marble, or a tomb. It takes me a moment to find the door handle, which I turn and tug. Locked, of course.

Are they going to let me asphyxiate in here with a camera running? Maybe this is one of those karmic things where you get what would've been coming to you if you hadn't escaped it. Had dying in my garage been my destiny? No, no, this is crazy thinking. If only my head weren't so buzzy and dizzy.

I pound on the door. "Let me out." I turn toward the room and plead to anyone watching online to rescue me. The engine keeps purring. The music keeps playing.

With my back to the door, I sink into a squat. Are the fumes stronger down here? No, wait, smoke rises, right? I'm too fuzzy to remember. I rest my head against my knees and close my stinging eyes. Even my throat burns. Whatever they're pumping in here is stronger than car fumes. When I fell asleep in my garage all those months ago, I didn't feel a thing.

Or did I? I've tried so hard to block it out, I've never really considered the details, even when I tried to recount it for the shrink.

What the hell had I been thinking that night? Everyone knows it's dangerous to sit in a garage with the engine running. The thought must have crossed my mind at some point that I should turn off the car. But the seat and the music and the heater had been so cozy. And I'd been upset. That's right, I'd been mad at Sydney. A little point that I hadn't thought about before now. We'd spent hours going over her lines for a play, yet at the end of the evening, instead of thanking me, she'd complained that her costume made her look fat. A costume that I'd altered for her, twice.

Was I mad enough to kill myself? That's ridiculous. But, maybe, just maybe, I'd done what I'd done in hopes of getting a little attention. That's also crazy, yet there's a tiny corner of my brain that wonders if there's any truth to it.

I slap the stone floor. This game, this speculation, it all sucks. I just want to go home and sleep, forget everything. Screaming, I hammer at the door, bruising my fingers to the bone. I'm angry at myself for getting into this mess, angry at NERVE for this awful dare, and angry at the Watchers for not saving me. Turning my hot face away from the door, I raise my middle fingers to the dark room. If they're going to let me suffer, I'm going to haunt them. But I'm not going to cry.

The door behind me clicks.

I rise, but it's difficult because my legs have gone numb. When I'm up, I turn the knob, and this time it opens. I push against the door, half expecting the world outside to have shifted into another horror show.

But I find myself back in the hall with the tiny lights along the floor, like in an airplane. The air is cold, but clean. I take huge gulps of it as I make my way up the ramp and to the door, the one that leads me back into the room with the other players. It pops open just as I reach it.

I squint against the bright light, which hadn't seemed so intense before I left for the last dare. Across the threshold, Ian's waiting for me, arms open wide. I stumble into them and let him hold me.

"You did it," he says.

I sigh. "Like I had a choice." My body and spirit have given up. If I had the strength, I'd march out the main door right now. But my knees can barely support me.

Ian must sense this, because he half carries me to our love seat, where I nestle against him, hoping to forget the rest of the world. His heartbeat feels so strong, so sure, so alive. When I lift my head to peek at the others, who've all huddled near the beer cabinet, it's clear that Jen and Daniella are even worse off than me, if that's possible.

NERVE pumps in more techno music. A glance at my phone shows that we still have another hour. How can that be? I can't do another minute, let alone an hour.

Guy and Gayle show up on the screen in party clothes, like we're at a New Year's Eve celebration. Guy says, "Congrats on making it through another round! Let's move along."

"No," I say.

He frowns and Gayle's eyebrows go sky high. A few of the other players turn to me, scowling as if I'd spit in church. Micki balls her fists. So does Ty. But Daniella and Jen are nodding their heads, causing their partners to give them death glares. For a few seconds, the panels flash our mug shots and

Watcher approval ratings. I don't need to check mine out to know it's gone lower. So what?

I take a long breath. "You just tried to kill me. I've had enough."

And then Guy reappears. "You're absolutely right."

I am?

He does his little finger wag. "Not about the killing, silly. That's just your nerves and the beer. Sounds like your mind played tricks on you. Amazing, where the brain goes when it feels trapped in the dark. But let's be sensible. You're all fine, right?"

No one answers.

Gayle steps into frame next to him. "The audience thinks you guys need some refueling for your spirits. We agree. So take a look at your phones."

How thoughtful, audience. I'll have to remember to send thank-you cards, laced with anthrax. Still, even though I don't want to do anything else NERVE asks me to, I'm curious enough to check out my phone, which now has a message titled LOOK WHO'S WATCHING! When I open it, there's a video from Eulie and Liv.

Liv starts with a high five to the camera. "I'm so proud of you, Vee! You're the bravest girl I know." Eulie joins her, laughing. "Even more of a star than you know who." They go on to tell me that all of our friends are rooting for me and that there will be some serious celebrating tomorrow. Obviously, they don't realize that I'll be grounded until summer, but it still makes me smile to know that not everyone hates me.

Ian and the other players watch clips on their phones too. Everyone's features soften, even Micki's.

Gayle calls to us from the screen, "Feel a little better, guys?"

I'm the only one who answers. "Not enough."

She smiles. "Then you haven't checked out what else is on your phone."

I look down to find another message. When I read it, I almost drop my phone. They've raised my grand prize to include a summer internship with one of the hottest design houses in New York. The rest of the players must have offers that are equally as tempting, because the room erupts in hoots and whistles.

Ian's face is flushed. "I don't believe it."

"What are they trying to bribe you with?"

He whispers, "An emancipation lawyer."

When I cock my head at him in question, all he says is, "It means total freedom. How about you?"

I tell him about my prize.

He's almost giddy, as if whatever happened to him in the room didn't matter. "It's worth another hour of whatever bullshit they can throw at us, right?"

"I don't know." Did NERVE try to gas me? In the light of the room, cuddled next to Ian, the thought seems insane. For one, they'd never get away with it. Right? I'm tired and stressed, and they messed with my head. It's what they do. But they also offer prizes that no one else can. With that internship and fashion school, I'd have it made.

Ian kisses my cheek. "Nothing can stop us."

I roll my eyes. "Yeah, we're totally invincible."

Guy claps us all to attention. "Is everyone ready to move on?"

The other players shout "Yes!"

I'm not crazy about the idea, but their bribe has worked. I nod.

He smiles. "Wonderful! Now then, let's enter the last phase of the grand prize rounds."

The display fades. We wait for our emcees to reappear. The techno music fades into the new age stuff you hear at a yoga studio, which puts me on edge way more than the synthesizers on steroids did, even though I've made the choice to play on. I try to inhale deeply, but can't seem to get a decent breath. A bead of sweat rolls slowly down my cheek. The blank display teases us. After a long moment, the letters scroll around our heads.

ALL YOU HAVE TO DO IS CHOOSE A VICTIM.

fifteen

The room buzzes with questions, except for Micki, who snickers. My head feels floaty again, like my brain's escaping. I grit my teeth to rein myself in.

They want a victim.

Why the hell did I fool myself into thinking they'd let me win a full ride to fashion school without driving me completely insane in the process? I try to rise on shaky knees.

Ian grabs my wrist with a gentle squeeze and whispers, "Don't throw away your tuition yet." He faces the camera. "You want us to choose a victim? For what?"

Ty laughs. "For fun, bro!"

The rest of us wait, staring at the display, waiting for Guy or Gayle to explain what the "victim" is being chosen for. But the screen remains blank.

Ian rubs his cheek. "Maybe it's a trick and the victim actually wins something."

The others smirk. I don't believe it either.

Micki points a fresh bottle of beer, her fifth, at me. "I vote for her. *V* stands for *victim,* right? Or is it *virgin*?"

Jen nuzzles Micki's neck. When she comes up for air, she says, "I'm voting for the virgin victim too."

What? I thought we'd kind of bonded over the chocolate earlier. Please, God, let her get caught on one of the safety pins jutting from her girlfriend's jaw.

I cross my arms against the hollowness I feel inside, and force myself to speak, although I barely trust that my voice still works. "This is crazy, you guys. Don't you get it? They're trying to turn us against each other for their amusement."

Ty takes a swig of beer. "Duh. But all we're doing is voting. It's not like we're actually going to do anything to you, right, everybody?" He holds his arms out, a beer in each beefy hand, and spins in a slow circle to face the others.

Micki nods. "*Riiiiight.* Unless the virgin doesn't vote and causes us to lose out on our prizes. Then, hell yeah, we'll do something to her."

Ian shakes his head in disgust. "If anybody tries to mess with her, they'll have to deal with me."

Micki flutters her fingers. "Oooo, tough guy. Think that'll get you *Ian* Virgin Vee's pants?"

Ty winks at me. "I'll give the cutie a break by voting for

her hero, Ian." He raises one of the bottles and finishes it off.

The room is silent except for the ringing in my ears.

Then Guy's voice comes over the speakers, even though the screen remains dark. "What about you, Samuel? Daniella? Ian? Vee?"

Daniella puckers her mouth and twists it side to side. "Is it true you're a virgin, Vee?"

I glare at her.

She shrugs. "Sorry 'bout that. Anyway, I'll be nice and vote for Ian too."

Samuel examines his hands. "Sorry, Vee. I'm going to vote for you. Just to make it a simple majority."

I give him a *thanks a lot, asshole* glower. He's going along with the herd for safety reasons, and I'm less of a threat than Ian. Of course, that's the best strategy for someone playing alone. But still.

Ian votes for Ty and I vote for Micki, as if it matters.

We settle into fidgety waiting. The other players return to the table and take their seats too, even though the music shifts into some vanilla pop crap they play in the all-ages dance clubs. We're long past dancing.

Ian's lips are near my ear. "They're just trying to psyche us out. You'll see."

I whisper back, "If NERVE sics these idiots on me, I'm out of here. We can all lose our prizes."

He kisses my cheek. "Fair enough."

Nothing happens for five long minutes. Unless you count Micki going for another beer, or the trembling taking over my legs and arms, which are covered in goose bumps. I wish NERVE would tell us the next dare and get it over with. Ian tries to soothe me with whispered encouragement, but he didn't earn the most victim votes.

"Is there a bathroom around here?" I say to the blank panels. They have to give us bio breaks, right? But I don't remember passing any other doors in the corridor.

Micki, whose bladder must be as large as the Puget Sound, given all the beer she's guzzled, points at me. "Don't even think about escaping, or I'll mess you up good."

Ian raises a hand. "Chill. We all want our prizes, with as little messing up as possible."

Gayle's disembodied voice says, "The restroom door is in the wall right behind you, Vee."

Of course, another hole in the wall. I turn around to face where the make-out closets opened up earlier. Sure enough, in the space to the left of the closets, a spiral lights up. On wobbly legs, I make my way around the love seat, noticing how the rest of the players avert their eyes, as if I'm no longer an entity. Oh God, isn't that the first step that people at war go through? Depersonalizing their victims?

I press the lit spiral, which causes a door to pop open. Behind it is a tiny bathroom, windowless, of course.

"If you're not out in five minutes, we're coming after you,"

Jen says, looking to Micki for approval, which is given in the form of a noisy kiss.

I close myself into the room, grateful when a vent automatically turns on to cover any embarrassing sounds. The door doesn't have a lock, but it's the most privacy I've had in hours. I sit on the toilet and put my head in my hands for the millionth time tonight. Now I'm the "victim." What does that even mean? Will they push me around like the Purity Promisers did? Or scratch my eyes out the way the hookers threatened to? Can they make me feel as worthless and guilty as Syd and Tommy did? As much as I try to resist, I begin to cry.

After a minute, I clench my fists. How stupid. The last thing I need is for Micki to barge into the bathroom and catch me crying on the toilet. Would the cameras reach in here? Oh hell, my insides cramp with the sickening realization that there could be cameras in here too. I examine the ceiling and don't see any, but that doesn't mean they aren't embedded in the walls around me. Why didn't I think about that before I used the toilet, dammit? How much has the audience seen? The audience who didn't bother saving me from that dark room with the fumes.

Keeping my skirt down, I pull up my underwear, and then flush the toilet and wash my hands. In the mirror, bloodshot eyes ringed in smeared makeup stare back. So much for freshening up earlier. I splash cold water on my face. It helps with the red in my eyes, but removes the last of my mascara, making me resemble the middle schooler Ian teased me about looking like earlier. I could grab my new cosmetics bag from the love seat to repair the damage, maybe create a new character for myself, but that's probably what NERVE wants me to do, so forget it.

There's a knock on the door. "Hurry up, I gotta go too," Daniella says in her high-pitched whine.

"Keep your thong on. I'll be out in a minute." My own voice is rough, but I feel my strength returning. Taking a deep breath, I open the door and narrow my eyes at her as I exit. I give the same glare to the others, except for Ian, as I plunk into my seat, silently cursing it out when it bounces under me.

"Someone's been crying." Micki laughs.

"Shut up," I say. "I'm tired."

She runs a hand along the tips of Jen's Mohawk. "Yeah, guess it's past your bedtime."

Ian whispers, "The more you respond, the more she'll harass you. Focus on me. We're going to walk out of here as winners. Imagine how we'll celebrate."

As I listen to him, I stare through the table at the crimson carpet. Its pattern subtly curls, leading to a point under the table's center. The swirls and whirls draw my eyes around and around.

My attention is broken when the door behind us clicks open.

Daniella, freshly iced with thick lipstick that would give ancient prostitutes some serious competition, exits the bathroom and takes her seat. Waves of musky perfume fill the room, causing the spot between my eyes to ache. NERVE couldn't have planned a more effective attack on our noses.

I resume my inspection of the carpet. Something about it bugs me. At the center point under the table, I detect what appear to be concentric rings of darker spots. I lean forward to examine them, gently resting my arms on the table so it doesn't swing.

The panel beeps and Guy says, "You guys are the last grand prize players left now. All Watcher eyes are on this room!"

Jen and Micki wave to the cameras. I feel like I need to use the bathroom again. Why aren't the emcees showing their faces anymore? It's creepy having their voices come at us in surround sound without any visuals.

Gayle says in a commanding tone, "Daniella, open the green cabinet."

Daniella bounces up, clapping her hands. "More goodies!"

Great, what now? Whiskey or arsenic? I don't want to know. With a frown, I focus my attention downward, toward those spots on the carpet. They're actually more like gaps, no, holes. Holes? With a punch to my gut I realize what they are. A drain. What the hell kind of VIP lounge needs a drain in the middle of rubbery red carpet that I'll bet is water resistant. I jerk my head up.

Daniella peeks into the cabinet, gasps, and slams the door back shut. With no apparent thought to her front teeth, she gnaws at her waxy lower lip

Ty slaps the table. "Enough with the drama. What is it?"

She gives him a lipstick-stained smile as she opens the cabinet with shaky hands, this time swinging the door open wide.

The rest of us catch our breaths too.

Hanging against the back of the cabinet are seven handguns.

Sixteen

Two seconds later I'm at the door.

But Micki is just as fast, pushing past Daniella and Ty. "You're not going anywhere, bitch!" She grabs me by my elbow, wrenching it backward.

Screaming, I strain toward the doorknob. "I'm not sticking around while a bunch of drunk monkeys play with guns."

Ian's next to us, trying to pry Micki away from me. "Let her go."

Her fingernails dig through my jacket into my arms. "This little chickenshit princess isn't costing us our prizes."

Jen and Ty join the fray, yanking Ian away from me and the door. He thrashes while I struggle to get away. But Micki's grasp is too tight. She spins me toward the floor, throwing me onto it and then herself on top of me. My spine screams under her weight.

Safety pins poke my cheek when she presses her face next to mine and spews hot, beery air into my ear. "Bet a little bitch like you would love it doggy style."

I wriggle beneath her, but can't break free. She jams my face into the carpet, which smells as rubbery as it looks and reinforces my suspicion that it was chosen for its washability. I shudder to imagine what fluids it's come in contact with.

The music morphs into metal rock, a deep bass pounding in time to my heart. With a grunt, I get an elbow free long enough to jab Micki's ribs. She yanks my hair in retaliation, bringing tears to my eyes but also raising my head so I get a quick scan of the room. Samuel's still seated at the table. Daniella huddles in a corner with her arms wrapped around herself, eyes bugging at the brawl around her.

To my left, Ian, Ty, and Jen dart and jab. The minute Ty puts down his beer and starts wrestling for real with Ian, we'll be done for. Ian must realize that too, because in a move straight from a Tarantino film, he leans against a wall and kicks into the air at Ty's chest, sending him backward into Jen, and both of them onto the floor. Yes! At least one of us can escape and end this horrible game.

Ian runs to the door and yanks at the knob. And then yanks it again. "What the hell?"

Micki's weight on me suddenly slackens, but my chest feels heavy as I watch Ian tug at the door. Something isn't right. By the time I get to my knees, Micki's thrown herself on Ian's back and is pulling his hair. He whips around hard enough to throw her off balance, launching a domino effect as she falls against me and I fall against Ty and Jen, who've just gotten up from their last tumble. We all crumple to the ground screaming obscenities. Somehow I end up on top of the pile like a ragdoll atop Rottweilers. I roll off and spring toward Ian.

His biceps bulge as he tries the door again and again. But it doesn't budge.

He jumps, swiping the air beneath the nearest camera. "You bastards locked us in! That's kidnapping."

Micki shoves herself between Ian and the door and tries the doorknob too. She laughs when it doesn't open. Who the hell laughs about being kidnapped?

The music transforms into an ice-cream truck melody, and then is drowned out by the *beep, beep, beep* of the panel, where a message rolls by. THE DOOR MUST BE JAMMED. WE'LL SEND A HANDYMAN OVER AS SOON AS POSSIBLE.

I yell at the screen, "You can't do this! We'll sue!"

WHO. EXACTLY. DO YOU PLAN TO PROSECUTE?

I point to Micki. "I can start with this bitch."

GOOD LUCK. SEEMS LIKE AN OPEN-AND-SHUT CASE OF SHE SAYS. SHE SAYS.

Does the audience see the messages from NERVE? Or just some edited version that protects the game administrators' butts? Maybe that's why we don't see the emcees anymore now that we're in handgun territory. The thought makes my blood rush downward.

I duck behind Ian, reach into my pocket for my phone, and punch 911. Micki's face goes wolf-like, and she lashes out at me, but Ian holds her back. It doesn't matter, though. The call is blocked. My grunt of disgust draws laughs from Micki and Ty.

I can't believe this. "Are you guys psychopaths? We're locked in here with guns. Doesn't that bug anyone but Ian and me?"

Samuel's huddled in his love seat. "They've probably removed the firing pins or loaded them with blanks."

It's all I can do not to jump on him. "You really want to bet on that?"

Ty grunts, "Chill out. No one's doing any shooting. It's just a game."

Daniella's got a hand to her mouth like she's trying not to cry, but she doesn't say anything. Jen and Micki nibble each other's lips and giggle. Do they know something I don't?

I try my phone again. Maybe I can delete the NERVE app and regain access, but it demands a password. Holding the phone up to the camera, I shout, "Get your program off of here."

Of course, there's no reply. I rub the tops of my arms, trying to soothe the panic that threatens to take over. The sleeve of my jacket has been torn loose, revealing deep scratches on my right shoulder.

I holler, "I need to see a doctor. Your pit bull got off leash."

Micki has a hand to her forehead. "You deserved worse."

FIRST AID SUPPLIES ARE IN THE YELLOW CABINET. OUR VIRTUAL DOC THINKS YOU ALL LOOK FINE. BUT WE'LL HAVE YOU CHECKED OUT WHEN THE HANDY-MAN OPENS THE DOOR.

The cabinet. I run toward it, not caring about first aid supplies, but wanting to block the others from the guns. I note that someone, probably Daniella, closed the green door they're behind.

Ty beats me to it, however, and hovers over me. "Oh no you don't."

I try to dart around him, but he's too large. "I need a bandage. And probably a rabies shot."

Ian's next to me. "C'mon, dude, we're all stuck in here. Let her get what she needs."

Ty holds an arm out. "I'll get it for her. Just in case some dumb-ass thinks they can grab a gun and shoot the lock off the door." He stares at me. "It wouldn't work anyway. They tested it on TV."

Great. That's probably the one piece of scientific data in his pea brain.

My arm aches. Maybe I really do need a rabies shot, or

at least distemper. "Okay, fine. I'm not going for a gun. Just give me something for my arm, okay? Then again, maybe you should let me bleed until I need medical attention and NERVE has to cancel the game." I bet NERVE will do no such thing.

Ty summons his gang for backup. We stand there face-to-face, twitching, while he opens the yellow drawer and rummages through it. He hands me a couple bandages and a few other supplies.

Back in our seat, Ian wipes my scratches with antiseptic pads before applying the bandages. Across the table, Jen holds an ice pack to Micki's head. Did *I* hurt her? Good.

Ty sits with his arms crossed, his glare daring us to make a move toward the cabinet. Daniella purrs and runs a hand through his hair, her bracelets jangling like jail keys. To Ian's and my left, Samuel remains silent, eyeing us over his glasses. We're all seated, like at the Last Supper, only no food and no saints.

The music shifts to elevator rock. Who's choosing the soundtrack? Satan?

OKAY PLAYERS. TIME TO EARN YOUR KEEP.

Again, our commands come only via text on the panels. As plastic as I found Guy and Gayle to be, without them, the room feels more isolated.

TY. PLACE THE GUNS ON THE TABLE. ONE IN FRONT OF EACH PLAYER.

My stomach goes to my feet. Ty stares at the panel with

a wrinkled forehead, like maybe he can't read. Or maybe he's grown a conscience.

YOU'LL EARN A HUNDRED-DOLLAR BONUS FOR YOUR EFFORT.

With a broad smile, he gets up. I hold my breath, praying that, like a magic trick, the weapons in the cabinet will have been replaced with doves. But as soon as he opens the door, it's clear that hasn't happened. Whatever bad luck's been biting my bony butt all night is here to stay.

I call out, "Don't do it, Ty. This is totally *Lord of the Flies*. NERVE wants to turn us into savages. Show them that you're your own man."

Ty addresses Ian. "Can't you control your woman, bro?"

Ian's face stiffens. "She's right. Don't do it, Ty."

"Pussy." He removes a gun and strokes it. "SIG Sauer P226. Sweet. A Navy SEAL's best buddy."

Keeping the gun at his side, he takes out a second one and places it in front of Daniella. The next two guns go to Jen and Micki, who leans in to examine hers with a low whistle. I flinch when she glances my way. Ty places guns in front of Samuel, then me, and finally Ian. He's laid mine and Ian's so that the barrels face us.

I cross my arms and start chanting loudly, "Whoever's watching, call 911. Whoever's watching, call 911." What are they going to do, threaten me with another consequence? Upgrade to machine guns?

I keep repeating the request. Even if NERVE blocked out my pleas when I was in the other room, they can't keep censoring me, especially now that all the other grand prize rounds are over. There'd be no show. Eventually, they'll either have to let us go or let the Watchers see us. Either way, the game is over. Screw fashion school.

TIME TO SHUT IT, VEE.

"Time to let me quit. I quit. I quit. I quit." I alternate this with pleas to the audience to call 911. Ian joins me in the chant.

LOOK AT YOUR PHONES.

I interrupt my chant to say, "There's no other prize you can offer. Fashion school and an internship aren't worth this. Nothing is."

Ty snarls. "Well, taking a trip to Ireland with my dad before he gets too sick is plenty worth it. So suck it up."

LOOK AT YOUR PHONE. YOUR PARENTS WOULD AP-PRECIATE IT.

What, they're bringing my parents into it again? I check my phone, which contains a long message. I read. It appears to be notes from my sessions with the shrink, stuff she was typing into her damn computer while I blabbed away. Details like what type of music was playing in my car that night. It's amazing how much info is in her notes. I thought I'd been so smart, trying to get her attention off of the garage incident by feeding her crap about how I felt invisible around Sydney, even going into that time when I was fooling around with Jason Walker and he called me her name by mistake. There's more humiliating material following that story. God, did I tell the shrink everything? Fat lot of good all those privacy forms I signed did. And to make things worse, there's a second message with details from a therapy session the shrink had with my parents, something about them not having intimate relations since—aw, no, they'd be mortified if this got out.

I look at the panels. Ian, who's been reading his phone, does too. His eyes are haunted.

WE'LL KEEP OUR MOUTH SHUT IF YOU DO.

I stop chanting.

NOW THEN, EACH PLAYER MUST PICK UP THEIR GUN. ANYONE WHO DOESN'T CLAIM HIS OR HER GUN FORFEITS IT TO ANOTHER PLAYER OF OUR CHOOSING.

Micki picks hers up first. Everyone follows suit. Except me.

I clear my throat. "It's not worth it. Let's just drink beers and hang out. This could still end up okay."

A crease forms between Ian's eyes when he glances my way. "Take the gun, Vee." Whoa, they must have even worse dirt on him than the crap they have on my family. Or did NERVE offer him another bonus? But what could be worth it? I wish I could get into his head and see what's motivating him.

My own thoughts, focused on the shiny black weapon in

front of me, send a shiver down my back. My mouth is dry. "This is crazy."

His eyes travel to the others around the table. "Yeah, it is. But if you don't claim it, you'll be totally unarmed."

Every breath I take threatens to turn into a wail that'll never stop. I force myself to speak through quivering lips. "Not taking a gun could be safer than taking one. Even these guys wouldn't shoot an unarmed person."

Micki smacks her lips. "Of course not."

YOU HAVE THIRTY SECONDS TO DECIDE.

Gayle's voice whispers over the speakers, "Be smart, Vee."

Too late for that.

A clock starts ticking down on the display. I gaze around the room. Micki and Ty caress their guns as if they're pets. Even Samuel seems to hold the gun like he's handled one before, which surprises me—must be all those video games. Daniella and Jen have theirs resting on their laps, while they tightly clutch their armrests.

The clock shows twenty seconds left.

"You don't have to point it at anyone, just claim it," Ian says.

"That's how they get you, baby steps," I whisper, although everyone can hear me.

Ian's voice is tight. "No one's going to make you fire it, but if you take it, that's one less gun for those guys to get their hands on."

Micki and Ty stare at me like pythons waiting for a rabbit. Maybe I should grab the gun and shoot out the cameras.

Ten seconds left.

A drop of sweat rolls down Ian's forehead. "Vee, please, I can't protect us alone."

I so do not want to. But how can I sit here defenseless? With three seconds to go, I grab the gun. It's heavy and greasy and totally does not feel fake. I place it on my lap, beyond caring if the oil stains my skirt. Micki grunts, a huge sneer on her face.

GREAT, GUYS! NOW SIT BACK AND ENJOY A SHORT FILM. JEN, PLEASE OPEN THE PINK CABINET FOR MOVIE TREATS.

She gets up, unsure of what to do with her gun, looking at Micki questioningly.

"Just hold it facing down," Micki says.

Jen does so and tiptoes toward the cabinet. I can only imagine what NERVE's sick idea of treats will entail. Probably something toxic. We haven't had any poisonous dares yet. But when she opens the yellow door, the buttery smell of popcorn fills the air and makes me want to puke. She pulls out a tub plastered with a brand name on its side and places it on the table before making a couple more trips to deliver boxes of candy that are also clearly labeled. Do the product sponsors actually think this'll sell more concession-stand items? Dumb question.

Jen calls out to Micki, "There's a cooler full of Red Bulls. Want one, baby?"

Of course, Micki and the same people who were downing beer earlier each take one. Alcohol and caffeine, a winning combination.

Ty and Micki are the only ones to grab at the popcorn, stuffing handfuls in their mouths. Samuel takes a box of candy with a shrug. Once Jen's back in her seat, the lighting dims and a movie comes up on the panels. Its title, *Gun Handling for Newbies.*

We spend the next five minutes learning how to load our guns, cock the hammer, pull the slide back, and aim with one hand or both. With each new piece of knowledge, I fight the urge to scream. We'll be shot. Our blood will flow down the drain, leaving the room tidy for the next batch of players. My knees shake so hard the gun might fall from my lap.

Ian takes my hand. "It's all for show. They're just trying to scare us." Trying? Even *his* face is pale, and the pulse in his hand drums against mine.

WE'LL GET TO THE FUN PART SOON, GUYS. BUT FIRST A LITTLE HOUSEKEEPING. SOMEONE STILL NEEDS A CONSEQUENCE FOR HER ACTIONS DURING A PRIOR DARE.

Seriously? What could possibly be worse than this? I want to kick myself as soon as the words form in my mind. It's one of those questions that always answers itself in a way you'll hate the moment you ask it.

In between Micki's whoops, the sound of chattering comes from behind one of the doors we used for the customized dares. With a pop, the panel opens and two people wearing blindfolds stumble into the room.

The gun in my lap feels ten pounds heavier when I realize who's joined us.

Tommy and Sydney.

Seventeen

My spirits plummet, but I jump up. "You guys, get back out while you can!"

They tear their blindfolds off and blink against the lights with dazed expressions. The door they just emerged from slowly closes on its own.

I race toward them, pointing toward it. "Run!"

Their heads whip with nervous expressions between me and the door, which clicks shut. Micki and Ty, who'd risen from their seats, probably to block me from escaping, sit back down wearing smug expressions.

Sydney blinks with a level of disorientation I've never seen on her. The confusion snaps into shock when she sees the gun dangling in my hand. "That's not real, is it?"

I tuck the weapon behind my back. "I don't know."

Tommy scans the room with a mixture of disgust and curiosity. He stares at me and shakes his head with an *I told you so* purse to his lips. The other players remain in their seats, some munching popcorn, as if my friends and I are the new show.

Syd struts forward so we're inches apart, her eyes boring through mine. "You've taken this way too far. How could you not quit after they got you to hallucinate that you were breathing carbon monoxide fumes? Shit, Vee." She grabs my arm and drags me toward the door they just came from.

I trail in her haughty wake. "How much have you seen? Did any of my requests to call 911 get through, or did you guys think that was part of the hallucination?"

She ignores me and knocks on the door. "Okay, let us out now."

The panels light up and beep, causing her to crane her neck backward to read the one above her head. I put a hand on her back, bracing her for a message that's sure to set her off.

THIS DOOR'S ON A TIMER AND CAN'T BE OPENED AGAIN FOR THIRTY MINUTES. UNLESS, OF COURSE, THERE'S AN EMERGENCY. THE PLAYERS CAN SHOW YOU WHERE THE DRINKS ARE. MAKE YOURSELF AT HOME!

Sydney slaps the wall. "I don't want to make myself at home. And, hello, guns *are* an emergency!" She tries to pry her fingers into the almost invisible seam along the door, but it does no good, so she runs to the main door and tries the knob. When that doesn't work, she bangs at the door and shouts, "You guys said Vee was in over her head and that Tommy and I should come pick her up. Now we have, so let us out or I'll call my dad. He's an attorney."

Micki laughs and asks the other players if they want another beer. She pretends to prance on high heels as she passes between us.

Syd pulls out her phone and swears when she sees that she doesn't have service. She marches to where I stand in the middle of the room. "Give me yours."

My chest is heavy. This is my consequence. It's not enough to put myself in danger or freak out my parents. NERVE's playing on my guilt, which doesn't take much with Capricorns, especially since mine was already near a breaking point before the grand prize round. I can hardly stand the thought that I'm responsible for my friends joining me in a hell they don't yet understand. If anything happens to them . . .

I hang my head. "None of our phones work, and no one's getting rescued or prosecuted. Not while we can entertain the Watchers. And now they've given everyone guns and made us watch a training video. I'm so sorry I got you into this."

Tommy's face is hard. He yells at Ian, who's risen from the love seat and come out from behind the coffee table. "It's your fault, you son of a bitch!" He takes a step forward.

Ian keeps his gun at his side, but his eyes go nuclear. "You don't want to come any nearer."

I dart in front of Tommy and hold out my hand. "Haven't you been watching? As long as we're stuck here, we're lucky Ian has our backs."

Tommy exhales loudly, pushing against me. "You call this having your back? You'd never have come in here on your own."

My palm presses into his chest. Surprisingly, it's as taut as Ian's. "No one's put a gun to my head. Yet. Ian's in this horrible grand prize round just as much as me. And now, unfortunately, so are you and Sydney. Oh God, I wish you guys hadn't come."

Sydney's hands are on her hips, the way they were in Act One, Scene Two. "A little late for that."

"Why didn't you call the police if you wanted to help me?" I ask.

She blows out in exasperation. "Police? For a game? Everyone knows it's all choreographed."

Now I'm exasperated. "You believe that?" I'm looking at Tommy. He should know better.

His cheeks are red. "They went skydiving in the Colorado grand prize round and all of the chutes opened. Your fear is manufactured."

"Trust me, manufactured fear feels the same as the organic stuff." I sigh. "We've all been duped."

He pushes past me toward Ian. "Well, your partner didn't help. He's like a kind of Web whore. I found a few nasty sites with images that I'm sure are of him. Just wait until I run it against some facial recognition software." He pulls out his phone and turns to me. "Here, I'll show you."

I grab at the phone. "I thought you didn't have service. Call 911. Now!"

Micki and Ty jump from their places as Tommy clutches his phone to his chest and his eyes bug. "I don't have service. I downloaded the video earlier." He clicks on something and holds the phone up in front of my face.

Ian's neck is red. "That's bullshit!"

There's a dimly lit video of what appears to be several barely dressed people wrestling, or whatever. I push it away. "This isn't the time to be checking out weird videos."

Tommy keeps the clip running. "You need to see who you've teamed up with and who you can trust."

Micki laughs and peeks over the back of her chair. "What's the matter? Virgin can't handle a skin flick?"

The wall panels beep, luring our eyes to them.

ENOUGH CHITCHAT. HERE'S THE NEXT TASK: POINT YOUR GUN AT EITHER WHOEVER YOU VOTED FOR AS THE VICTIM OR ONE OF THE NEW ARRIVALS.

Sydney's stilettos come an inch off the floor. "What the—"

A yelp escapes from my lips, and it feels as if all of my blood evaporates. Is this how I'll die? Or get one of my friends killed? Is that what the audience really wants to see? My throat is tight. Why didn't I stay after the play to greet Mom and Dad? Any decent daughter would have.

Micki and Ty turn around and use their seat backs to rest their arms and aim. She holds her gun with two hands, Ty with one, straight and sure. The holes in the gun barrels stare at me and Ian, unblinking.

Samuel takes a big breath before raising his gun. "Sorry, Vee. But I promise I'll never pull the trigger."

"That makes me feel so much better." My voice has risen an octave. I consider running to the bathroom for cover and taking my friends with me, but the door doesn't lock.

"Pick up your gun," Ty says to Daniella.

She crosses her arms around her chest. "I don't know. This is getting too creepy."

Ty's jaw goes tight. "Thought there was more to you."

She turns toward us slowly, biting her lip, and then picks up the gun with two hands, one on the grip and one under the barrel. Thanks to the film, I know the terminology. Will that be the last knowledge I ever pick up?

Daniella whimpers and uses her shoulder to wipe her cheek. Her wobbly movements cause her bracelets to jangle, jangle, jangle, and cause my guts to twist.

"Good enough," Ty says.

Micki whispers something into Jen's ear before nipping at her lobe. Jen sighs and picks up her gun too. That's one more barrel pointed at me, one more at Ian.

I turn to him. A pulsing vein bulges from his neck. Slowly, he picks up his gun and aims at Ty.

The room goes so quiet I can hear the buzz of the overhead lights.

I want to melt onto the carpet, nasty as it is, but I need to think. "Sydney and Tommy, this isn't your fight." I point to the main door. "Go stand over there."

I begin walking around the table, back to my love seat, which is on the far side of the room from where I've directed Tommy and Sydney to go.

But they follow me.

I turn and say, "No. You'll just give these jerks a bigger target. I know you're smart enough to see that."

Tommy leans in and whispers, "Also smart enough to have called the police before we got here. It's only a matter of time before they get to this floor. All we need to do is stall."

I want to sing in relief. Did NERVE hear him? I'm not sure if that would be bad or good. I whisper back, "I should've known. You're amazing, Tommy. Now, please, go stall over there. I promise to check out any video you want after we get out of here."

He takes Sydney's arm, trying to nudge her in that direction, but it's no use, of course. She pulls away and places her hands on my shoulders, as if she's oblivious to the fact that she's directly in the others' gun sights.

Her eyes are moist, yet her makeup is still perfect. "Vee, even though you've behaved like a bitch and a half tonight, I came to help you, not huddle in some corner."

"You know what, Syd? You're right, I've been horrible. Somehow, I'll make things up to you. But if you truly want to help, then please stay out of the way. Really. Please, please, please do it for me."

She doesn't budge. How can I get her to protect herself when she's hardwired to stick up for me?

The lights begin to dim.

I push her toward the door. "Go now, before they turn off the lights and you're stuck standing in the crossfire. Then you're no help to anyone."

She trembles, whether in fear or frustration, I can't tell. But finally, common sense sinks in. She trudges away. Tommy follows, glancing back toward Ian and me.

I head to the love seat, bumping into the stupid table along the way, which causes it to swing with a groan. Samuel puts out his free hand to stop it, keeping his gun arm pointed at me. Instead of sitting, I get behind the love seat and crouch, using its back the way the others have to hold my gun. The flimsy back cushion probably wouldn't stop a bullet, but it makes me feel better to hide behind a shield. Over it, I aim at Micki, who aims back with a sneer. I can hardly believe I'm pointing a weapon at another human being.

Ian's still in the center of the room, out in the open. As

the lights dim further, he comes around the table too, taking a spot behind Samuel's love seat. Why didn't I think to tell Tommy and Sydney to hide there so they'd at least have some cover? Just another way I've failed everyone I care about tonight. My friends look so vulnerable huddled near the door.

Although the other players would probably hate to admit that Ian and I have the right idea, the two couples across the coffee table get out of their seats to take up positions behind them, the way we have. I'm sure that Samuel would like to get behind his seat, but since Ian's there, he hurries around the table to join Daniella and Ty behind theirs. So, we're like two armies, five against two, aiming over our love seats and across the coffee table border.

It's only taken a minute for us to assume our positions, but we must've made NERVE impatient, because the beeping starts up again.

COCK THE HAMMER ON YOUR GUN.

The panels display an animation of a gun being cocked in case we don't remember from the video.

My stomach drops. I press my thighs together to keep my legs from shaking, and I say, "Do you really think you can get away with this? If these guns are loaded and one of us gets shot, that's the end of your game, for good."

NOT THE END. AN ADVERTISEMENT. The words flash quickly on the panel across the room, the one that Ian and I face, but not on the one to our right. Sydney and Tommy crane their heads toward the message I saw, but I don't think they were fast enough to read it.

I speak to the camera, "Are you kidding? Even if no one can find you, who'd want to play your game after that?"

The other players look puzzled. Is the panel above my head, the one they're facing, not working?

The panel across from me blinks quickly. PEOPLE WHO LIKE TO WIN WILL ALWAYS PLAY.

A dark corner of my brain knows this is true, no matter how badly I want it not to be. Look what I've done tonight in the hopes of winning fashion school tuition.

If I can't appeal to NERVE, maybe I can find a shred of logic in the other players, who probably think I've lost it, since they only heard my end of the conversation. "C'mon, you guys. Let's stop. They want us to shoot each other. As an advertisement. You think I'm exaggerating? Look at the carpet under the table, in the center. That's a drain. Know what it's for? To hose down this room. From our blood."

Micki sneers. "No, it's probably to wash out the piss, from babies like you who wet their panties."

She rubs her thumb against the back of her gun, creating a loud *click*. Jen closes her eyes for a long moment, and then, keeping her gaze averted from mine, cocks her hammer too. Ty does the same. Ian too. *Click, click, click.*

Ty raises his eyebrows at Daniella. "What're you waiting for?"

"Are these loaded?" she calls out.

WHAT DO YOU THINK? Now all of the panels are back in action. Have there been messages tonight that the others have seen that I haven't?

Jen's shoulders shake. "I don't have any gun experience. What if it goes off?"

Ty scowls. "It won't unless you pull the trigger, idiot. Cocking the hammer just shifts it from double action to single action."

Samuel adds, "Which is only a problem if it's a real bullet."

What, he still believes the guns aren't lethal? What does our audience think? No police have crashed in to save us. Does everyone really believe this is a big game of paintball or something? That we'll walk out of here with nothing more than a few bruises? There are sadists watching who want it to be real. My friends, at least, must be watching in horror. And helplessness, because no one knows where we are.

I don't remember what the video said about double action and bullets in the chamber, but I know that cocking the gun is one step closer to shooting it. And Daniella realizes that too. Mascara runs down her cheeks. But, ultimately, the fear of becoming the next victim if she screws up the grand prizes must get to her, because she cocks her gun.

"Vee?" Ian says.

I feel the same way Daniella does, not wanting to touch the hammer, to point this thing with less of a net. On the other hand, if something crazy happens, I need to protect myself. And my friends. Holding my breath, I flick my thumb against the knobby protrusion at the back of the gun. *Click.*

Micki's upper lip takes on a sheen that wasn't there before. Good. A red veil shadows my vision.

"How long do we need to stay like this?" Jen calls out in a squeaky voice.

No answer from NERVE.

Ian says, "All the game told us was that we had to cock our guns, not how long we had to leave them cocked. We've completed that part of the dare, so now let's flip the decocking levers and lower our weapons before anything stupid goes down."

Samuel nods. I wish he'd say something.

We all look toward the panels, expecting NERVE to chime in.

Ian focuses on the players across the table. "How about I count to three and we decock them at the same time? Let's quit before we pass the point of no return."

He takes a breath. "One."

Jen raises her eyebrows at Micki, whose gaze remains firmly on me.

"Two."

Sweat drips down my spine. The room is quiet, no music, not even the squeak of a chair.

Ian inhales deeply. Will we be the only ones to decock our

guns? My breathing is so shallow, I think I'll lose consciousness at any moment.

"Three."

I move my thumb to the lever, but before I click it off, my world goes dark. The room's lights have gone out. Strobe lights flash on. People scream. And shots fire.

eighteen

Instinctively, I duck. The metal of the gun is heavy and slippery, yet I keep it propped on the seat back way above my head. My heart hammers in my chest like it's trying to escape, and, as my hearing returns, I detect twangy music that you'd find at a square dance. Yee-haw. Clearly, some sicko's idea of a joke.

My right arm is stiff, almost numb, so I slowly lower the gun to the floor, tempted to drop it. But I might need it to protect myself, against all of those other guns, which I'm sure are still pointed my way, even in the dark.

"Is everyone okay?" I ask the room in a soft voice, not wanting to startle anybody into more gunfire.

In the space to my left, Ian says, "Yeah."

I speak louder, over the banjos. "Tommy? Syd?"

There's a rustling in the far corner of the room, and then Sydney's voice, which always projects crystal clear: "We're fine."

I exhale in relief.

"Aren't you going to check on us?" Micki says in a singsongy voice.

"I figured you survived, seeing as how I didn't fire my gun."

She grunts. "Like hell you didn't, or maybe your pretty boy's the one who shot at us."

There's a sound of Ian shifting his body. "No, some of us can control our trigger fingers."

Ty laughs. "That's not what she said."

Samuel speaks up, for the first time in what seems like hours. "There were five shots. I didn't fire. And the sound didn't come from next to me. So it had to be you guys."

Ian's voice is angry. "My gun is cold; wanna come here and check it?"

Of course, Micki adds, "Knew he had a cold gun, to go with his frigid girlfriend." God, is everything tied to sex with that girl? And why doesn't she just admit that she freaked out and fired? Unless . . . With a tremor of anger, I realize another possibility.

I clear my throat so that my next words are as clear as Sydney's. "Maybe NERVE fired the shots. Or maybe they injected the smell of gunpowder into the air vents along with a recording of shots. Either way, they wanted to scare us into shooting. Don't you guys get it? This is the finale."

Everyone's silent for a moment. On some level, they must know that what I've suggested is a likely scenario.

Ian says, "In the dark, with the strobe lights, we couldn't tell who was shooting or not."

Sniffling, Jen says, "Assholes. Turn the lights on, already. Your audience can't see us in the dark anyway." I hadn't pegged her for the crying type. But then, I hadn't pegged myself as the gun-toting type.

"Smells like piss in here," Ty says.

Is that a faint ammonia odor mixed in with the scents of firecrackers and popcorn? Ugh.

NERVE must be doing something tricky with the lighting, because although I can't see any glow overhead, I begin to make out the shape of my arms. I sit up, mostly to get away from the nasty carpet, but also to take a peek at the shapes emerging in the semi-darkness: the love seats, the shifting heads peeking back at me. The coffee table is invisible, but eventually I can spot the thick cables connecting it to the ceiling.

OKAY. NO EXCUSES. YOU NEED TO RE-AIM YOUR WEAPONS NOW. AND, TO BE CLEAR, YOU MUST HOLD YOUR AIM FOR THE LAST TWENTY MINUTES OF THE GAME.

I remember watching a grand prize finale last month, the one with the kids standing at the edge of the roof. Which I was sure had a net below. As the players trembled, NERVE kept cutting to highlights from the previous dares. That's what they must be doing now with us. All for sadistic entertainment.

As my pupils dilate, I detect Ty rising above the back of his love seat barricade, his gun pointing in Ian's direction. He hisses something at Daniella, who slowly joins him. Jen and Micki aim their weapons toward me, well, my love seat, same difference. So does Samuel. Ian raises his gun toward Ty.

I hold my gun in my lap, deciding what to do. Running my fingers over it, I locate the decocking lever. Should I flick it? But I have to protect myself, and I'm sure no one else has decocked their gun, even though NERVE hasn't said anything about keeping them cocked. There's really no choice, is there? If I want to defend myself and my friends, I have to be a combatant in this sick game. I rise up onto my knees and take aim over the seat.

We wait. Again, the lights dim and the music goes silent, causing minute sounds to become noticeable—the buzz of electricity, a pipe rushing from a floor above us, rapid breathing, bodies shifting. The darkness is impenetrable, like a living creature that reaches into my eyes, my nose, my mouth. I want to yank it away, but it's got me in its clutches. My chest wall threatens to burst open to release my wildly pumping heart. I hiccup, unable to control my breathing or the sounds I'm making. Someone across the divide laughs. Micki.

Ian shifts to the end of his love seat that's closest to mine and whispers, "Put your head down for a minute. Concentrate on long, slow breaths."

I do as he says, keeping hold of my gun and its aim. I don't care about the damn dare, but if Micki starts shooting, I have to fight back. I breathe deeply. After a minute, I think I have my wits under control. But my head throbs, so I let one hand free from the gun to rub my temple. This is all a horrible fantasy, right? I try to imagine myself someplace else.

Suddenly a lecture my science teacher gave on quantum physics comes to mind. Something about a cat. Schrödinger's Cat. It was a story about how events remain in the realm of probability until they actually happen, or maybe until someone witnesses them happening. This scientist named Schrödinger claimed that if his cat were in a box, no one could know for sure whether it was alive or dead until they opened the box to find out. But now I wonder if the Watchers won't learn of our fate until someone opens this evil box.

No, stop it. I need to use my mind in a way that slows the out-of-control beating in my chest. The darkness around us could be anywhere, anytime. I could be alive or dead. Okay, I choose alive. While I'm at it, I choose the darkness to be a gentle blanket on a moonless night, where I rest a few feet from a boy who's warm and sweet. When he holds me, his heart beats strong with what I tell myself is passion, not fear.

I've almost got myself believing in this romantic fantasy

when the faint light appears again. Across the room, three guns still point at me. Fantasy over. Tears well in my eyes along with a hopeless weight in my belly.

Which only gets heavier when Sydney produces a theatrical sigh and says, "Okay, that's about four minutes. Time for a scene change. I'm sure we can do something more interesting than point guns in the dark." There's a tremor to her voice I've never heard before.

I wish she'd be quiet. But has she ever been one to silently endure?

Ty snorts. "You're welcome to come sit over here and show me what you got in mind. I've got a free hand."

Frantic whispering comes from Syd and Tommy's corner.

My skin feels like bugs are crawling all over it. "Stay where you are, Syd," I call out. I'd go over there and tackle her if it wouldn't cause several guns to alter their aim.

"What's your name?" she says.

"Ty, like in *tiiiiime* to party!"

I sit up tall. "Syd, do not even think of moving."

Leave it to Syd to try and turn the game around. But this is way bigger than a school play. She can't charm her way out. Or mine. The thought of Ty placing any of his fat fingers on her makes me want to gag. And what about Daniella? She could get jealous, and discover that holding on to a gun has its benefits after all.

Micki groans. "God, Virgin Victim's friend is even more

annoying than the virgin is. Maybe we should shift our aims."

I speak up. "Yeah, that sounds like what I'd expect from you, aiming at the people who can't defend themselves. Just remember whose weapon will be pointed at your head."

I can't believe I just said that, but Micki maintains her aim on me instead of swinging it toward Sydney. I hate that Syd's here, so defenseless. My brave, stubborn best friend, who's been wearing that silly corset so long that her back must be aching.

I wipe my eye. "Syd, just stick with Tommy, okay?" He must've told her about contacting the police, right? Unless he's afraid she'll blurt it out in a dramatic moment.

Tommy says, "Seems like we should get weapons too."

No! What the hell is he thinking? Especially when police should be here at any moment. Or is that what he's banking on? Which means his request is just a way of playing tough. Who's he trying to impress? This audience isn't worth it.

I call out to him, "There are enough guns in here already. No one needs to add more for their sick show."

A dagger of pain shoots down my right arm. Maybe from gripping the gun so long. I don't know how many minutes more I can hold on to this slimy weapon. How much longer do we have, fifteen minutes? And if I'm getting tired, what about the others? All it would take is for the strobes to go back on, or another bang to startle someone into pulling a trigger. The more tired we get, the easier it'll be to make a mistake.

The room fades to pitch-black.

I whisper to Ian, "We've got to end this as soon as possible." Before someone's aching arm cramps up. Before Sydney gets with Ty and stirs up a heap of trouble. Before NERVE introduces something that sends us over the edge. Which I know they'll do.

Ian whispers back, "I'm working on a plan."

I ask, "What? Dive to the floor and hope for the best?" I don't mean for that to come out so snarky, but hopelessness can bring out the worst in anyone.

He grunts. "I'm assuming there was no window in the bathroom, right?"

That's the best he's got? "Of course not. No windows anywhere in this twisted theater." As I say the words, a combination of images flood my mind: stages, audiences, windows, guns. We're the actors in this sick production. Our scummy Watchers could be based anywhere in the world, kicking back with cocktails. Making bets. Waiting for blood.

Imagining the audience watching our show makes my pulse quicken with the promise of an idea. What is it? I can't shake the feeling that I'm on the edge of something, like when my mind's eye takes a pile of fabric and sewing notions and coalesces them into a design. *Think.* I wish I could examine our surroundings better. Maybe we could make one of the doors open somehow. How many openings have we seen so far? Nine? I squint, trying to make out anything in the dark.

NERVE's probably using night-vision cameras to broadcast close-up shots of us. They think they can capture our anxiety. It's a turn-on for them. I'll bet the sickest viewers wish they could be here in the room with us, smelling our fear. I envision spectators cheering for gore, like at a Roman arena, the emperor enjoying the kills from his gilded seat.

I stop short. That's it.

Someone in the audience would've demanded the best seats. Someone always does. The wall to our left has paneling that's different from the other walls. And it only has one door, a regular one, in the corner, unlike the other walls, which have all kinds of weird hidden openings. As Ian and I made our way to the room at the beginning of the grand prize round, we passed those chairs lining the hallway. The front row.

Suddenly, I'm certain that the silk wall-hanging in the corridor outside is more than decorative—it's a drape, the grand drape, now raised for this sick show. And the shiny wall next to the door isn't a wall, it's a one-way window. We have Watchers only feet away. I feel it as surely as if they were breathing down my neck.

Should I share my suspicions with Ian? What if any of what Tommy said is true? Did Ian manipulate me into this for Web fame? Maybe Micki was right about there being a plant for NERVE in here. How else could he pay for private school? Syd thought he was shady too, and she's a great judge of character. Or is she? How great a judge can she be, when she chose me for a best friend? A best friend who doubted her loyalty and signed up for a treacherous game that might kill us both.

Ian's been my rock tonight. And I need someone to help me break out of here. Tommy could be mistaken about seeing Ian on creepy Websites, just like he was wrong to think he could count on the police to show up in time. He saw what he wanted to see online, not what was there. But he's the smartest guy I know. Could he really have gotten it wrong? I pull at my hair. There's no time to figure out the truth. I need to act on my gut.

Behind a cupped hand, I whisper my suspicions to Ian, praying he's on my side.

"That's crazy," he says, but his voice hints at his uncertainty. "And even if it's true, what do we do about it?" At least he's whispering, not broadcasting my ideas.

I shake my head, frustrated that he doesn't see things as clearly as I do. Or maybe he doesn't want to. Will he go so far as to stop me?

I say, "We shoot through the window."

He's silent for a moment. "Gunshots would either penetrate it and hit someone on the outside, assuming there are people there, or they'd ricochet back at us. Neither option is acceptable."

I'm not so sure the audience doesn't deserve bullets

coming through the window at them, but I'll accept his point for now. "How about ramming a love seat into it?"

"They're bulky and not on wheels. I don't think we could get the momentum to push one through the wall."

We have nothing else in the room to throw except beer bottles and popcorn boxes. Unless you count the other players, a couple of whom I wouldn't mind throwing through the window. If only we could pick up the weird glass table.

My breath catches.

We don't need to. Attached to its cables, it's like a missile. And, since there aren't love seats on either end, there's nothing to block it. I whisper to Ian. He resists at first, but what's the alternative? We trade a few ideas for how to put the plan into action without causing the others to shoot us. As soon as we have something figured out that doesn't sound impossible, I hear a tiny *click*.

"What's that?" I ask.

"I decocked my gun," he says.

My chest contracts. I feel vulnerable. But he's right. Escaping will be worthless if we accidentally shoot people in the process. And NERVE never specified that we had to keep our guns cocked; so as long as we maintain our aims, they shouldn't expose our actions with messages about violating the integrity of the dare. I decock my gun, but keep it pointed Micki's way.

"Ready?" he asks.

254

I don't have time not to be. Any second now, Sydney could strut over to Ty, which would piss off the players next to him. And NERVE might blast the music or set off the sprinklers, startling someone into shooting.

I rise up next to Ian and say, "Showtime."

He leans close to me. "I need to tell you something first. I don't know what kind of sick video-editing of me Tommy did while he jacked off, but it's totally fake."

I can't begin to figure out what's true and what isn't. Tommy's capable of creating any kind of video he wants. Whatever Ian's done online doesn't matter anyway. What does is that we need to make an escape attempt. Now. But I understand wanting to make things clear, for the record.

I whisper back, "My real name is Venus. I just want you to know, in case . . . And you have to protect Syd, no matter what."

"We'll get through this, Venus." He presses his lips to mine.

Will we? Will Syd and Tommy? What I wouldn't give to be backstage watching Sydney and Matthew's stage kiss. It could go on forever and ever if they wanted.

I take a deep breath. "Okay, action!" I say, wishing we had the time to let Tommy and Sydney in on our plan.

We move to our right. Ian begins to laugh quietly and then louder, which sends a chill through me even though I was expecting it. No one shoots. So far, so good.

"What's so damn funny?" Ty asks.

"Us," Ian says. "We're acting like scared little rabbits in the dark. There's nothing we can do, so why not give our audience the show they want? Maybe if we're good enough, they'll add on to everyone's prizes." He moves past me.

I grab his shirt with one hand and keep the other one aiming at Micki until we make our way around the love seat and hit the table. Ian squeezes my hand and then lets go, moving to the side of the table near our enemies, while I stay on this side and reach in the air until I find the cable that the glass plank is attached to. Hopefully, Ian's doing the same on the other side. If he's going to betray me, it'll be soon.

"Anyone for a little swinging?" Ian says, giving the table a push.

Micki shouts, "We're supposed to be aiming, moron."

I grit my teeth, but try to keep my voice cheery. "Some of us are able to play and aim at the same time."

"What are you guys doing?" Syd asks.

I yank my cable in time with Ian. "If NERVE is happy with our performance, maybe they'll give you and Tommy a break."

Between Ian and me, the heavy glass sways side to side. I hold my aimed gun close to my chest so the cables don't smack it.

Ian laughs again. "Anyone want a ride before Vee and I climb on and start rockin' this thing?"

Samuel's voice trembles. "Those cables might not support all the extra weight."

I groan. "You calling me fat?"

Ian and I push the table harder. The cables creak.

"Last call," Ian shouts. "C'mon, Micki, you and Jen could show us how it's done." As he talks, the table taps the wall. Hopefully, no one notices.

"Fuck off," Micki says.

Will NERVE swoop in and stop us somehow? Or, maybe the mystery of what we're doing is raising the Watcher approval ratings to levels that satisfy the product sponsors.

"Next push," Ian whispers.

This is it. If my plan fails, I have nothing else. No other way of saving my friends. My knees feel weak with the weight of what we're up against. They start to buckle, the way they did when I tried out for the play. The way they wanted to when I poured water on myself in the coffee shop. The way they always threaten to do when I'm the center of attention. I try to straighten them. This is my time to be strong. For once, I need to perform.

When the table comes back to us, I heave in a deep breath, gather my strength, and wrench the cable with every ounce I'm worth. Will Ian make this last push too or suddenly yank his side to a stop, showing his true allegiance?

But the table flies. With cables wailing, it slams into the wall, which I'm praying is a window after all.

An ear-splitting crash reverberates through the room. And then I hear the loveliest sound of the night, the screams of the audience on the other side of the glass wall.

Welcome to our show, assholes.

nineteen

"What the hell?" Micki shouts.

"Ooops," Ian says.

I catch the cable as best I can on the return swing, and we push again, causing more piercing cracks of glass hitting glass. A burst of gunfire goes off. I duck as the strobes and more gunfire boom around our heads. Is it real? The screams sure are.

Between the flashes, a steady stream of light penetrates the room from the hallway. Is this the thrill the front-row Watchers were seeking? I feel a rush of hatred toward the audience, who's hovered so closely by but hasn't rescued us.

Even when the strobes stop, the light from the hallway casts a dim glow in the room. This makes our task easier and harder, since Ian and I can see what we're doing, but we can also be seen.

Ty rises from behind his love seat. His gun wavers between Ian and me. "What are you ass-wipes doing?"

"What NERVE told us to," I say. "Didn't you get the message on your phones?" Ian and I catch the cable and give it another push. Even if the other players don't quite realize we've violated the integrity of the dare, NERVE must. It's only a matter of time before they respond with another consequence or something worse. With no reason to maintain a fake aim, I tuck my gun into the back of my skirt's waistband so I can have both hands free for the next push.

The table hits the wall of glass again, about two feet from the floor, and widens the hole to about a foot across. More light. More screaming. I wish the table had blasted all the way through to the hallway, crashing into our worthless audience, who sound like they're running for cover.

The panels above flash a message in giant letters. INTEGRITY VIOLATION! AIM YOUR GUNS AT ANOTHER PLAYER NOW OR EVERYONE LOSES THEIR PRIZES! A long horn blares.

Micki jumps up, frowns at the hole in the wall, but keeps her gun on me. "They're trying to escape again. When we're eight minutes from winning our prizes!"

Eight minutes from getting killed in a grand finale slaughter is more like it. Ian and I get in one more slam before he rushes to my side of the table. A chunk of glass falls away from the wall, leaving an opening of about a foot and a half in diameter.

Micki yells, "Stop or I'll shoot, you assholes!"

Ian grabs my cable and we give the table a lopsided push. "We aren't even holding our guns. You going to shoot us in cold blood?"

I hold my breath. Will she?

Her face is a mask of rage. "I'm giving you one more chance to stop screwing with the table and get back into the dare."

Ty's next to her. "Me too."

Ian and I make another unbalanced push, which hits the glass wall with less force than the previous ones.

I swallow. "There's no way you or NERVE could convince the whole audience that you shot Ian and me in self-defense when we aren't holding our weapons. Plus, Tommy called the police before he got here. You really think you'll get away with it?" I glance at Jen and Daniella, hoping that they'll join the good guys, but both of them hold their guns more or less in my and Ian's direction.

"*You* really think you'll screw me over?" Micki lunges over the love seat.

I scoot alongside the table away from her. But instead of firing, she yanks the cable Ian had, preventing it from doing more damage to the glass. That's my cue to run toward the hole in the wall.

Ian's right behind me, and Tommy and Syd are next to us. I kick at the edge of the opening, causing another chunk of glass to fall off. The hole comes up just past my knees and is about two feet wide, with edges that look like they could cut through bone.

Down the hall, a Watcher yells, "Move it! The little shits are getting loose!"

Micki launches herself at Ian while I kick at the hole's bottom, breaking another chunk free. Sydney's trying to kick the wall too, but her stilettos are useless. Tommy just stands there looking stunned until Ty grabs him with a sickening crunch.

Tommy groans. "Stop! This isn't what we signed up for. You need to end it now."

Hell, he and Syd didn't sign up for anything except rescuing me. But neither Ty nor NERVE gives a damn.

Ian wraps his arms around Micki's torso and swings her back and forth so that her flailing legs whip into Ty, who's pulled Tommy away from the wall. Jen yanks Syd by the hair and they spin off into cat-fight mode. Daniella slouches nearby with her hands to her ears. Is she crying? As long as she isn't attacking.

I kick at the glass wall. Ian keeps swinging Micki, and either her feet or Tommy's hit Ty in the groin, because he doubles over and drops Tommy in a heap.

I call to Samuel, "Help me." I free another chunk, wishing I'd worn heavier shoes.

Samuel shakes his head. "Don't ask me to throw away my future, Vee."

Is he for real? "If we stay, there is no future, dumb-ass. You don't think NERVE will throw something worse at us in the next five minutes? It only takes seconds to kill someone."

My next kick is harder and breaks away a chunk of glass the size of Samuel's face. This brings the hole all the way down to the floor. Ty begins to straighten up. Tommy's on the floor in front of him, but it doesn't look like he'll be able to hold anyone off. Ian swings Micki back and forth again, which might keep Ty away from me, but only for a few seconds more. I'm out of time.

To protect my hands, I pull my arms as far into my sleeves as I can before I get on all fours. Then I crawl out, trying to pad softly on the remaining glass. The top of the hole scrapes at my jacket, but the thick brocade keeps my back from getting sliced. I enter the deserted hallway. Going to the right would lead to the closed door at the end, which could be an exit or an execution chamber. Heading to the left would lead to the reception area, where Watchers may be lurking, waiting to ambush me.

Before I can decide, something yanks my ankle and twists my leg around. I flip onto my butt and gaze into Ty's bulging face through the opening. He has a clear view up my skirt, but his eyes are on mine, burning with anger. Around his face, the wall, which on this side is a giant window, displays the room in perfect focus. Above the window are several screens, each with a different camera shot of the game room.

Ty pulls at my leg. I use the other to kick him in the face. He gasps, but his grip on my leg barely loosens. I try kicking again, but he's ready for it and grabs my other ankle. With a smile, he lowers his heavy chest onto my feet, pressing them into the rubbery carpet. On my side of the window-wall, glass shards scrape through my tights into the backs of my thighs.

Ty pins the bottom six inches of my legs beneath his forearms. "I can lie here all night, you know. Or maybe I'll just drag you back in here."

Oh God, there's no way I'll make it back through the opening without getting sliced up. I stretch to my right in an effort to grab the silk wall-hanging for support, but it's been pulled off to one side like a curtain, too far to reach. I twist my arm behind myself to try and pull out my gun, but my jacket and skirt are twisted around it, trapping it in my waistband. Thankfully, the pocket with my phone has landed on my stomach. I reach inside. Can I dial 911 fast enough? Will the reception work now?

Ty must figure out what I'm up to, because he almost crushes my ankles as he shifts his weight to get onto his knees. He tugs my feet, causing my butt to slide a few inches closer to the room, and more glass to graze my legs. I dig through my pocket, even though I can't imagine making a call in time. That's when my fingers brush against something next to my phone, the campaign button. Oh, thank God for Jimmy C! I grab the button and, without pausing to think, snap it open and jam the pin into Ty's cheek.

He screams as I jab his forehead and other cheek. "You fucking bitch!"

Although my kick to his face hadn't been enough to force him to let me go, the little campaign pin carries more power. While Ty grabs at his cheeks, I pull my legs from the hole and scoot backward over glass shards that crunch under my butt and dig into my palms. Getting up, I quickly check my hands. Only one piece punctured skin, causing a sharp pain at the base of my left thumb. But the backs of my thighs sting with what must be half a dozen small cuts. I brush at them quickly. Nothing more I can do now.

Ty starts to crawl through the hole, his face contorted in rage, but his broad shoulders won't clear the opening without serious damage.

Ian yells, "Run, Vee! If one of us escapes, the game is over!"

After all of my struggle to get free of the room, I still hesitate for a second, wanting to be with Ian, Sydney, and Tommy, but unsure how. Leaving them feels like the worst kind of abandonment. But getting help is our best hope.

Ty gets up and kicks at the hole, breaking away another piece. "You're dead, bitch."

I run.

"I'll find the police!" I holler back as I dash left, toward the reception area. The corridor suddenly goes dark. My shoulder wails in pain when it slams into a wall. I clutch it and keep running, spurred by the thumping and crunching sounds behind me.

A shot rings out, startling everything into silence.

No, no, no!

"Get back here, bitch, and take your next consequence or whatever the game tells you to do," Micki yells. "Or the next bullet goes into one of your friends."

My mouth goes dry. Would she do that? She didn't shoot in cold blood before, but now she's more desperate.

Sydney shouts, "Go, Vee!"

Ian joins in. "The game is already over."

Is it? What'll Micki and Ty do if I keep going? What'll they do if I return? My brain tells me that Ian's right, but it feels like betrayal. Glass shatters behind me. Ty must be almost through the wall. I flail in the dark, bumping into something with sharp corners. The concierge desk. I'm almost out of here. Then I remember my phone. I fumble it from my pocket, panting with hope. A quick glance makes me groan. Still no service.

But at least I can use the phone's display as a tiny flashlight, which reveals the main door. Behind me comes grunting and yelling, and then another gunshot.

Oh God, oh God, oh God. But if Micki's done the unthinkable, going back will only make things worse. I open the door that leads to the small entry area in front of the elevators, and I'm blinded by the light, even though it's still set to a moody level. There's movement in front of me—the elevator door to the left begins to close on a car full of six or so Watchers. Their clothes are colorful, but their faces are gray. One man, in his fifties, with slicked-back hair and a tailored leather jacket, blows me a kiss.

Son of a bitch. I recognize him as the chaperone from the Purity Promisers, who threw Ian and me out onto our butts.

I leap forward, pull out my gun, and jam it into the last inches of narrowing space between the doors. Steel crushes against steel, and the Watchers shriek as they move toward the walls of the elevator. Not such a fun show anymore, huh? And then, with a little bouncing motion, the elevator doors give up and open.

I point my gun at the guy who blew me an air kiss. "You, throw me your phone."

He shrugs. "We left our phones with the chauffeurs. NERVE doesn't want anyone charging for game videos except them."

Damn. Do I force them out of the elevator and take it down by myself to look for police who may or may not be searching the building? I can't afford the time. Another plan takes shape.

I swallow. "Fine, then get out. Just you."

The man leans against the elevator wall, crossing his arms and kicking a leg out. He smiles, actually smiles. The bastard. "You won't shoot me."

I prop my foot in the elevator in case the doors decide to close again. Should I force one of the others out? They're all equally deserving. But this guy's smugness is more than I can tolerate.

I steady my aim. "But these bullets are fake, right? So why not shoot? Nothing will happen." I cock the gun.

He licks his lips. "Part of the fun is not knowing just how real the weaponry is. But I'd take bets on what you will or won't do with it. Violence is not in your profile."

I nod. "Do you really want to bet that my profile isn't a whole hell of a lot different than it was a few hours ago? If I find out that any of my friends have been hurt, it won't bother me a bit to aim for parts of your body that are near and dear to you. So, c'mon."

He glances down at his groin and then looks up with a smile, which sends my creep-o-meter sky high. "Don't threaten me, little girl."

"One," I say, aiming for his knee.

A chunky woman next to him gives his elbow a nudge. "Just go with her. NERVE will square things away. They don't want to lose their biggest supporters."

His face goes scarlet. "Shut your bovine mouth."

"Two," I say, moving my gun sight up his leg. The door starts to close until I kick against the side, causing it to bounce open again.

The man stares venom into me.

"Fine," I say, tightening my finger on the trigger. "Thr—"

"Okay, you little bitch." He strides forward so quickly I'm afraid he'll grab my gun.

"Slower! Or I'll shoot you now. Trust me, it'll feel good after what I've been through." Surprisingly, at that moment, I believe it would. And he must see it in my eyes, because he does as I say. God, what have I become?

I back up as he exits the elevator and glowers before me. We stand face-to-face until the elevator doors close. His skin is taut, like he gets regular facials, and those "casual" pants cost at least five hundred dollars. All that money, and he wastes it on perverted entertainment. Making him squirm will be a pleasure.

"We're going back to the room," I say. "Walk."

I let him take a few steps in front of me, and he opens the ornate door. Inside, it's still dark, but the light from near the elevators shows Ty, clutching his arm and stumbling in the reception area. He must've gotten turned around in the dark. His face breaks into a smile when he sees us. I squint, trying to see into the blackness of the corridor behind him, but it's a void.

I step behind the man. "Go back, Ty, or I'll shoot this guy. He's one of NERVE's high rollers, even had a cameo on one of our dares. So you can forget about winning any prizes if he gets hurt."

Ty laughs. "Who do you think you're kidding?"

The man straightens. "Do not even think about taking one step out of there. If she shoots me, there'll be hell to pay for all of you."

"But—" Ty falters. "My arm is—"

"Now," the man says, clearly used to giving orders.

"Who got shot?" I ask.

"I didn't bother checking," Ty says. Asshole.

I peek around the man's side to make sure that Ty starts heading back down the corridor. Something dark drips from his elbow. Well, he knows where the first aid supplies are. From somewhere in front of him come the sounds of shouting and thrashing.

"What's next, princess?" the man asks.

"Prop the door open quickly," I tell him. We need the light. He does.

"Now walk through the waiting area and down the hallway, toward the room. No quick moves, but don't drag your ass either."

He struts forward. I keep a few paces behind him, pointing my gun at his butt and shining the light from my phone. Every few steps, I peek around him to make sure no one else has entered the hallway. Yells come from the game room. Has NERVE sent in reinforcements?

I call out, "Syd, Tommy, Ian, are you guys okay?"

"We're fine," Sydney shouts back. "As long as psycho girl doesn't shoot the ceiling anymore."

A breath explodes from my chest. Thank goodness. When we get to the room, I say, "Go back inside, Ty."

"Why? I thought you wanted the game to be over."

"Do it," the man says.

Ty ducks through the cave-like opening in the glass. Even though the lights are out in the game room, the panels above the one-way window reveal various images in muted shades of green, confirming my earlier suspicion that NERVE was filming us with night-vision cameras. Micki and Ian pick themselves off of the floor, where they must've been wrestling. They cock their heads my way, as if they're trying to make out what's going on here in the corridor.

"What the hell?" Micki crouches so her eyes are even with the hole. Why didn't she follow Ty out? Does she think there's a chance the game will continue as long as she remains inside? What kind of prize did they offer her on top of the Harley? Ownership of a dog-fighting emporium?

My voice is steel. "Ian, Tommy, and Sydney, c'mon out."

Micki straightens up and grabs a gun from Jen. "My next shot won't be a warning." On one of the panels above, I see her aim at Syd.

The man speaks up. "If you don't do as Vee instructs, none of you will receive any prizes. I can make sure of it."

Ty pokes his head back through the opening. "Who are you, like the NERVE boss?"

"No, but they'll want to keep me happy, I assure you."

There's silence. No doubt they're waiting for NERVE to confirm what the man said. But NERVE's probably too busy assembling an army. The panels remain focused on the players in the room.

Micki's voice is harsh and she still aims at Syd. "Doesn't seem like anyone's backing you up, Mr. Investor. Maybe they don't care if you get shot."

The man begins to tremble. "But I care. And I have the means to make sure you earn your prizes."

There's movement and murmuring in the room.

Ty speaks up. "How can you guarantee it?"

"If she shoots me, I can guarantee you won't get anything. And if she doesn't, I always reward those who assist me. Just as I punish those who don't."

Micki's snarly voice rises. "But we're the ones with the guns. Maybe NERVE just wants us to shoot you ourselves. And then Virgin and her friends." She turns to point her gun through the opening in the wall at the man.

Ian says, "Are you high? Whatever happens in this room will be broadcast. And stored on video. You want to spend the rest of your life behind bars, or as the bitch of whoever owns the video so you can avoid prison time?"

I steady my aim. "Besides, we'd shoot back, which would be self-defense. Not that it matters, since I don't see any cameras out here in the hallway. I'm the only one not being filmed." My voice is hard and my veins are like ice.

Ty says, "I don't know."

"Well, I do," I say. "I'm done playing. I'm giving this ass-hole the punishment he deserves. And screwing you guys out of winning anything at the same time."

The man's body stiffens. "I'm pulling out my wallet. It's filled with cash and credit cards. Use them." He takes out the wallet and sets it on the floor.

Micki stares at the hole in the wall, probably calculating whether she could dash through and beat my head in before I shot the guy. Or her.

Tempted as I am to prod her, I let her think. She may be vicious, but I don't believe she's stupid.

And then her shoulders slump and she lowers her gun. "Get out of here, shitheads." Jen tries to hug her, but she shrugs away.

A few moments later, Tommy ducks through the opening, followed by Syd and Ian.

Before we head out, I motion toward the man's wallet. "Take out your driver's license."

"Why? You can't buy anything with that."

No, I can't. And I wouldn't. The thought of buying any prizes with this creep's cash makes me ill.

I say, "Just do it." Now he can see how it feels to have his privacy invaded.

He kneels down to remove a card before placing the wal-let back on the floor. In the limited light from my phone and the overhead panels, I can't tell for sure if it's his license or a membership card to Pervs Anonymous, but he has to know I'm not fooling around. He stands up and holds it out toward me.

No way I'm getting close enough for him to knock the gun from my hand, so I have him hand it to Tommy. With me in the lead, but walking backward so I can keep my gun trained on the man, we march out. Ian brings up the rear, pointing his gun at the man from behind.

Out by the elevators, I kick up the doorstop and yell, "Anyone leaves before we're out of the building and this guy gets shot in the ass." No one ever died from a butt shot, I tell myself. As I slam the door shut, I imagine hands in the dark grabbing for the man's wallet.

Ian reaches to press the button for the VIP elevator, but I shout for him to stop. "This whole lounge has been taken over by NERVE. If they send backup, or those chauffeurs down there are armed, they'll come through the private entrance."

Ian hits the button for the "housekeeping" elevator. We all jerk upright when the bell rings, our wary eyes waiting to see whether someone's headed our way. The doors open to an empty car. Thank God. But I'm still not convinced NERVE won't have a firing squad waiting for us below, even in the dance club.

As we move toward the elevator door, the man asks, "Are my hostage duties complete?"

I pause. If we run into someone from NERVE, will this guy give us leverage? I don't think so, or they would've rescued him already. On the other hand, if there are police below, paid off or not, it won't look good for me to be dragging a hostage at gunpoint.

"You can stay up here," I say.

We get on board, and I hit the button marked "Club," saying a silent prayer that we don't need an access code to go down.

The door closes and the car moves. As soon as it does, Sydney and Ian collapse onto me in a group hug. It hardly seems real that we've escaped from that room. How long before the other players finally give up and leave?

Over Syd's shoulder, I spy Tommy looking uncomfortable in the corner. I feel a pang of sympathy for my wingman, even though he filmed me during the dare at the school theater. But he came to rescue me, right? Once Sydney and Ian let me go, I approach Tommy and give him a hug too. He seems surprised, but grabs me in an embrace that isn't too awkward until I lose my balance and shove an arm into his side. A vibration suddenly shudders at his hip. I jerk my arm away. What the hell?

Tommy takes a step back, and pushes me away from his body. His face flushes and his eyes dart down to his hip.

I grab at him. "Your phone works. I just felt it. Answer it!"

His mouth smiles, but his eyes don't. "They must've just

turned it back on." He pulls the phone out of his pocket with shaky hands and reads a text.

I check my own phone, which still comes up as blocked, and I tell Ian and Syd to do the same. All blocked, except for Tommy's, even though we're in an elevator.

"Why aren't you calling 911?" I ask.

He fumbles with the phone. "Uh, yeah. I will."

"C'mon, how hard is it to press three numbers?" And why is he so hesitant? Then the chaos of the past few hours seems to settle in my brain, leaving a clear trail to what I hadn't seen before now. "Where are the police, Tommy? Did you even call them?"

He stares at his phone. "Of course I did. They must've gotten the wrong address or something. GPS isn't as exact as people think."

"But you are." Everything that happened tonight sharpens into crystal focus, like that one-way glass into the room. "Give me your phone, Tommy."

He pokes at the display. "I said I'd call."

"Humor me."

"Humor me," he mimics in a high voice. "You sound like a character in one of those plays you couldn't get cast for."

"I want the phone now, Tommy."

"Give it to her," Ian says. He presses the close button to keep the elevator doors from opening.

"Shut up." Tommy wipes some sweat from his forehead.

"Vee, I came here to bail you out and you don't trust me?"

"I don't know what you came here to do. But the fact that you didn't come with the police was stupid. Stupid isn't in your profile, Tommy. Neither is daring. But calculating is. I'll bet you're the one who told NERVE about why I was mad at Sydney. Liv and Eulie never would've betrayed me like that. And how many people could've told NERVE about the sticker on my car's stereo knob? You asshole!"

He sneers. "As if I'm the biggest asshole tonight." He shakes his head in disgust.

The flame within me goes white. And then in a martial arts move I'd rehearsed with Sydney when she had a role in that ninja play, I slice my leg through the air and sideswipe him in the crotch.

When he goes down, I grab the phone out of his hands. It's loaded with texts from NERVE, confirming my suspicions. "Son of a bitch. You betrayed me for a big-screen TV?"

He looks up at me with bloodshot eyes. "Screw the TV. We've got three at home. You aren't the only one tired of living backstage."

I stand as close to the door as possible and enter the numbers that will end this. Tommy doesn't move from his corner while I tell the police about the guns in the VIP lounge.

"Told you he was full of shit," Ian says.

Tommy slams the wall and scowls at Ian. "NERVE only

chose you instead of me because they knew you'd break Vee's heart."

Sydney cocks her head at Tommy. "You tried out too? How come no one mentioned that you posted a video?"

Tommy glares at her.

I can barely keep myself from spitting on him. He screwed me over because NERVE picked Ian instead of him? Pathetic.

Ian lets the elevator door open to a nondescript corridor. Peeking my head out, I see a nearby door that throbs with deep bass and another door at the far end of the hall. I duck back into the elevator to demand the NERVE investor's driver's license from Tommy, who throws it at me. I tuck it into my pocket and exit into the hallway with Syd and Ian.

As the elevator doors close, I say over my shoulder, "Game over, Tommy."

twenty

"Which door?" Ian asks me.

Sydney, for once, awaits my decision too.

The far door might lead to an immediate exit, but it could also send us straight into a bunch of NERVE psychos, and who knows how long it'll take for the police to show up? I open the door to the music, which leads onto a balcony overlooking a large dance floor. Ian and I glance at each other and quickly tuck our guns into our clothes.

As we descend a winding staircase, the crowd seems to ignore us. We probably look like underdressed, underage kids who snuck in, never mind my scratched-up jacket and bleeding hand. On the main floor, I grab a napkin from a table to press onto my wound. The scratches on my thighs will have to wait. We bump and jostle through people laughing and drinking as though this is just a typical Saturday night. All I focus on is the exit sign.

When we're halfway across the room, a woman points our way and screams, "Hey, those are the NERVE players!"

The music instantly softens, and everyone turns our way to stare. One guy fumbles with his phone and asks, "What are you doing here? Is the game done? They've been playing flashbacks since you crashed a hole in the wall. That was awesome!"

I rear back. "You were watching?"

"We all were." He points up to a large screen that's playing a clip of Ty and Daniella in the closet, lit by night-vision so they're green. Not something I'd want to watch in full color anyway.

I get in the guy's face. "You saw us trapped in there with guns? Why the hell didn't you help us?"

"They have producers and stuff looking out for you, right?" He points his phone at me and hollers to his friends, "Yo, I told you they were in the room upstairs. I totally recognized the table!"

Everyone around us presses in to get a better look, shouting our names and laughing. Two girls ask for my autograph, and their dates start to hoist me into the air until Ian stops them.

My body stiffens. How can they act like they know us? It's hard to get my head around the fact that while I feared for my life a few floors above them, they saw us as just one more form of entertainment, hardly worth a second thought.

Ian and Syd try to pull me to the exit, but I shrug them away, pushing through the waves and the "Hey, Vees!" until I'm next to the DJ. The screens above us have shifted to a clip of Ian in a small room, eyes fixed on a grainy video. All I can make out is a tall man slapping a little boy and dragging him into a pickup truck before the camera angle shifts to the image of Ian, alone in his dare room, watching the footage with a stricken expression. There's no way someone made a family video of that, is there? No wonder his prizes were all about escape. I turn to stare into the eyes of the real Ian at my side, who swallows and blinks.

"That little boy wasn't you, was it?"

He shakes his head. "But he may as well have been."

The DJ welcomes us with a big smile. "We have VIP guests here tonight, folks!" he says into his microphone.

VIP, yeah, right. I grab the microphone and ask him to turn off the music. Because I'm a temporary celebrity, he actually does what I say. The crowd turns toward us, some still dancing to the tunes in their heads.

After helping out with so many school performances, I should know how to use a mike, but it still feels awkward. I blow on it to make sure it's on and say, "Hi. I'm Vee."

"Hey, girl!" a dozen or more club-goers shout back.

I point to the screen. "You just saw me playing NERVE

and probably thought it looked like a fun way to earn some cool prizes. Here's the truth. We almost died up there. The game is real. Whatever you do, don't apply and don't watch it next month. Or ever."

A few people have gone to the bar to order another drink and chat. The rest of the crowd stares at me, some smirking, some whispering with their buddies, some looking puzzled. I recognize the woman from the bowling alley, with the red curls of a soprano. She was on our side before, maybe she'll get her friends to listen. Instead, she pulls out a camera and points it at me. Everyone around her does the same. The room becomes a swarm of arms in the air holding cell phones for a better shot.

I could have been killed, and their response is to film me? It's all I can do not to throw the mike at them or bust out crying. In that moment, the myth that every time your picture is taken, a part of your soul is stolen strikes me as a certain truth, because I feel my spirit being sucked out of me, into hundreds of all-seeing lenses that simply want to capture my fear, my anger, my performance.

I stand there, numb, dumb, and empty.

The DJ turns the music back on, and when Ian and Syd push me forward, I don't argue. We claw our way through a swarm of people yelling at us to describe the dares, to give them our phone numbers, our Web pages, our smiles for yet another picture or video. People yank on my jacket, grab my arms, even pat my head like I'm a poodle. Without warning, my body rises off of the floor, carried along by a churning sea of Watchers. I thrash and scream for them to put me down, until I end up on the floor with a heavy thump. One guy rubs his chin where I slapped him and calls me a stuck-up bitch. How many times have I heard that word tonight? It no longer matters.

Ian finds me in the chaos and pulls me along. When we're almost to the exit, the door swings open and two policemen enter, asking to speak with the manager. As much as I wanted them to come earlier, I can't stomach the idea of anything that'll keep me in this zoo a moment longer. It's not like there's anyone still upstairs, right? And if they are, they're just drinking the rest of the beer. Still, I should at least give them the NERVE investor's license and the gun. I reach into my pocket and am stunned to discover that both are gone. Did they fall out or did NERVE get someone to pickpocket me? A tremor rips through me with the thought that those assholes are calling the shots even now. Are these policemen on their payroll too?

Maybe Ian and Syd are having similar thoughts, because we scramble into the icy air outside, rushing with our heads pointed downward until we reach the VIP parking spot. I'm surprised that no one's slashed the tires on Ian's Volvo. But I'm not surprised that there's no trace of Tommy's car.

Since Syd got a ride here with him, she gets into the Volvo.

Even if she'd driven herself, she's not ready to be alone just yet.

But I feel more alone than ever. Thousands of people must have watched us tonight, and most of them never gave a thought to the fact that the players were real, live people.

A Watcher runs to the car and pounds on the window, begging for one more picture. I shake my head and look away. Through the glass, he screams, "Who the hell do you think you are?"

I have no idea.

Ian pulls another of his getaway car maneuvers to ditch a couple of diehard Watchers, and then we drive in silence. Even Sydney seems to be grappling with some inner turmoil, huddled in the backseat with her arms tightly crossed. Is she kicking herself for letting Tommy bring her into the final dares? Fooling the girl who's supposed to be such a great judge of character? Speaking of character, I have to know about Ian for sure. It's not like I really believe he's a plant for NERVE or some kind of Web exhibitionist. But can I trust my own beliefs?

I peek at him from the corner of my eye. "Can I ask how you afford private school?"

He seems taken aback, but then nods as if he gets the reason for my question. His shoulders slump. "Financial aid. And I deliver a lot of pizzas. Cool, huh?"

I brush his arm. "I'm sorry you didn't win your freedom."

"Hell, any game that gives its players guns is probably not the kind that'll ever really let you go free."

Sydney clears her throat. When I glance back at her, her fingers quickly sign, *He's a keeper.*

Something tells me she's right. Everything Ian's done tonight proves he's a great guy, right? But what if it was all for show? What if his real dare was to break my heart, like Tommy said?

My head hurts. I should call my parents, but more than anything I want to close in on myself, to reclaim a sliver of the privacy I've lost. The rest of the ride sinks into silence until we reach Sydney's house.

When she gets out, I do too.

I hang my head. "I'm so, so sorry about everything."

She sighs. "I think I get why you signed up. The important thing is you saved us. We're all good."

I look up. Even though I doubt Ian can hear our soft voices from inside the car, she signs, *sister.*

I sign the same thing back to her and wait outside until she enters her front door.

Ian wants to drive me to my house, but I tell him to take me to my car at the bowling alley. Some stubborn part of me wants to end this night the way I started it, under my own control.

Back at the bowling alley, the neon lights have been turned off. No more Purity Promisers, no more Watchers. Just an almost empty lot that holds my car and a beat-up van.

Ian's eyes look way older than they did when we met here all those hours ago. "How about I follow you home, just to make sure you get there okay?"

"That's really sweet, but you're just as tired as me. Go home and call me tomorrow. Or today, I guess. Once we've had some sleep."

He grins. "I don't have your phone number."

There's a whole world of folks who've seen me terrorized and knows my bra size, but my partner doesn't even know my number. Crazy. We exchange digits.

He leans over and kisses me softly. "The one good thing about tonight is you."

I nod and get out of the car, wanting to believe him, but fighting the nagging doubt that he's being so sweet because there's some kind of post-game prize involved. Maybe someone's filming us from that van. Ugh. If this is life in the paranoid lane, it's exhausting, but I'm too tired take the exit ramp right now. Guess I'll find out Ian's true feelings in time.

When all bets are off.

twenty-one

One month later

I am not a morning person, but I'm learning to be. The calmness of dawn offers a daily promise that all things will shift back to normal. But, like Schrödinger's Cat, the only way to find out will be to poke my head out of the box. I wait until after I've eaten and dressed to turn on my phone, tempted to prolong the peacefulness for a moment longer, but eager to see if anything's changed.

One message in particular catches my eye, but it's almost lost among the hundreds of texts and dozens of connection requests. A typical day's accumulation. Which means life's still crazy. For now, I've got the attention of a whole bunch of people.

So I'll use it.

I broadcast my weekly message to every new phone number and ThisIsMe page I've collected in the past seven days. Most people will probably ignore it, but some, hopefully enough, won't.

> DEAR WORLD,
>
> I ALMOST GOT KILLED PLAYING NERVE, JUST SO THEY COULD MAKE A PROFIT. THEY THINK THEY CAN GET AWAY WITH ABUSING PLAYERS BECAUSE NO ONE REALLY CARES AND NO ONE CAN FIND THEM. BUT THEY'RE WRONG.
>
> THEY CAN'T HIDE, NOT FROM ALL OF US.
>
> SO USE WHATEVER COMPUTER SKILLS YOU HAVE, WHATEVER SKILLS YOUR FRIENDS HAVE, AND HUNT THESE BASTARDS DOWN.
>
> I DARE YOU!

After I send the message, I put away my phone, and won't check messages until tomorrow morning if I can manage it. My Apparel Design teacher calls me a Luddite. I call it keeping my sanity.

I pull my hair into a ponytail and head for the garage. Although I'm grounded nights and weekends from now until I'm old enough to vote, I'm allowed to go out for morning exercise three times a week. So I get into my car and drive to a local trail, where a sensible gray Volvo waits for me.

Ian's next to it doing quad stretches, dressed in athletic shorts and a T-shirt that show off tan, toned arms and legs. I'm getting a little buff myself from our regular workouts, and have decided that biceps make a lovely fashion accessory. When I reach Ian, we kiss for a long moment and then take our spots on a curb to tiptoe into calf stretches.

"We may have a hit," I say, referring to the message on my phone earlier.

"On him or her?"

"Gayle, who's real name is Jordan, if the facial recognition software is right."

He smiles. "Yay, Tommy."

After apologizing profusely, Tommy's earned his way back into a wary friendship with me, and has been a big help in spearheading my fight against NERVE. I truly believe he had no idea things would go to the extremes they did. And it's not like he was the only one who acted against character and better judgment that night.

Ian and I move to a tree next to the trail and lean against it for some more leg stretches before we take off running, settling into an easy pace. On the first week after the game, our morning jogs had been bombarded with Watchers, videoing us for their after-games and weird system of credits. Tommy even located a GPS tracker stuck to my car's bumper.

The police haven't helped much. Insufficient evidence, they say. The other players insist that the guns were plastic and the drinks were juice. I'm sure they've received some type of payoff for their cooperation. And the creepy investor, who had crashed the Purity Promisers' event, isn't saying anything either.

But we're fighting back. And I've heard from a ton of folks who want to help, including a Watcher who captured video footage that included a brief snippet of our hosts in the grand prize round. It's a video of a video, so the image is grainy, but Tommy did what he could to clean it up enough for facial recognition software to compare it against millions of other images on the Internet. Of course, Guy and Gayle were probably paid to entertain like the rest of us. But if there's any way they can provide a lead to who the big money-makers are behind the game, it's a lead worth pursuing.

Ian and I jog past a cluster of honeysuckle that scents the trail with the promise of summer. I breathe deeply but jump back when a skinny guy springs out from the next tree, pointing a camera.

Ian slams to a stop in front of him. "Dude! You don't have to ambush us. If you'd have asked to take our picture, we would've let you."

And it's true, since we've learned an interesting rule about fame. Those who seem desperate for it are the people that others least want to see. So Ian and I make a point of posing for pictures when asked. The more we put ourselves out there, the less popular we hope to become.

But this guy didn't ask. So he'll get a consequence. Ian and I pull out our phones and start filming our Watcher.

He puts his hands in front of his face. "What'chya doing that for?"

Ian smiles. "It's for a new site called LOOK WHO'S STALKING. Smile."

The guy runs away, cussing. That worked better than usual. My own footage is probably shaky and blurry, since I'm still stuck with a piece of crap camera. But there are worse things than dealing with lousy video equipment.

A mile into the trail, we stop at a long wooden bench. Ian takes me onto his lap and pulls me into a kiss that's warm and yummy, but I can't help scanning the trees around us, wondering if we're truly alone.

We've tried finding more privacy on our morning get-togethers, but both Ian's house and mine are out of the question. And even when we've parked in the most remote of locations, we've been interrupted by nut-jobs clinking their cameras against the windows. I can understand why that other player, Abigail, escaped to the backcountry of Virginia for a week. As much as I want to shut down NERVE, a tiny part of me hopes they'll play the next round as scheduled this Saturday, if only to shift the focus to another set of players. It's a terrible wish, I know.

When a pair of joggers passes us, we rise up to resume our run. The day promises to be clear and sunny. Maybe Syd and I can go out at lunchtime with some kids from the photography club to work on her headshots. And I'm using my free nights to work on my portfolio. To hell with NERVE; we're making our own dreams come true.

All too soon, the workout's over. Ian and I part with a long, slow kiss before I get into my car. As I drive off, I notice that the car smells like a diner, like someone's been eating bacon in it. Did something come in through the vents? I quickly peek to make sure that no one's hiding on the backseat. It's empty, but I still feel a tiny quiver in my shoulders. Will this shaky feeling ever go away?

When I get home, Mom and Dad greet me with relieved smiles, the way they do every time I go running. I know it's taken all of their willpower to trust me even this tiny bit, so I'm going to do what I can to earn it. One unexpected result of coming clean to them about what happened with NERVE is that they got a chance to see just how badly I want to live. I think they finally believe that what happened in the garage was an accident. Maybe if I'm really lucky, they'll make an exception to my prison sentence so I can attend a Habitat for Humanity event with Ian next month.

Mom points to the hallway. "Did you order something? That was sitting outside when I went out to water the plants."

As if I have the money for anything but saving for college. I check the table near the front door, where a package rests. It's way too early in the morning for a delivery, isn't it? Maybe it was out there since yesterday. The return address is printed with the gold-embossed name of a high-end department store in New York. The postmark is also from New York, so chances are good it isn't a bomb. There goes my overactive paranoia again.

I open the box to find an inner box amidst a sea of biode-gradable packing material. Inside, there's a velvet bag with a designer logo that I recognize from hours of staring at it online. With shaky hands, I pull a pair of flamingo-colored shoes from the bag. The shoes that NERVE dangled in front of me for my dare in the coffee shop. That's strange. They'd made it clear that I lost all of my winnings when I escaped from the grand prize dares. Is this some kind of mistake?

I find a little silver envelope tucked into one of the shoes. Inside is a note that causes me to kneel slowly onto the cold floor.

I'll never get tired of watching you, and can't wait to see you play again.

I stare at the shoes, which become uglier by the second. Well, some woman in a shelter is going to be walking around in style really soon. I get up to drop the shoes into Mom's "donation" box. As I pass through the living room,

I'm startled by a familiar sound. It's my phone, summoning me. But not with my generic, chiming ring tone.

Instead it calls with the chanting of a spoiled child.

CURTAIN

Acknowledgments

I've had loads of help and encouragement to make this book happen. My heartfelt thanks to my family and friends, both near and far, who've cheered me on these many years as I've pursued this dream of novel-writing. Your support and excitement fueled me through many challenging days.

To my editor at Dial, Heather Alexander, whose guidance helped push this story farther and sharper than I thought possible. Also to Andrew Harwell, whose vision for *Nerve* influenced this book long after he left the project.

Many thanks to my agent extraordinaire, Ammi-Joan Paquette, whose keen eye and savvy input helped me whip this manuscript into shape, and whose cheerleading never wavers. Every writer should be so lucky.

A heap of thanks to my many critique partners, who've seen this story morph from its rough beginnings into something publishable. To my local writers group, who are ready to hash out ideas at a moment's notice, and have been with me for five manuscripts (and counting!): Annika de Groot, Lee Harris, Christine Putnam and Lesley Reece. To my online critiquers who challenged me to find a better beginning for this story, which is how I ended up placing Vee in a theater: Kelly Dyksterhouse, Kristi Helvig (who also beta-read),

Joanne Linden, Mary Louise Sanchez, and Niki Schoenfeldt.

To my sisters and niece who jumped in to read and provide input when I got angsty: Mary Ryan, Rachel Ryan and Madeline Anderson (whose surgically attached phone gave me the idea for a story where phones play such an integral role). To my brother-from-another-mother, Tim Beauchamp, whom I can call 24/7 to get input on whatever technical details are stumping me. In this book, it was gun usage. Any errors about firearms that may've ended up in the manuscript are my doing, not his.

One of my biggest champions from my very first manuscript was my dear friend Lisa Berglund, who KNEW I'd be published someday. The only cloud in the blue skies of that finally happening is that she isn't here to celebrate with me. If there's a book club in heaven, I'm sure she's leading it.

Finally, thanks to my husband and kids, who've supported me through countless evenings where "Mom's gotta go to the coffee shop and write." They encourage me so much and are active participants in my writing, from drawing pictures of how they think a scene should look to debating story ideas. I love them beyond words. And by my calculations, owe about 1,509 home-cooked meals.